EMBASSY TO CONSTANTINOPLE

EMBASSY TO CONSTANTINOPLE
The Travels of Lady Mary Wortley Montagu

INTRODUCED BY
Dervla Murphy

EDITED AND COMPILED BY
Christopher Pick

NEW AMSTERDAM
New York

© 1988
Published in the United States of America, 1988 by
NEW AMSTERDAM BOOKS of New York, Inc
by arrangement with Century Hutchinson Ltd, London.

NEW AMSTERDAM BOOKS
171 Madison Avenue
New York, NY 10016

This edition designed and produced by
Playne Books, Avening, Gloucestershire, Great Britain

Editing, Photography and Design
Gill Davies Gail Langley Marc Langley
David Playne Karen Wilson

Typeset in Plantin on Scantext by Playne Books

Printed and bound in Great Britain by
Butler and Tanner

ISBN 0-941533-41-7

Contents

The Ambassador and his Delegation crossing the Second Court of Topkapi Saray attributed to Antonio Guardi and studio, c.1735-45. Leading the procession are the Head Chamberlain and the Chief Usher, who carry their long silver staffs of office.

INTRODUCTION

Everybody allows that the talent of writing agreeable letters is peculiarly female —
Jane Austen, Northanger Abbey.

The letters of Lady Mary Wortley Montagu have long been a favourite 'quote-mine' for historians, biographers, essayists and travel writers. Yet to most general readers she herself has never seemed more than an astringent commentator on the side-lines — almost a disembodied voice. In our own day, with its over-fondness for labels, she has been referred to as a 'pioneer woman traveller and/or feminist', though it is impossible to squeeze her into either category without distorting her personality. Any reader of her letters must think of her, primarily, as an *individual*: strong-willed, warm-hearted, keen-witted, high-spirited, often unpredictable, sometimes downright eccentric — a woman who rarely allowed her many disappointments and misfortunes to provoke recriminations or self-pity. She was at once stoical and imaginative, gullible and shrewd, childishly vain and touchingly humble, sincere and loyal in her affections but occasionally indiscriminate in her choice of friends. As the years taught her to value wisdom above knowledge she became wryly self-mocking. And nowhere in her own writings — feline as she could be in her snap judgements — is there anything approaching the scurrility with which she was repeatedly tormented by Pope, Horace Walpole and their (often anonymous) hangers-on.

'I prefer liberty to chains of diamonds.' Lady Mary was not striking a pose when she wrote thus in 1758; by then she had been choosing liberty, in a variety of situations, for more than half a century. This preference was linked to her appreciation of solitude, which co-existed (as it does more often than people realize) with an equal appreciation of good company and sophisticated entertainments. As a twenty-year-old, she wrote from the family seat at Thoresby, in Nottinghamshire, to Miss Anne Wortley:

> *I am now so much alone I have leisure to pass whole days in reading... I am trying whether it be possible to learn Latin without a master... I find the study so diverting, I am not only easy but pleased with the solitude that indulges it. I forget there is such a place as London, and wish for no company but yours.*

Forty-four years later she wrote from her exile's home in Gottolengo, Italy, to her daughter, 'I know by experience it is in the power of study not only to make solitude tolerable but agreeable'. Urging a good education for her granddaughters, she added, 'Every branch of knowledge is entertaining and the longest life is too short for the pursuit of it'.

Our perception of Lady Mary is restricted almost entirely to what we can see of her character as reflected in her letters and it has been suggested that we see only a flattering self-portrait. Yet much may be deduced from a copious personal correspondence with intimates, spanning fifty-four years. However posterity-conscious a writer may be, the bedrock of personality gradually emerges from beneath the carefully cultivated verbal lawn. And one of the most endearing traits revealed in Lady Mary's letters is her determination to make the best of almost all her personal relationships, unpromising though they might be. It seems she gave up only on Pope, whose implacable enmity for her was as abnormal in degree as it was baffling in origin.

In 1689 Evelyn Pierrepont was elected to Parliament for East Retford and his twenty-one-year-old wife bore their first child, Mary. The young family's worldly prospects were good and soon became better. Five years earlier Sir John Evelyn had left his Wiltshire estates to his daughter, Elizabeth Pierrepont, who was to pass them on to her youngest son Evelyn should he prove worthy of such a substantial inheritance — which he made it his business to do. On the paternal side, his father and both his brothers died young, which meant that in 1690 he found himself Earl of Kinston and his baby daughter became Mary Pierrepont. The new Lady Kingston rapidly produced two more daughters, Frances and Evelyn, followed in 1692 by the essential son, William. She died a year later and is known to us only as a breeding-machine. The four children were then dispatched to their paternal grandmother, described by her cousin John Evelyn (the diarist) as a 'most excellent and prudent lady'. Thus Lady Mary's first remembered home was West Dean Manor, near Salisbury. The large Jacobean house stood amidst elms, overlooking stepped terraces and a well-wooded park criss-crossed by canals in fashionable imitation of a Dutch landscape. Deer wandered through the park and the canals were fed from a lake-like fish-pond, surrounded by dense, dark yew-groves. High hedges of bramble and hawthorn sheltered the recently enclosed nearby fields and the manor's sheep grazed on more distant downs. Apart from luxury goods, West Dean was self-sufficient and Lady Mary and her siblings spent their childhood in a domestic atmosphere of secure prosperity. Yet at that time their country — beyond the tranquillity of its great estates — was tense, confused and apprehensive.

Lady Mary's birth-year also saw the birth of modern England. In 1689 Parliament denied the Divine Right of Kings and altered succession to make possible the replacement of the Catholic Stuarts by the Protestant Hanoverians. This development caused the political atmosphere to become peculiarly opaque during Lady Mary's youth. From our vantage point, the years 1689-1714 may seem not very significant. We know that when George I came lumbering across from Hanover he was tolerated (for fear of something worse) and thereafter the apparent placid eighteenth century proceeded on its elegant way. But during the reigns of William and Mary, and Queen Anne, the people of England lived in suspense. Many feared — and the Jacobites hoped for — a new century scarred by revolution and war.

Coincidentally, 1689 was also the year when England's annual consumption of beer, as assessed for excise, broke the record at fifty-one gallons per head of population. This news bothered Queen Mary and King Billy; it seems no one told them that for centuries ale and beer had been protecting the populace — men, women and children — from water-borne diseases. Royally encouraged Societies for the Reformation of Morals proliferated throughout the kingdom, 'a vast number of lewd and disorderly persons' were brought to justice and beer consumption dropped spectacularly. But this edifying phenomenon was short-lived. It had in fact been caused not by a revival of virtue but by an abrupt decline in the economy — and soon a fate worse than beer overwhelmed the masses. On the recommendation of their Dutch allies in what was popularly known as King Billy's War (1689-97), they became addicted to cheap gin. During the 1680s England's average yearly consumption of spirits had been less than half a million gallons; by 1710 the figure was over two million and by 1740 eight million — sobering statistics, given a population of about six million. For this crisis, England's land-owning legislators were largely responsible; they had put an absurdly low tax on gin because distilling enriched them by expanding the market for corn. A 1751 Act attempted to control the situation, yet in the 1760s medical men estimated that gin-swilling was causing one-eighth of London's adult deaths. Hogarth's 'Gin Lane' and 'Beer Street' were not exaggerations but pictorial statements of fact.

Our view of eighteenth-century England recalls George Savile's aphorism: 'Time hath thrown a Vail upon the Faults of former Ages, or else we should see the same Deformities we condemn in the present times'. The Age labelled 'Augustan' by Goldsmith was also — we have been taught — the Age of Reason. Bigotry had waned; people were no longer beheaded for treason or burnt at the stake. Stability, harmony and a peacefully increasing prosperity were the ideals. Various wars were indeed happening somewhere out there; and John Company was inadvertently acquiring an empire to replace the soon-to-be lost North American colonies. But at home all was (was it not?) calm and rational. Standards were being set by Pope's poetry, Gibbon's prose, Baskerville's printing, Chippendale's furniture, Adam's palaces, Brindley's bridges, Wedgwood's china. The poised, richly apparelled leaders of this cultivated society were painted by Kneller, Gainsborough, Reynolds, Lawrence, Stubbs — though they acquired their other paintings abroad, having more regard for Continental artists than for the native breed. Of course we know there was also a lot of squalor, violence and injustice around: Hogarth, Rowlandson and Gillray

Audience of the Ambassador with the Grand Vizir, probably painted over twenty years after Montagu's return from Constantinople by Antonio Guardi and members of his studio in Venice.

weren't simply imagining things. But even today we do tend to overlook the Inclosure Act and to criticize those degenerates who, having fecklessly crowded into London, went quickly to the bad on strong drink and weak women.

The Inclosure Acts made possible estates like West Dean and Thoresby, while leaving very many yeomen farmers landless and depriving the rural poor of free protein, grazing and fuel — which from time immemorial had made the difference between 'just enough' and 'destitution'. This 'rationalization' of farming not only satisfied the greed of the great land-owning families (its immediate motive) but contributed to England's evolution as a modern nation. The scandal was that those Acts were enforced so ruthlessly. In 1798 Arthur Young, the rector's son who devoted his life to agricultural reform, noted sadly – 'The poor may say and with truth, "Parliament may be tender of property: all I know is that I had a cow and an Act of Parliament has taken it from me."'

Professor Basil Williams has explained that during the first half of the eighteenth century 'the chief function of government was held to be "the Preservation of property"...however oppressive such a system might be to the weaker members of society...'. Hence the infamous Black Act of 1723, which created almost fifty new capital offences, was passed by Parliament in four weeks without serious debate or division and remained in force for a century. Its sole purpose was to defend the property of the privileged. Sir Leon Radzinowicz, the legal historian, has written that 'There is hardly a criminal act which did not come within a criminal code with anything like so many capital provisions as there were in this single statute.'

After 1723, any man who shall unlawfully and wilfully hunt, wound, kill, destroy, or steal any red or fallow deer, or unlawfully rob any warren or place where conies or hares are usually kept, or shall unlawfully steal or take away any fish out of any river or pond ... or shall cut down or otherwise destroy any trees planted in any avenue, or growing in any orchard, garden or plantation, for ornament, shelter or profit ... shall be adjudged guilty of felony, and shall suffer death as in cases of felony, without benefit of clergy.

When Elizabeth Pierrepont died in 1698 she left a huge fortune (some £12,000) to her youngest granddaughter, Evelyn, and £1,000 to Frances but nothing, inexplicably, to Lady Mary. Evelyn then went to live with an aunt, Lady Cheyne, while the others were cared for by servants, either in their father's London house or at Thoresby. Lady Mary's architectural tastes were formed by her adolescence in this superb Palladian house with its well-stocked deer-park, sixty-five acre lake and three-quarters-of-a-mile-long canal which fed many fountains in vast formal gardens. But to her the most important of all her father's possessions were his town and country libraries, where she indefatigably made up for her governess's much-scorned deficiences.

One pities that nameless woman; most governesses would have seemed deficient if required to cope with a thirteen-year-old who so admired Ovid's *Metamorphoses* that she was determined to teach herself Latin—and who had already digested, among much else, the plays of Beaumont and Fletcher, Dryden, Rowe, Lee, Otway, Congreve, Molière, Corneille, plus numerous bulky romances in French and English, including *Grand Cyrus, Pharimond, Almahide, Parthenissa*. By 1703 Lady Mary's own writings were already voluminous and she then copied them into an album entitled *Poems, Songs &c. Dedicated to the Fair Hands of the Beauteous Herminsilde by her most obedient Strephon*. However, the Preface revealed a reassuringly normal mixture of adolescent defensiveness and shy pride —

> *1 Question not but here is very many faults but if any*
> *reasonable Person considers 3 things they wou'd for-*
> *give them*
> *1 I am a woman*
> *2 without any advantage of Education*
> *3 all these was writ at the age of 14*

By the age of fifteen Lady Mary had filled another album with *The Entire Works of Clarinda.* In a prose allegory, describing Strephon's quest for true love, she affirmed —showing the influence of all those Restoration comedies—that 'Love and marriage are irreconcilable enemies'. A year later she was longing to be rich enough to found an Anglican convent for learned ladies, with the foundress as self-appointed abbess. This ambition must have been inspired by the controversial writings of Mary Astell, a Newcastle merchant's 'bluestocking' daughter then based in Chelsea who later became one of her close friends. Even as a daydream, it would have appalled her solidly Whig family.

Meanwhile, throughout the uneasy 'half-Stuart' decades, Lord Kingston had been manoeuvring to establish himself as a political leader. Parliamentary democracy still lay in the womb of time and, as Charles Chenevix Trench has pointed out in *George 11:*

> *Politicians had no parliamentary salaries, direc-*
> *torships, or trade union emoluments to sustain them...*
> *Election to Parliament, preferably as a county mem-*
> *ber, was the plum, attained only by a fortunate few.*
> *There was no better lottery than the House of*
> *Commons to push one's fortune... Those who gave*
> *steady support to the Ministry expected to be*
> *rewarded for their services, not in cash but in jobs for*
> *themselves and for their protégés.*

Those jobs allowed men to help themselves from the till of public revenues, through their control of military, excise and Church finances. The top posts offered limitless opportunities; that of Paymaster-General made it possible for immense fortunes to be accumulated by, among others, the Earl of Ranelagh, the Duke of Chandos and Sir Robert Walpole. This system resembled the political administrations of various non-European societies which have always believed that a man's first duty is to his family. In 1748 Lady Mary emphasised this point to her daughter, Lady Bute, whose husband had recently become a trusted friend of Frederick, Prince of Wales:

> *I am very glad you are admitted into the conversa-*
> *tion of the Prince and Princess. It is a favour that you*
> *ought to cultivate for the good of your family, which is*
> *now numerous, and it may one day be of great advan-*
> *tage. I think Lord Bute much in the right to endeavour*
> *the continuance of it, and it would be imprudent in*
> *you to neglect what may be of great use to your child-*
> *ren. I pray God bless both you and them...*

We get the same message from a 1751 epitaph quoted by G.M. Trevelyan:

> *Here rests all that was mortal of*
> *Mrs Elizabeth Bate,*
> *Relict of the Reverend Richard Bate*
> *She was honourably descended*
> *And by means of her alliance to*
> *The illustrious family of Stanhope*
> *She had the merit to obtain*
> *For her husband and children*
> *Twelve several employments*
> *In Church and State.*

By 1700 the Church had become shamelessly Erastian, an easily manipulated State prop led by venal bishops who drew annual salaries ranging from £3,000 to £7,000 plus perks. Thousands of parsons, usually half-starved and quarter-educated, lived on less than £50 a year — and hundreds on less than £20. During election campaigns Bishops were expected to exert themselves, as unscrupulously as might be necessary, on behalf of candidates sponsored by their ecclesiastical patrons. In the House of Lords their votes were then of major importance and by 1730 the bench had been so skilfully packed that Walpole could count on twenty-four out of twenty-six episcopal votes. The suppression of the convocations of the lower clergy — a measure true to the political spirit of the age — meant that for some 150 years there was virtually no communication between the bishops and cathedral clergy and their rural 'brethren'.

(These convocations, which had dealt energetically with religious matters in the sixteenth and early seventeenth centuries, also served as a safety valve for the grievances of lower clergy. But they were firmly downgraded at the Restoration, losing many privileges including that of voting clerical subsidies.)

Not surprisingly, Lady Mary seldom referred to religion unless pragmatically in a Tory/Whig context. Like most of her aristocratic Whig contemporaries, she valued the Established Church not as a fount of spiritual sustenance but as a useful device for maintaining law and order by intimidating the lower classes. Her magistrate cousin, Henry Fielding an eloquent champion of those classes dryly noted:

Heaven and hell, when well rung in the ears of those who have not yet learned that there are no such places, are by no means words of little or no signification.

When living in Avignon (1742-6) Lady Mary was startled to hear that Selina, Countess of Huntingdon, had become patroness of the rabble-rousing Wesley brothers and George Whitefield. But she had too keen a sense of humour to support the Duchess of Buckingham, a notoriously deadly female who in 1743 excoriated the defiant Countess:

I thank your ladyship for the information concerning the Methodist preachers. Their doctrines are most repulsive, and strongly tinctured with impertinence, and disrespect towards their superiors. It is monstrous to be told that you have a heart as sinful as the common wretches that crawl the earth. I cannot but wonder that your ladyship should relish any sentiments so much at variance with high rank and good breeding.

When Lord Kingston become Marquess of Dorchester his eldest daughter was seventeen and it then occurred to him that she should acquire some political accomplishments, like Italian and drawing — and carving, too, since she was now of an age to preside over his frequent marathon dinner parties. A carving master gave her lessons thrice weekly and soon she was exercising her new skill, which in that era demanded both the tact of an ambassador and the brawn of a butcher. Although prevented from joining guests at the table, she had many other opportunities to enjoy the company of her father's friends. These included Dr Samuel Garth (the Yorkshire physician, poet and translator of Ovid), dramatist William Congreve, Richard Steele and Joseph Addison — the last two close friends of an aspiring young politician named Wortley Montagu.

Mr Edward Wortley Montagu was a grandson of the first Earl of Sandwich. His father, the Honourable Sidney Montagu, had married an heiress named Anne Wortley, a ward of the Earl, and taken her name as part of the 'deal'. In confusing consequence, his son was known sometimes as Wortley, sometimes as Montagu and sometimes as Wortley Montagu. Contemporary pedants seemed to favour 'Montagu' but Lady Mary settled for 'Wortley'.

History does not record the couple's first meeting but Wortley's younger sister Anne, one of Lady Mary's closest friends, seems to have introduced them. At first their courtship proceeded unremarkably, if a trifle more slowly and cautiously than was usual when an eligible young man fell in love with a suitable young woman. Wortley seemed much impressed by Lady Mary's learning, wit, beauty and poise. He sent her fervently complimentary letters, in his sister's name and handwriting, and the replies, ostensibly addressed to Miss Anne Wortley, were not calculated to lessen his fervour. By the time Lady Mary went to London for the winter season of 1708 Mr Wortley was tacitly recognized as her suitor. Some of her contemporaries may have thought him rather too elderly: he was then aged thirty. But in most respects he seemed 'ideal', a gravely handsome, genuinely scholarly and adequately wealthy young man who had gone from Westminster School to Trinity College, Cambridge, and so on to the Middle Temple, being called to the bar at the age of twenty-one. A three-year Grand Tour followed, during which he was accompanied for much of the time by his intimate friend, Joseph Addison, then on a pension of £300 from the Earl of Halifax. The amiable Addison was not noted for original thinking but his flair for regurgitating other people's new thoughts in easily digested forms made him a valuable ally of politicians.

In 1705 Wortley had been elected to Parliament for the Borough of Huntingdon, a Whig seat controlled by his cousin Lord Sandwich, and during the winter of 1708 Lady Mary heard his being much praised for a recent speech supporting a Bill to naturalize Huguenot refugees. It is unsurprising that by then she wanted to marry him, though it is impossible to determine whether she was in love with Wortley the man or merely in love with love. She had however, been bred to respond to the stimulus of Whig politics and had acquired a taste not only for the company of cultivated men but for the multitudinous intrigues, conducted with wit and erudition, which filled their conversations and almost filled their lives. She would not have been unmoved by the fact that Addison dedicated the second volume of the *Tatler* to Wortley. And she was very moved by the fact that when she admitted to ignorance of Quintus Curtius (he who recorded Alexander's Asia Minor campaigns), Wortley sent her a magnificent edition, flatteringly inscribed in verse. Surely here was a man who valued her hard-won intellectual accomplishments and with whom she could never be bored...

Wortley's informal, slow-motion courtship continued throughout 1709. At the end of the year his sister Anne's sudden death deeply distressed Lady Mary; but the couple still met regularly — at Court, or at the London houses of mutual friends — though their tête-à-tête opportunities were fewer. This perhaps suited Lady Mary, who seems to have found it easier to deal in writing with a relationship that had gradually become more intense and frustratingly complex. Wortley was proving not only fairly hesitant but moodily jealous, insultingly suspicious and irrationally possessive. They had by now discussed the possibility of marriage but numerous signs suggested that Wortley's total lack of humour would endanger a permanent relationship by always exacerbating minor squabbles. Yet at this stage it was plain that beneath the surface discords both were as deeply in love as their natures allowed.

To her devoted yet dilatory suitor the twenty-one-year-old Lady Mary penned a series of notably honest and realistic letters. Every phrase, every adjective, every nuance seemed designed either to prove the sincerity of the writer's feelings or to bring Wortley to the altar with the minimum of delay — but only if that could be done without deceiving him on any level, emotional, intellectual or economic. On 25 April 1710 she wrote:

> *One part of my character is not so good nor the other so bad as you fancy it. Should we ever live together you would be disappointed both ways; you would find an easy equality of temper you do not expect, and a thousand faults you do not imagine. You think if you married me I should be passionately fond of you one month and of somebody else the next. Neither would happen. I can esteem, I can be a friend, but I don't know whether I can love... Make no answer to this. If you can like me on my own terms, 'tis not to me you must make your proposals. If not, to what purpose is our correspondence? However, preserve me your friendship, which I think of with a great deal of pleasure and some vanity. If ever you see me married, I flatter myself you'll see a conduct you would not be sorry your wife should imitate.*

Reading such letters, Wortley may well have felt intimidated by the subtle strength of Lady Mary's personality. When she rebuked him for putting her in 'a pretty pickle' by using indiscreet channels of communication, which had led her father to suspect the closeness of their friendship, he implied that if only he could be sure of their life-long compatability he would gladly approach Lord Dorchester. A fortnight later Lady Mary ended another long letter imperiously, 'Either think of me no more, or think in the way you ought'. Cowed, Wortley at last overcame his doubts and soon after made a formal proposal to Lord Dorchester.

Both sides appointed lawyers and lest Lady Mary might attempt to influence the negotiations she was exiled to West Dean, unvisited since her grandmother's death. Lord Dorchester deemed Thoresby too close to Wharncliffe Lodge, Wortley's Yorkshire home; evidently he respected his eldest daughter's ingenuity and tenacity.

Other men might be able to treat their female offspring as mere marketable commodities — cards to be adroitly shuffled in the aristocratic pack to give the dealer the best possible hand for the preservation and increase of family property. But already there were ominous indications that Lady Mary would, somehow, assert herself as a free spirit. And very likely Lord Dorchester had diagnosed Wortley as too malleable a creature to ignore his beloved's views on the marriage contract.

The Marquess was adamant that his daughter must have a fixed establishment in London — not just lodgings rented for each season — and that Wortley's estate must be entailed on her first-born son. Wortley was no less adamant (but much more reasonable) in his refusal to 'entail blind'; and he insisted that he could not afford to invest £10,000 — the minimum outlay — on an appropriate 'fixed establishment'. Neither man would give in and during the next few months their argument, only thinly disguised, was developed in the pages of the *Tatler*. The issue of 18 July condemned that degradation of women inseparable from mercenary marriages:

> *Her first lover has ten to one against him. The very hour after he has opened his heart and his rent-rolls he is made no other use of but to raise the price... While the poor lover very innocently waits, till the plenipotentiaries at the inns of court have debated about the alliance, all the partisans of the lady throw difficulties in the way, till other offers come in; and the man who came first is not put in possession, until she has been refused by half the town.*

At the end of July Lady Mary was still semi-imprisoned at West Dean, but Wortley had devised ways of keeping up their correspondence. On 28 July he informed her that negotiations had completely broken down; even had the lawyers created further room for manoeuvre neither man was inclined to compromise. She swiftly replied that her father was already wheeling and dealing with another suitor, but Wortley chose to ignore this warning. He complained of feeling unwell, his appetite was waning, he must go to take the Spa waters... From Harwich he wrote asking for letters during his two months' absence in Belgium and Lady Mary obliged with six — which he failed to claim until his return to England. And he never once wrote to her.

While Wortley was abroad England was shaken by a political crisis. Henry Sacheverell, a Jacobite High Church clergyman, was tried for preaching a seditious sermon and *not punished*. After this portent, the Whigs expected their overwhelming defeat in the autumn election. Wortley however was among those re-elected and on hearing that news he hastened home to help make life difficult for the new Tory Parliament. He arrived in London on 20 October and Swift reported in his *Journal to Stella* that he had shared a bottle of wine that evening with Addison and Wortley. In such circumstances a modern MP might hurry to consult with his constituency officials and party whips; but both Swift and Addison (who by then was secretary to Ireland's Lord Lieutenant) were as involved as anyone could be in the contemporary political upheavals. During the Augustan Age England's literary and political worlds were intertwined as never before or since — to poetry's detriment. As David Cecil has observed in another context:

> *The greatest poets concern themselves with the most important issues raised by the human condition. But they seldom identify these with topical public events of their time. Chaucer tells us nothing of what he thought about the Peasants' Revolt, nor do we hear Shakespeare's views about the conflicts stirred up by the Reformation...*

Whatever Wortley's defects as a suitor, he had remarkable integrity — at least by 18th-century standards — as a politician. In December 1710 he put forward his Place Bill for a second hearing; had it become law it would have greatly reduced Parliamentary corruption by forbidding any Member to accept a Ministry pension — 'pension' being a contemporary euphemism for the sort of bribe that bought indiscriminate loyalty. Significantly, this bill was passed by the Commons but defeated in the Lords.

Wortley now resumed his correspondence with Lady Mary and on both sides it became increasingly tetchy. He longed to marry her, but as a prudent businessman would concede nothing to Lord Dorchester. She was made edgy by his jealous snooping on her social engagements and resented his indifference to the risks she ran for his sake. Her father frightened her, badly: ''Tis so very dangerous for me to write to you, I tremble every time I do it'. Lest gossip might circulate, she refused to meet Wortley at Corticelli's warehouse or Colman's toyshop — well-known rendezvous for illicit lovers. Their stressful courtship by now resembled a Richardson novel, as Lady Mary herself remarked many years later when reading the newly published *Clarissa*. All their meetings had to be strictly (no longer half-playfully) clandestine, which unpleasantly heightened tension; neither was of an age or disposition to enjoy the drama of furtively snatched conversations during carefully arranged 'chance encounters'. Nor was there any reason to hope for a happy ending — unless someone changed the rules of the game.

At this stage some of Lady Mary's letters suggest that her solitary years of reading and day-dreaming in the library at Thoresby, may have engendered conflicting ideals and emotions. She sometimes quoted from Prior's ballad of Henry and Emma, a tear-jerker about an heiress who eloped with a bandit-lover. Possibly she rather fancied the role of Noble-minded Bride whose Pure and Ardent Love scorns the trammels of marriage-contracts. To choose love without a settlement would of course be extremely hazardous. Her father and family might (probably would) punish elopement by rejection. And if her marriage then failed and Wortley refused to support her...? Yet she was irresistibly attracted by this high-risk choice. It would be a spectacular spurning of the hated conventions and also a signal that she was nobody's chattel, that she had staked her claim to life-long personal liberty — in a garret, if necessary. When questioned about her dowry she denied knowing the figure and added, 'People in my way are sold like slaves; and I cannot tell what price my master will put on me'.

Early in 1711 Lady Mary was outraged by her father's take-over of his too-submissive heir's future. While still a legal 'infant' her beloved brother William was married to the sixteen-year-old Rachel Baynton, an illegitimate daughter of John Hall, whose immense estates had been settled on the young Lord Kingston — at the expense of Hall's legitimate heirs. The marriage contract required Lord Dorchester simultaneously to settle his own estates on his son, having provided an £8,000 dowry for each of his daughters. These shenanigans needed the 'Marquess of Dorchester Estate Act', which received the Royal Assent in May 1711. But, as Lady Mary was wont sententiously to observe, 'Neither riches nor power can secure real happiness'. At the age of twenty William died of small-pox, leaving an eighteen-year-old widow, two children and a shattered father. Subsequently Lady Kingston ('a poor silly soul', in Lady Mary's view) lived openly with the alarmingly unstable Lord Scarborough, by whom she had two sons in the confident expectation that one day he would marry her. When he suddenly stated that he had no such intention she completely lost the power of speech and died within twenty-four hours. Lord Scarborough became engaged to the Duchess of Manchester a few years later but committed suicide just before their wedding-day. On hearing this news Lady Mary commented, 'I confess I look upon his engagement with the duchess not as the cause, but sign, that he was mad'.

In March 1711 Lord Dorchester forced his wayward daughter to promise never again to communicate with Wortley and once more she was banished to West Dean; evidently his lordship had been hearing gossip. Rightly disregarding this enforced promise, Lady Mary informed Wortley of these developments and challenged him to resume negotiations with her father. Jealous doubts were again tormenting him; his beloved had many other eager admirers and could hardly be expected to eschew all male company for his sake. In an effort to reassure him she wrote:

Perhaps I have been indiscreet; I came young into the hurry of the world. A great innocence and an undesigning gaiety may possibly have been construed as coquetry and a desire of being followed, though never meant by me... I know not anything I can say more to show my perfect desire of pleasing you and making you easy than to proffer to be confined with you in what manner you please. Would any woman but me renounce all the world for one, or would any man but you be insensible of such a proof of sincerity?

Wortley received this letter in Yorkshire; he had retreated to his home territory, announcing to friends that he was planning a new bachelor life far from London and the possibility of ever again meeting Lady Mary. Having decided that their friendship must end, because she did not love him, he wrote on 2 May, 'Adieu, dearest L.M. This once be assured you will not deceive me. I expect no answer'. His suspicions may have been confirmed when

'L.M.' took his farewell seriously enough to remain silent for five months. But then came a brief note explaining that her autumn return to town would be delayed because of smallpox in the house next-door to her father's in Arlington Street.

Meanwhile Addison had been urging Wortley to 'put his hand to the plow' — that is, to help oppose the Treaty of Utrecht, which the Tories were determined to sign with France. After six months in Yorkshire, where his neighbours were chiefly interested in hunting and coal-mines, Wortley was susceptible to Addison's persuasion and by the end of the year the two friends were sharing lodgings — and a good cook — in Kensington. Lady Mary was also back in Arlington Street, but there were no more clandestine communications until March 1712. Then Wortley wrote suggesting a meeting because he had 'for some time been grieved to hear you was to be confined to one you did not like, and in another country'.

In April 1710 Lady Mary had written: 'I will never think of anything without the consent of my family'. Two years later, this docility had evaporated in the heat of her fear of a suitor who sounds as though he had strayed backwards in time from the Drones Club. The Honourable Clotworthy Skeffington, son and heir to Irish Viscount Massereene and about eight years her senior, had been very attentive during the past two seasons; Wortley had often complained of having seen him 'pressing close to her' in the Drawing-Room (at Court) and escorting her to assemblies, operas and the park. In fact Lady Mary found him peculiarly unattractive and he had received no encouragement as a suitor. But now he had made an offer which delighted Lord Dorchester: a fixed London establishment, 'pin-money' of £500 a year and £1,200 a year should Lady Mary be widowed.

There were moreover no entailment snags; the future Lord Massereene would automatically be succeeded by his eldest son. Yet Lord Dorchester was not being as smart an operator as he liked to imagine. Wortley, though much given to bewailing his relative poverty, had a fatter present income and rather better long-term prospects than had Skeffington, whose extravagant habits were to necessitate the sale of the family's oldest estate and who, according to his father-in-law, left his affairs 'in no good condition' when he died in 1757.

Before the signing of the contract Lady Mary made one last desperate appeal to her father, protesting that she could never love, or even tolerate the proximity of, this Irish suitor. She begged to be allowed to remain single: for life, if Lord Dorchester so insisted. He replied that she could of course make her own decision, but he would indeed insist on her never marrying *anyone* else and would leave her a meagre £400 a year. He urged her to discuss the problem with her relatives, who predictably chorused that a sensible woman doesn't have to be *in love* to be happily married. Lady Mary then gave her father the impression that she would after all obey him, while simultaneously giving Wortley the impression that if he took no action she could be bullied into becoming Lady Mary Skeffington.

Soon elopement was being discussed. Wortley suffered agonies of ill-tempered indecision, Lady Mary winced at the thought of living in England as a pitied or mocked 'poor relation'; already her younger sister Evelyn was securely married to Lord Gower with a 'fixed establishment' in London and a choice of country seats. She unrealistically suggested that they should settle in Naples: the idea of living abroad had always appealed to her. In Italy, she argued, comparative poverty need not prevent their enjoying a life of modest comfort. Reliable sunshine, Mediterranean vivacity and Classical remains would augment married bliss and more than make up for absent luxuries. She was naïve enough to believe Wortley when he seemed to share her enthusiasm for a romantic exile, though it would have required the abandoning of his burgeoning political career and the neglect of those time-consuming but lucrative coal-mines on which his family's prosperity depended.

In July 1712 Lady Mary was sent to the family's Acton villa, where her brother was then living with his wife and baby — the future second Duke of Kingston. On 19 July her close friend, Mrs Hewet, wrote to the Duchess of Newcastle: 'Lady Mary Pierrepont is not yet married but is to be very soon...' Elaborate celebrations were planned; already Lord Dorchester had spent £400 on her wedding-clothes. Then came a postponement; someone noticed an ambiguity in the wording of the marriage contract and an amended version had to be sent to Ireland for re-signing.

Even at this stage, Wortley remained less than resolute — half-committed to an elopement but still bewailing the loss of the Pierrepont dowry. That loss would, he ungallantly pointed out, enrage his own father, who knew the Wortley Montagu heir could have first choice from among an array of substantially endowed if unexciting Yorkshire maidens. In reply Lady Mary acknowledged:

I am as sensible as you yourself can be of the generosity of your proposal. Perhaps there is no other man that would take a woman under these disadvantages, and I am grateful to you with all the warmth gratitude can inspire...

But then she crisply pointed out that she too was sacrificing wealth for love — not only the ample Massereene settlement but the £8,000 that would have rewarded her for obeying her father.

On Monday 11 August Lord Dorchester briefly visited Acton to order Lady Mary to go to West Dean on 18 August and remain there until her wedding-day; he may have heard rumours that made him more than usually mistrustful of his daughter. At once she wrote to Wortley:

My father has been here today. He bid me prepare to go to Dean this day sennight [week]... Tell me what you intend to do. If you can think of me for your companion at Naples, come next Sunday under this garden wall, on the road, some little distance from the summer house, at ten o'clock. It will be dark, and it is necessary it should be so. I could wish you would begin our journey immediately; I have no fancy to stay in London or near it. I will not pretend to justify my proceeding. Everybody will object to me, why I did not do this sooner, before I put a man to the charge of equipage, etc.? I shall not care to tell them, you did not ask me sooner... I shall not be surprised if you have changed your mind, or even if you should change your mind after you have consented to this. I would have no tie upon you but inclination; I have nothing to do with your word or your honour etc. The scheme I propose to myself is living in an agreeable country with a man that I like, that likes me, and forgetting the rest of the world as if Naples were the Garden of Eden. If there is any part of this scheme that does not agree either with your affairs or inclinations do not do it.

Wortley agreed to this plan, yet the incessant bickering that had marked their singular courtship continued on paper throughout the next week, apparently intensified rather than soothed by their imminent union. On the Friday Wortley was still suspiciously brooding, 'If you are likely to think of cuckoldom you are mad if you marry me'. Yet again Lady Mary dealt with her lover's paranoid jealousy, and then wondered, 'Are you sure you will love me for ever? Shall we never repent?' On the Saturday she urged Wortley to abandon any secret lingering hopes he might have of eventual financial benefits. Her father would be unforgiving — 'Reflect now for the last time in what manner you must take me. I shall come to you with only a night-gown and petticoat, and that is all you will get with me.' She then suggested a timetable change: it would be better if Wortley collected her early on Monday morning.

There is some uncertainty (and a whiff of Restoration comedy) about the events of the next four days. Wortley did not obtain the special (bann-evading) marriage licence until Sunday the 17th, probably by way of preserving secrecy. But it seems he was unsuccessful in this endeavour. Lady Mary received an agitating letter from him early on the Sunday morning and replied immediately:

If my F. knows of it, tis past. I shall be sent to Dean early tomorrow morning, and hindered tonight. He comes today. I am coward enough to apprehend his rage to a degree of being ready to swoon. I know he may make me do what he will.

Someone warned Wortley just in time that Lord Dorchester had been told about his corresponding with Lady Mary all week. His lordship invaded Acton that forenoon, in the expected rage, and ordered his son to supervise Lady Mary's journey to West Dean on the following day. Throughout that Sunday, she hoped for a reply from Wortley to her early morning letter: but none came. At dawn next day she crept out on to the balcony, presumably with her night-gown and petticoat in the 1712 equivalent of a plastic bag. When her lover's coach had not appeared by seven o'clock she gave up and was soon being escorted to West Dean by Lord Kingston.

Wortley's non-arrival at the pre-arranged time has never been explained. In view of Lord Dorchester's discovery of their correspondence, perhaps he judged that a coach noisily arriving outside the Acton villa in the dawn quietness might prove an unsound elopement technique. When he arrived later in the morning he was distraught to find Lady Mary gone and rode hard in pursuit, accompanied by a servant. He spent that night at an inn, unaware that the West Dean party were fellow-lodgers; they had arrived shortly before him and Lady Mary — understandably suffering from nervous exhaustion — had retired early.

Next morning (19 August) the pursuit continued but now Lady Mary was aware of being pursued and contrived to scribble several short notes to encourage her lover. At this point one has to suspect sympathetic fraternal collusion. On 20 August she wrote to Wortley from West Dean, lamenting the inn misfortune:

We have more ill luck that any other people. Had you writ in your first letter where you intended to be etc. I could have ris up by myself at four o'clock and come to your chamber, perhaps undiscovered... After my woman was up she watched me so much it was impossible; she apprehended you was in the house... Had I not been sick and gone to bed sooner than usual I should have seen your gentleman and then he would have told me where you was... If you are still determined I still hope it may be possible one way or other. I have since asked my brother what he could have done if I had been married in that way. He made answer, he durst not have taken me with him; we must have stayed in the inn, and how odd that would have been!

There is no official record of when and where Lady Mary actually became Wortley Montagu. However, on 15 October 1712 her sister, Lady Frances, wrote to a friend from West Dean:

A week after her arrival to this place she went off with Mr Wortley Montagu and was married at Salisbury. My father is not yet reconciled to her. She writes everybody word she's perfectly happy, and it seems has found Paradise (as she terms it herself) when she expected but Limbo.

That Paradise was soon lost — if it ever in fact existed. On neither side is it possible to disentangle the motives for this patently foredoomed marriage and it is futile to speculate about what, precisely, went wrong. But *something* went very wrong very quickly and within two months of the elopement Wortley was spending long periods away from his bride, attending to coal-mining or political interests. Naples was mentioned no more and Lady Mary sat pregnant and lonely and disillusioned in various country houses belonging to Wortley's friends or relatives — often empty but for the servants — where she could live cheaply while avoiding the critical scrutiny of her own circle. She rarely complained about her solitude but could not conceal the deep hurt inflicted on her by Wortley's apparent indifference to her welfare and callous refusal to reply to her letters. By the time their son was born, in May 1713, it must have been plain that marriage would provide none of the affectionate companionship and mutual intellectual enrichment to which she had looked forward.

Why, many people asked, had Wortley agreed to an elopement? True, Lady Mary was beautiful, witty, intelligent, politically well-connected and, for a woman, unusually erudite. But marriage to her, without a dowry or contract of any kind, represented economic lunacy — and on economic issues Wortley was known to be very far from lunatic. Was he then, in his own cold-fish way, as much in love with her as he ever could be with anyone? Or, more likely, did Skeffington's near-victory cause his possessiveness to overcome his parsimony? Jealousy is a well-known aphrodisiac.

In 1729, by which date Wortley had developed the habit of writing maxims in imitation of La Rochefoucauld, he mused: 'We are apt to fall in love with those whose professions, we are persuaded, will make us secure of their affections; but when we think we have the desired security we are apt to lose the passion'. It seems probable that Wortley did not have much physical passion to lose. Nor perhaps did Lady Mary, despite her later reputation. She was intensely emotional, 'enthusiastic in her friendships', frankly dependent on affection. But more than once she expressed her distaste (fastidious, rather than puritanical) for the casual liaisons then so popular in fashionable London.

Lady Mary's fortitude, resilience and determination to enjoy life were severely tested by her marriage — and not found wanting. At its worse, being Lady Mary Wortley Montagu was preferable to being Lady Mary Skeffington; all her life she remained gratefully conscious that Wortley had accepted her 'with night-gown and petticoat'. Remembering her vehement pre-marital pledges, she refused to be embittered by her husband's frigid detachment and was for many years as good a wife as he would allow her to be.

Elopement without a contract had meant entrusting herself to Wortley's generosity — never his most conspicuous characteristic. He was, however, an honourable man and in this respect at least gave her no cause for reproach. And so she discovered that her relatives had been right when they asserted that a woman could be happily married, or at least happy *and* married, without being 'in love'.

Having so often assured Wortley that she could cope on a modest income, Lady Mary felt bound to cultivate frugality as one of her chief virtues. When she went house hunting in the summer of 1713 — unaided by Wortley, then engaged in a 'very disagreeable and fatiguing' fight for a Parliamentary seat — she decided on settling in Middlethorpe, a village so close to York that friends could come for short economical visits instead of expensive din-

Audience of the Ambassador with the Sultan, attributed to studio of Antonio Guardi, c.1735-45.

ners. Next she arranged furniture removal by water — much the cheapest method because England's roads had been neglected since, literally, the Romans left. In winter or wet weather they were impassable to wheeled traffic and goods had to be transported by expensive pack-horse trains. (Apparently some law of nature decrees that when imperial powers withdraw roads collapse; it happened too when the Ottomans left the Balkans and the Europeans departed from Africa.)

By mid-September Lady Mary and Wortley, with their infant son (another Edward Wortley Montagu), were together in their own home for the first time. Wortley had recently lost his seat despite lavish spending, which Lady Mary had advised him was unwise in the prevailing politi-cal climate, and so he was able to spend much of the next year with his family, when not seeing to the Montagu mines. This period was particularly dangerous for miners and challenging for mine-owners. Shafts were being sunk more deeply every year by engineers who as yet lacked the necessary expertise and were gaining it through grim experience. In 1708 and 1710 horrific explosions in north Durham, close to the Montagu properties, had killed hundreds of men and destroyed many nearby houses. In 1712 a machine for pumping water out of mines had been invented in Lancashire (the first genuine steam-engine) and Wortley was keenly investigating its possibilities, both as a safety device and a profit-booster. As G.M. Trevelyan has pointed out:

The ownership of mines and an interest in their working was not deemed beneath the dignity of the greatest noblemen of the land, for in England, unlike most countries of Europe, all minerals except gold and silver have been treated as the property of the owner of the soil.

The following year was momentous for England — and also for Lady Mary's family. In July, to the consternation of all good Whigs, Lord Dorchester allowed his daughter Frances to marry a leading Tory — a thirty-seven-year-old widower, the Earl of Mar, then a Secretary of State for Scotland strongly tainted with Jacobite sympathies. Lady Mary was incensed but not surprised; she guessed the reason for her father's aberration. And sure enough he himself had remarried within a week of the Mar wedding. His bride, the youngest daughter of the Earl of Portland, was only a year older than Lady Mary and had long been assiduously wooed by the elderly Marquess, whom she had firmly refused to marry until all his daughters were off the Thoresby and Arlington Street scenes.

Then on 1 August 1714, the last reigning Stuart died. At once the Elector of Hanover was proclaimed King — but would all his new subjects accept him? Tension rose throughout the kingdom and from Middlethorpe Lady Mary wrote to Wortley, in London:

I cannot forbear taking it something unkindly that you do not write to me when you may be assured I am in a great fright, and know not certainly what to expect upon this sudden change... This morning all the principal men of any figure took post from York for London, and we are alarmed with the fear of attempts from Scotland, though all Protestants here seem unanimous for the Hanover succession. The poor young ladies at Castle Howard are as much afraid as I am, being left all alone without any hopes of seeing

their father again this eight or nine months. They have sent to desire me very earnestly to come to them and bring my boy... During this uncertainty I think it will be a safe retreat, for Middlethorpe stands exposed to plunderers... We are alarmed with a story of a fleet being seen from the coasts of Scotland and an express went from thence through York to the Earl of Mar.

Lady Mary spent a month at Castle Howard, seat of the Earl of Carlisle, who as one of the Lord Justices had to welcome the Elector to London. By the beginning of September everyone had calmed down; it was generally agreed that an immediate rebellion was unlikely. Back in Middlethorpe, Lady Mary was cheered by the news that her father had come round to Wortley and received him as his son-in-law. In the words of Robert Halsband (Lady Mary's most recent biographer, to whom I am much indebted), 'No belated dowry or settlement came from him; victory brought only the moral advantage of family unity'. However, family unity was to be important during the months and years ahead.

At Court and at Westminster, Lady Mary noted, Queen Anne's death was followed by a vicious frenzy of 'shoving and thrusting who shall be foremost'. From Middlethorpe she tirelessly encouraged her husband's political ambitions and sent him detailed practical advice on the running of his new election campaign. Given her background, it would have been odd had she not entered the electoral fray with sword unsheathed. She had matured in an atmosphere of vigorous Whig versus Tory debate and her own energy, dammed up behind the conventions of time, sought release through her husband's career. Repeatedly she showed more acumen and craftiness than Wortley, Addison and Swift combined. In another age, she might well have been England's first woman Prime Minister.

Towards the end of September, Wortley's campaign

manager reminded him:

No modest man ever did or ever will make his fortune. Your friend Lord Halifax, Robert Walpole, and all other remarkable instances of quick advancement have been remarkably impudent... A moderate merit with a large share of impudence is more probable to be advanced than the greatest qualifications with it... 'Tis my interest to believe (as I do) that you deserve everything and are capable of everything, but nobody else will believe it if they see you get nothing. I cannot see why you should not pretend to be Speaker [of the House of Commons]. I believe all the Whigs would be for you, and I fancy you have a considerable interest among the Tories. The reputation of being thoroughly of no party is (I think) of use in this affair, and I believe people generally esteem you impartial...

Those comments suggest what future events confirmed; Wortley was an astute, hard-working businessman but not 'impudent' enough to be an eighteenth-century political achiever. This may have been one of his attractions for Lady Mary during their courtship, but plainly it exasperated her when a shift of the kaleidoscope offered him valuable opportunities for advancement. If her judgement was accurate—'I believe people generally esteem you impartial' — this fills out our picture of a man of integrity and helps explain the antipathy that always existed between Wortley and Robert Walpole. By 1714 Walpole had been Secretary at War and Treasurer of the Navy, and had been expelled from the Commons on corruption charges. Which did not prevent him, such was his 'impudence', becoming England's first Prime Minister and amassing prodigious wealth while running the country for some twenty years.

The next four months were action-packed. Following the coronation of George I in October, Lord Halifax became First Lord of the Treasury and offered his cousin an appointment as one of the four junior Commissioners. Wortley thought any non-cabinet post beneath him but sulkily accepted under pressure from Lady Mary. He then stood for Westminster, a seat controlled by the Court, and was returned to Parliament in January 1715. His wife was glad to exchange Middlethorpe and frugality for a prominent position at the Court of St James. Papa had just become Duke of Kingston-upon-Hull and was soon to be appointed Lord Privy Seal — his rewards for energetically supporting the Hanoverians. Wortley was not only a royally sponsored M P but heir-presumptive to the Earldom of Sandwich. She herself was already much respected in literary circles and could now cultivate the company of Alexander Pope, John Gay, William Congreve, the Abbé Conti and the Addison/Steele set. Before long she had also befriended both the King's mistresses and was working on the Prince and Princess of Wales. The only shadow was cast by Lord Mar; as one of the several ineffectual leaders of the '15 Rebellion he had to flee from Scotland to France in February 1716, leaving Lady Mary's favourite sister to fend for herself in London.

Then, in mid-December, this sweet year turned sour. Since her brother's death in June 1713 Lady Mary had dreaded smallpox above any other disease and now it threatened her own life. She resigned herself to death, or at best disfigurement. Two of England's most distinguished physicians were summoned, her old friend Dr Garth and Hans Sloane. But they could not save her renowned beauty. At the age of twenty-six she was suddenly no longer physically attractive; she had lost her eyelashes and her skin was deeply pitted. From now on her fame would depend on her literary achievements and her reputation as an often malicious but always diverting wit.

Lady Mary could never bring herself to defy convention

by publishing under her own name, yet she was certainly not displeased when 'the town' guessed the source of her satirical poems and essays urging social reforms. She and Pope became close friends and together with Gay, were soon ensnared by the notorious 'Mr Edmund Curll, Bookseller'. His unsavoury machinations embroiled the trio in a series of literary/Court squabbles that to them seemed momentous though to us they seem petty enough. Then quite unexpectedly, in April 1716, Wortley was nominated Ambassador to Turkey — a five-year appointment.

Lady Mary, elated at the prospect of 'going farther than most other people go', at once switched her attention to choosing a chaplain and a surgeon, ordering twenty suits of servants' livery and training a venturesome Yorkshire girl as her son's nurse. She had always relished books of travel and often reminded Wortley, 'I love travelling...'

The Ambassadorial party left London on 1 August and on 5 August she was writing hyperbolically from the Hague, 'The place I am now at is certainly one of the finest villages in the world... Nothing can be more agreeable than travelling in Holland'. But in the eighteenth century even Ambassadorial parties encountered considerable hardship when crossing Europe — especially in winter. All the Wortley Montagus' wealth could not ensure a consistent standard of comfort or entirely insulate them from 'the common people' and the Kingdom of Bohemia shocked Lady Mary —

...the villages so poor and the post houses so miserable, cleanstraw and fair water are blessings not always to be found and better accomodatoin not to be hoped. Though I carried my own bed with me, I could not sometimes find a place to set it up, and rather chose to travel all night, as cold as it is, wrapped up in my furs, than go into the common stoves, which are filled with a mixture of all sorts of ill scents.

First impressions of Vienna were also disconcerting; Lady Mary had been unprepered for that mixture of squalor and splendour surrounding the Imperial Court. Suddenly this self-possessed young Englishwoman, herself one of the ornaments of the Court of St James, sounds almost provincial. The nobility, she noted with horrified astonishment, occupied apartments 'divided but by a partition from that of a taylor or a shoemaker... Those that have houses of their own let out the rest of them to whoever will take 'em..' Moreover, five-and six-story multiple tenancy palaces shared certain problems with our own inner-city tower-blocks — 'The great stairs (which are all of stone) are as common and dirty as the street'.

Inside those apartments, however, all was 'surprisingly magnificent'; in England nothing comparable could be found. As Lady Mary lists the 'prodigious' possessions of the Viennese nobility her excited delight disarmingly recalls a Mid-West tourist trying to describe Chatsworth.

Meanwhile Wortley had embarked on the first stage of his extraordinary delicate mission. For two years Turkey had been at war with the Venetian Republic and Austria's Emperor, bound by treaty to assist Venice, was about to deflect his forces from their Mediterranean Spain-watching duties — which would, in England's view, wreck the European balance of power. At the end of Queen Anne's reign England had been left friendless in Europe; the Treaty of Utrecht, so strenuously opposed by the Whigs, merely alienated the Dutch and Austrians without achieving its purpose; to improve Anglo-French relations. So now Wortley's task was to mediate between Vienna and Constantinople.But unfortunately nothing in his temperament or previous experience fitted him to be a successful diplomat; and he was repeatedly double-crossed by Abraham Stanyan, England's ambassador to Vienna who longed to replace him in Constantinople. Nor did it help that both he and Lady Mary soon came to sympathise strongly and openly with the Turks.

On entering the Turkish Empire Lady Mary at once effortlessly adapted to 'a new world where everything I see appears to me a change of scene'. She learned to speak the language 'passibly', took 'great pains to see everything', was charmed by the 'civility and beauty' of naked Turkish women in the bagnio *(hamman),* found the wearing of the yashmak 'not only very easy but agreeable' and made friends with educated Turks of both sexes. Her enthusiastic descriptions of Constantinople and its surroundings recall another, fictitious, English Embassy to the Porte. (Did Virginia Woolf read these letters before writing chapter three of *Orlando?)* Of Lady Mary, too, it could be said that 'The English disease, a love of Nature, was inborn in her, and here, where Nature was so much larger and more powerful than in England, she fell into its hands as she had never done before'.

Their author's enterprise, curiosity and open-mindedness partly explain why these Embassy letters bear the hallmark of classic travel-writing. Important too was the eighteenth-century ex-patriates' mental and emotional isolation from their own culture. Modern travellers who wish genuinely to isolate themselves — the better to absorb other cultures — must deliberately make an effort to escape from the tentacles of hi-tek communications. Of course Lady Mary did not see this particular freedom as the luxury it seems to us. Writing from her Pera home, on 4 January 1718, she complained to Miss Anne Thistlewayte that most of her friends in England assumed she 'knew everything' and so neglected to keep her up to date on London gossip. She added —

Why they are pleased to suppose in ths manner, I can guess no reason except they are persuaded that the breed of Muhammad's pigeon still subsists in this country and that I receive supernatural intelligence.

However, future generations of readers were to benefit from Lady Mary's total immersion in Turkish life; being almost completely cut off from the familiar, she could more easily respond to and interpret the unfamiliar.

According to the terms of his appointment, Wortley should have remained in Turkey until 1721. Instead he received official letters of recall from an embarrassed Addison — recently made Secretary of State — on 28 October 1717. A soothing private letter implied complimentary reasons for this rather abrupt recall and promised Wortley a good London post as Auditor of the Imprest. This neither deceived nor consoled Wortley and his wife, who were equally reluctant to leave Turkey. In an attempt to reverse London's decision, Wortley blundered into a series of crass string-pullings which stregthened the general impression that he was singularly unsuited to be a diplomat. After much bickering about who should pay the expenses of the return journey, Wortley and Lady Mary reluctantly sailed from Constantinople in June 1718. By then they had two children; Mary, the future Countess of Bute, had been born five months previously.

In a letter to the Abbé Conti, Lady Mary defended the Turkish way of life —

These people are not so unpolished as we represent them. 'Tis true their magnificence is of a different taste from ours, and perhaps of a better. I am almost of opinion they have a right notion of life; while they consume it in music, gardens, wine and delicate eating... we are tormenting our brains with some scheme of politics or studying some science to which we can never attain or if we do, cannot persuade people to set that value upon it we do ourselves.... We die, or grow old and decrepit, before we can reap the fruit of our labours. Considering what short-lived, weak ani-

mals men are, is there any study so beneficial as the study of present pleasures?

On their zig-zag way home North Africa ('that barbarous country') was visited and Lady Mary contributed her mite to the evolution of what is known as 'British racist stereotyping'. Near the ruins of Carthage she paused to rest and —

While I sat there, from the town many women flocked in to see me and were equally entertained with viewing one another. Their posture in sitting, the colour of thier skin, their lank black hair falling on each side of their faces, their features and the shape of their limbs, differ so little from their own country people, the baboons, 'tis hard to fancy them a distinct race, and I could not help thinking there had been some ancient alliances between them.

Lady Mary would be astonished to know that 250 years later such an observation — crudely ignorant but not ill-natured — could get her into trouble with the law of her native land.

Wortley's mission to the Porte — like Lady Mary's involvement in London's literary scandals — seemed more important at the time than it does today. As Robert Halsband noted —

None of the newspaper reports or official documents mentioned the Ambassador's wife, yet her part in his Embassy was to make her famous throughout Europe, and her journey to the East would be remembered long after his mission was forgotten.

After the failure of the Embassy to Constantinople Wortley, according to the *Dictionary of National Biography,* 'never took any conspicuous part in politics, and devoted himself chiefly to saving money'. He blamed his lack of political advancement on the fact that he had refused 'to oblige Lord Sunderland on the Peerage Bill and

after to declare himself a friend of Sir Robert Walpole'. No doubt Addison's death in 1719, at the age of forty-seven, also hampered him. From this point on he becomes a shadowy figure in Lady Mary's story, only glimpsed occasionally through a haze of casual reference.

Lady Mary could plausibly be portrayed as tough, cynical, scheming: a woman with a tongue like emery paper and a heart of flint. But this image is inconsistent with the crusader who returned from Turkey vowing to 'take pains to bring this useful invention into fashion in England'. The invention in question was inoculation against smallpox and the pains required to introduce it to England were considerable. In several Turkish towns Lady Mary had closely studied the operation and from Adrianople she wrote to a friend describing it in detail and explaining, 'you may believe I am very well satisfied of the safety of the experiment since I intend to try it on my dear little son'. In April 1718 she did so, successfully, and back home that autumn she launched her pro-inoculation campaign. For several years it provoked public debate of extreme, almost unbelievable, ferocity. The participants were physicians, politicians, princesses, parsons, poets, apothecaries, surgeons and several members of the Royal Society. Lady Mary had her daughter inoculated in London, where numerous doubting Thomases could witness the operation and observe its after-effects. Princess Caroline, by then a close friend of Lady Mary, had two of her daughters inoculated in 1722, which prompted a further spate of sermons denouncing inoculation as a defiance of God's will. One William Wagstaffe published a pamphlet characteristic of the debate which ended:

Posterity perhaps will scarcely be brought to believe, that an Experiment practiced only by a few Ignorant Women, amongst an illiterate and unthinking People, shou'd on a sudden, and upon slender

Experience, so far obtain in one of the Politest Nations in the World, as to be receiv'd into the Royal Palace.

In retaliation Lady Mary published an anonymous pamphlet beginning:

Out of compassion to the numbers abused and deluded by the knavery and ignorance of physicians. I am determined to give a true account of the manner of inoculating the smallpox as it is practised in Constantinople with constant success and without any ill consequence whatever. I shall sell no drugs, nor take no fees, could I persuade people of the safety and reasonableness of this easy poeration... I shall get nothing by it but the private satisfaction of having done good to mankind.

When the 'progressives' at last won, Steele led the applause for Lady Mary's courage and tenacity. In *The Plain Dealer* he congratulated her for having won a victory that would save many thousands of British lives, as indeed it did. After her death a cenotaph commemorating her introduction of inoculation to England was erected in Lichfield Cathedral.

Concurrently with this public controversy, Lady Mary was going through a private crisis. She had become a victim of the celebrated French blackmailer, Toussaint Rémond de Saint-Mard — a friend of the Abbé Conti but described in the Duc de Saint-Simon's *Mémoirs* as 'an intriguing fool'. Foolish though he may have been, his intriguing trapped Lady Mary. His letters to her, which she showed to Wortley, proved that he was never her lover; yet their relationship left her perilously exposed to the nastiest sort of scandalmongering. It also indicated that despite her veneer of sophistication she could very easily be taken for a ride by any courtly rascal 'literary' enough to charm her. Many years later, in Italy, there was a not dissimilar involvement with a young and charming aristocratic thug by the name of Count Ugolino Palazzi. By 1722 Lady Mary had somehow extricated herself from the Rémond trap (the details are not known) but her nervous efforts to conceal this unfortunate friendship only served to publicize it and in the years ahead her enemies rejoiced to have such effective ammunition.

By 1724 Alexander Pope, not long before Lady Mary's most intimate literary friend, was among those enemies. She herself never could (or would) explain why they fell out but numerous theories circulated, one with a gloriously incongruous suburban flavour. According to a certain Miss Hawkins, Pope lent sheets to the Montagu household and these were returned unwashed.... Whatever the cause, Pope's enraged sneering stained Lady Mary's reputation during her lifetime and has proved an indelible dye.

Despite the eighteenth century's reputation as the Age of Reason, when everybody who was anybody kept their emotions under control, objectivity was not in fact a top priority. Lady Mary's own character assessments were often more like assassinations, too witty and elegantly phrased to seem offensive (unless one happened to be the victim), yet wildly unreliable. Among the generality of pen-wielders this was less the Age of Reason than the Age of Savagery; those lacking natural good manners were restrained by no rules, no inhibitions, no standards of 'fair play'. Writing to her sister, in June 1725, Lady Mary gossiped about 'the reigning Duchess of Marlborough' and then concluded, 'we continue to see one another like two people that are resolved to hate with civility'. But hating with civility was not the norm. When Pope's *Essay on Criticism* antagonised the critic, John Dennis, his published revenge included taunts about Pope's physical deformity. (Because of severe congenital curvature of the spine he was scarcely four and a half feet tall.) Again, when Queen Caroline had slowly died an agonising death, showing rare courage throughout a series of primitive operations, Pope publicly mocked the most humiliating physical symptom of her disease with a vicious crudity which it is hard to forgive — even after making all allowances for the standards of the time and his own tormented psyche. It seems cruelly unjust that this same Pope's attack on Lady Mary in the *Dunciad*, where he alluded to the Rémond scandal and insinuated that she had infected a French lover with a venereal disease, must be seen as 'the first step in the degradation of her reputation', as Robert Halsband has put it. Some months earlier, Henry Fielding her cousin had praised her as an intellectual feminist in the dedication to his comedy, *Love in Several Masks*. And an anonymous pamphleteer, engaged in defending those libelled in *Miscellanies* (a journal published in London in the 1760s) had described her as 'Renown'd for Wit, Beauty, and Politeness, long admir'd at Court; author of many pretty Poems scatter'd abroad in Manuscript; a Patroness of Men of Wit and Genius...'. But unluckily for Lady Mary, Pope's pen was mightier than any other.

Lady Mary's bluntness can often seem off-putting, even callous, to our ears. When Lord Sandwich's daughter-in-law had a stillborn child, the recently-wedded Lady Mary noted in her journal:

Lady Hinchinbroke has a dead daughter — it were unchristian not to be sorry for my cousin's misfortune; but if she has no live son, Mr Wortley is heir — so there's comfort for a Christian.

Although this directness shocks at first reading, it was a mark of honesty rather than insensitivity; Lady Mary was only putting into words what many, perhaps most, people would have secretly felt in similar circumstances. An illuminating phrase comes into the most poignant of all her letters to Wortley, written when she was painfully confronting the emotional aridity of their marriage:

I have concealed as long as I can the uneasiness the nothingness of your letters has given me, under an affected indifference, but dissimulation always sits awkwardly upon me.

Across the centuries, we feel the truth of that last statement. Lady Mary could seem wildly self-contradictory in her various dogmatic assertions of principle and brief but vivid bouts of introspection. This left her wide open to charges of striking melodramatic postures, of being smug, devious, hypocritical, affected — or at best no more than a tiresome chameleon, so anxious to make a good impression that in different circles she could persuade herself that she believed different things. Yet a careful reading of all her letters, in chronological sequence, suggests quite another interpretation of her character. Some of her most passionately proclaimed beliefs do seem to cancel each other out, not because she was dissimulating but because she was born too soon. Essentially she was a career woman, who needed the freedoms twentieth-century Englishwomen enjoy. Born 250 years later, she might have been a politician, a diplomat, an academic, a scientist, a writer (most probably the last). Born in 1689, she often had no choice but to go against her 'instinctive conscience' and natural inclinations.

One of her strongest inclinations — a veritable compulsion — was the urge to write. Her *Embassy Letters* are in fact a travel book rather than genuine *letters*, as sent to her friends. Like many another travel writer, before and since, she found the letter framework conducive to immediacy and informality. From Constantinople she had explained to her sister, Lady Mar (by then living in Paris, sharing her husband's political exile):

I am resolved to keep the copies, as testimonies of

my inclination to give you, to the utmost of my power,
all the diverting part of my travels, while you are
exempt from all the fatigues and inconveniences.

Back in England she used those copies, edited and polished and interwoven with extracts from her journal, to compile one of the best narrative travel books ever written by an Englishwoman. Then she showed the manuscript to Mary Astell, the pioneer feminist, who implored her to publish at once, by way of strengthening the much-derided feminist argument that an educated woman could be the intellectual equal of any man. But Lady Mary, though she greatly admired Miss Astell's stance, was an aristocrat first and a feminist only when feminism did not clash with her primary loyalty. And so she felt bound to lock away her precious manuscript for forty years.

To Lady Mary, writing was 'one of the most distinguished prerogatives of mankind, when duly executed', but it had latterly been degraded by 'trifling authors (who) write merely to get money'. In 1753 she reported from Italy that Lord Cornbury had asked for her 'sincere opinion' of his poetry.

I was not so barbarous to tell him that his verses
were extreme stupid (as, God knows, they were)... I
contented myself with representing to him that it was
not the business of a man of quality to turn author,
and that he should confine himself to the applause of
his friends and by no means venture on the press.

'Snobbery' is too feeble a word for the ageing Lady Mary's class prejudice. She considered 'our English writers (generally) very low-born' and criticised Swift and Pope for being ungrateful and disrespectful towards their patrons:

Had it not been for the good nature of these very
mortals they condemn these two superior beings were
entitled by their birth and hereditary fortune to be

only a couple of link-boys. ('Link-boys' were
employed by such as Lady Mary, before the days of
street lighting, to carry torches of pitch and tow.)

Although Wortley was no longer among the Whig leaders, his wife continued active behind the political scenes. By the 1720s most people had had to commit themselves either to the Court of St James or to the 'Alternative Court' at Leicester House. Typically, Lady Mary attended both; but, perhaps because of this ambivalence, she never held a Court post. During the mid-1730s her intimate friendships with Lord Hervey and Maria Skerritt (then Walpole's mistress, later his wife) inspired her to produce — anonymously, as usual — much muscular political journalism, including 'An Expedient to Put a Stop to the Spreading Vice of Corruption'. In that seditiously satirical essay she wondered, 'How can we prevent this contagion after it has gained so strong a head that it passes among foreigners for a part of our constitution?' She proposed the abolition of Parliament, after which the English could enjoy the respectability of being governed by their virtuous King (George II) and honest Minister (Robert Walpole).

Parliamentary venality was by then quite out of control, partly because the Lords and Commons regarded themselves (except of course during election campaigns) as the best judges of the public interest and so all their proceedings were as confidential as modern Cabinet meetings. Many argued that, through lack of scrutiny and criticism, both Houses were in danger of becoming as irresponsible as the worst of the Stuarts. Yet the public's interest in Parliamentary proceedings could not be stifled and was bravely catered for by the *London Magazine*, *Gentleman's Magazine* and *Historical Register*; these printed reports of important debates, evading punishment for breach of privilege by using transparently fictitious names. In 1738

William Pulteney, Earl of Bath, referred to such reports and observed grimly: 'To print or publish the speeches of gentlemen in the House looks very like making them accountable without doors for what they say within'. Indeed yes—and that would never do! But some of Lady Mary's acquaintances thought otherwise, as she zestfully recorded in 1739. At a sitting of the Lords on 1 March, the Opposition were all hyped up to force Walpole to go to war with Spain:

> It was unanimously resolved there should be no crowd of unnecessary auditors; consequently the fair sex were excluded, and the gallery destined to the sole use of the House of Commons. Notwithstanding which determination, a tribe of dames resolved to show on this occasion that neither men nor laws could resist them. These heroines were Lady Huntingdon, the Duchess of Queensbury, the Duchess of Ancaster, Lady Westmorland, Lady Cobham, Lady Charlotte Edwin, Lady Archibald Hamilton... I am thus particular in their names since I look upon them to be the boldest asserters and most resigned sufferers for liberty I ever read of. They presented themselves at the door at nine o'clock in the morning (and) the peers resolved to starve them out; an order was made that the doors should not be opened till they had raised their siege. These Amazons now showed themselves qualified for the duty even of foot-soldiers; they stood there till five in the afternoon, without either sustenance or evacuation, every now and then playing volleys of thumps, kicks and raps against the door, with so much violence that the speakers in the House were scarce heard. When the Lords were not to be conquered by this, the two Duchesses (very well apprized of the use of stratagems in war commanded a dead silence of half an hour; and the Chancellor, who thought this a certain proof of their absence, gave order for the opening of the door; upon which they all rushed in and placed themselves in the front row of the gallery. They stayed there till after eleven, when the House rose, and showed marks of dislike...by noisy laughs and apparent contempts... You must own this action very well worthy of record... I look so little in my own eyes, who was at that time ingloriously sitting over a tea-table...

The gaiety and vitality of Lady Mary's correspondence transcends without concealing her many personal disappointments and griefs. By the age of fifty she had suffered a joyless marriage, the early death of a devoted only brother, great distress on behalf of a favourite sister (Lady Mar) who went mad in her thirties and became Lady Mary's legal responsibility, bitter anxiety when a worthless only son repeatedly let the side down, disguised loneliness when a stodgy only daughter grew so like her father she was less than satisfactory as either companion or as correspondent, angry disillusionment when spiteful literary associates sabotaged her good name. And then there was Algarotti ... The only man she had ever ached for as a lover proved to be an opportunist homosexual.

This episode in Lady Mary's life was both undignified and therefore uncharacteristic. She first met the handsome, twenty-four-year-old Venetian Count Francesco Algarotti in 1736, when she was (dangerously) aged forty-seven. After a brilliant student career at the University of Bologna he had impressed Voltaire with his understanding of Newton and Locke. He arrived in London in March and within weeks had organised his nomination for membership of the Royal Society. Queen Caroline enjoyed discussing science and philosophy with him; Lady Mary's close friend, Lord Hervey, at once fell madly in love with him—and so, soon after, did Lady Mary. In both cases 'madly' is the *mot juste*. When Algarotti announced his (temporary) departure from England, Lord Hervey swore that he desired never to be parted from him and Lady Mary proclaimed, 'I shall love you all my life...'. Algarotti was used to sexually enslaving both men and women and it perfectly suited his purposes to have two rich, distinguished English aristocrats so infatuated that they abandoned every inhibition, at least in writing. During his London stay the hapless Lady Mary had communicated frequently:

> *I no longer know how to write to you. My feelings are too ardent; I could not possibly explain them or hide them... I see all their folly without being able to correct myself. The very idea of seeing you again gave me a shock while I read your letter, which almost made me swoon. What has become of that philosophical indifference that made the glory and the tranquillity of my former days? Forgive the absurdity that you have brought into being, and come to see me...*
> *(August, 1736)*

> *How timid one is when one loves! I am afraid of offending you by sending you this note though I mean to please you. In short I am so foolish about everything that concerns you that I am not sure of my own thoughts. My reason complains very softly of the stupidness of my heart without having the strength to destroy them... All that is certain is that I shall love you all my life in spite of your whims and my reason.*
> *(September, 1736)*

After Algarotti's departure for Venice the other two angles of this bizarre triangle were unable to maintain their long-established friendship intact; Lady Mary did her best, but Hervey's jealousy defeated her.

In December 1736 she wrote to Algarotti:

> *If you seriously wish to see me it will certainly happen; if your affairs do not permit your return to England mine shall be arranged in such a manner as I may come to Italy. This sounds extraordinary, and yet is not so when you consider the impression you have made on a heart that is capable of receiving no other.*

Algarotti ignored this pathetic suggestion and was not seen again until March 1739, when he borrowed money from Lady Mary to travel to England. In her case absence could hardly have made the heart grow fonder, but when he reappeared it was certainly no *less* fond. This seems odd, if Lady Mary's infatuation was what our clinical judgement might suggest — an acute case of hormonal imbalance, aggravated by twenty-five years of married lovelessness.

In 1739 Walpole's Ministry was beginning to look shaky and Algarotti found that Lord Hervey's influence had dwindled since Queen Caroline's death. He therefore moved on to the Earl of Burlington's villa at Chiswick, near enough to Lady Mary's Twickenham home. They discussed her Italian plan and by May it seemed that he had accepted it; they would settle in Venice and he promised her unimaginable happiness. (Shades of that unrealized idyll in Naples!)

When Lord Burlington under-exerted himself on Algarotti's behalf he was discarded in favour of Lord Baltimore, then about to sail to Russia on his yacht to represent the Prince of Wales at the marriage of the Princess of Mecklenburg. Algarotti eagerly accepted his invitation to join the mission; it was to last for several months and they sailed on 10 May, leaving Lady Mary excitedly preparing for her own journey to Italy. When she left London on 26 July 'the town', including Wortley, understood that she was going abroad for health reasons. Only Hervey knew the embarassing severity of her infatuation and of her arrangement with Algarotti. Her friendship with Hervey — one of the most important in her life —

had by then been mended and it is to the immortal credit of His Lordship (a much-maligned character) that the nature of her relationship with Algarotti remained a secret until Byron found some revealing letters in Venice. On 17 July 1818 the poet wrote to his publisher, John Murray:

The three French notes are by Lady Mary — they are very pretty and passionate — it is a pity that a piece of one of them is lost. — Algarotti seems to have treated her ill — but she was much his senior — and all women are used ill — or say so — whether they are or not.

While travelling with Lord Baltimore, Algarotti was noticed by the Crown Prince Frederick of Prussia—an eminently suitable patron—and Lady Mary did not see him again until March 1741. Then they both lived in Turin for almost two months, but not, apparently, together. In May Algarotti hastened back to Frederick's Court. And that was that, for fifteen years. Robert Halsband has diagnosed:

During her unhappy weeks in Turin, she forced herself to recognize that her romantic scheme had been an impossible self-induced, perhaps self-indulgent, vision.

The couple next met in 1756; Lady Mary was sixty-seven. Algarotti had retired to Padua for health reasons and they enjoyed a casual friendship based on mutual literary interests. Lord Hervey had died in 1743 and sometimes they affectionately recalled his 'gentle shade' — he who had so loyally kept Lady Mary's secret.

Even without an Algarotti in her life, Lady Mary would probably have emigrated in middle age; she had never found her inherited world entirely congenial and the notion that she 'abandoned husband and home' for Algarotti is a mawkish over-simplification. In 1738 she had written to a friend, then travelling abroad:

We are as much blinded in England by politics and views of interest as we are by mists and fogs, and 'tis necessary to have a very uncommon constitution not to be tainted with the distempers of our climate.

Sixteen months later, when newly arrived in Venice, she reported:

Here it is so much the established fashion for everybody to live their own way that nothing is more ridiculous than censuring the action of another... We have a clear bright sun, and fogs and factions are things unheard of in this climate.

Lady Mary took her grandmotherly duties seriously and several times attempted matchmaking by remote control. Living in Venice, she met many more young Englishmen than would ever have come her way in Twickenham. The English upper classes (and those aspiring to join them) regarded themselves as cultural *nouveaux riches*, by European standards, an awareness almost entirely lost sight of during the smug Victorian Age.) Thus thousands of young men were despatched annually, in the care of tutors, to spend a few years imbibing taste and learning from countries lucky enough to have Classical pasts and artistically active presents. But most of those archetypal cultural-vultures were quite unsuitable for Lady Mary's purpose. To Lady Pomfret she commented on the 'boys and governors' who swarmed through Venice:

Here are inundations of them broken in upon us this Carnival, and my apartment must be their refuge, the greater part of them having kept an inviolable fidelity to the language their nurses taught them. Their whole business abroad (as far as I can perceive) being to buy new clothes, in which they shine in some obscure coffee-house where they are sure of meeting some waiting gentlewoman of an opera queen, who perhaps they remember as long as they live, return to

Fragments at Ephesus by Luigi Mayer. European visitors can be seen sketching at what remains one of the richest archaeological sites in Turkey.

View of Constantinople from the Asian bank of the Bosphorus by Luigi Mayer. On the 10th April 1718 Lady Mary wrote:'The Asian side is covered with fruit trees, villages and the most delightful landscapes in nature. On the European stands Constantinople, situated on seven hills. The unequal heights make it seem as large again as it is (though one of the largest cities in the world), showing an agreeable mixture of gardens, pine and cypress trees, palaces, mosques and public buildings raised one above another.'

England excellent judges of men and manners.
Three months later, the situation was even worse:

> *This town is at present infested with English, who*
> *torment me as much as the frogs and lice did the palace*
> *of Pharoah, and are surprised that I will not suffer*
> *them to skip about my house from morning till night*
> *— me, that never opened my doors to such sort of*
> *animals in England.*

After Lady Mary's departure from England she and her husband never met again, though Wortley spent an occasional month or two on the Continent. However, they continued to correspond with civility — indeed, with growing cordiality — and the last of Lady Mary's regular letters arrived at Wharncliffe a few days after Wortley's death in 1761. He had tended his inheritance so obsessionally that he left £1,350,000 — most of it to Lady Bute and then to her second son, who was to take the name of Wortley. To his own good-for-nothing son he left £1,000 a year and to Lady Mary £1,200 a year, to be added to young Edward's bequest after her death. He willed that no more than £150 should be spent on his funeral and no more than £100 on his monument. A cousin, Elizabeth Montagu, hoped that his fortune might 'make his heirs as happy and illustrious as the getting it made him anxious and odious'. James Stuart Mackenzie, brother of Lord Bute and then Minister to Turin, described the will as 'a most extraordinary one, especially with respect to my poor little neighbour here, to whom the testator has indeed been most unkind...'. His 'poor little neighbour', though badly shaken by this 'ill fortune', observed all the proprieties of widowhood and never once allowed her upper lip to unstiffen. But within a few months she had sold her two Italian houses and embarked on the long journey home.

France and England were at war, so Lady Mary travelled through Germany and Holland. In Rotterdam,

Portrait by an anonymous Greek artist of a wealthy lady of fashion. This was either a Greek lady or an imaginative portrait, since the artist would not have seen any Turkish woman unveiled. Her dress was not dissimilar to Lady Mary's own 'Turkish habit', which she described in her letter of 1 April 1717 to Lady Mar (see page 109). Lady Mary also commented that 'I never saw in my life so many fine heads of hair. I have counted one hundred and ten of these tresses of one lady's, all natural.'

where her maid's illness and freak storms delayed her for over two months, she lodged with an amiable Anglican clergyman. When she showed her *Embassy Letters* to the Reverend Benjamin Sowden he echoed Mary Astell's pleas of forty years earlier. Lady Mary had told Miss Astell the manuscript was 'condemned to obscurity' during her life; now she must have realized that not much of that life remained. To her new friend she presented the autograph copy of *Embassy Letters,* having inscribed on the cover: 'These two volumes are given to the Rev Benjamin Sowden, minister at Rotterdam, to be disposed of as he thinks proper. This is the will and design of M. Wortley Montagu'. No doubt Lady Mary foresaw that her daughter and son-in-law could never accept the idea of having a female author in the family. Also, Lord Bute was about to become, for ten and a half months, one of England's least successful Prime Ministers — and who knew what awkward memories his mother-in-law's letters might stir up? Taking all possible future snags into account, it made sense to entrust Mr Sowden with the task of posthumous publication.

After an absence of almost twenty-three years, Lady Mary arrived in London in mid-January 1762 — not the best season to return to England from Italy. Lady Bute had rented a small house for her mother, off Hanover Square, but Lady Mary found it hard to adjust to a radically changed, and from her point of view, friendless London. Soon she was considering a return to Venice, but though so many complimented her on not having aged, she was in fact mortally ill. On 21 August 1762 she died of breast-cancer — having, according to Horace Walpole, 'expressed great anxiety' on her death-bed that the *Embassy Letters* should be published.

Hearing of Lady Mary's death, the Rev. Mr Sowden courteously sought her family's permission to publish the letters that had been left in his care for this purpose. The Butes said 'No!' In their terrified imaginations, those two volumes represented a cavernous cupboard packed with menacingly macabre skeletons. When Lady Bute attempted to retrieve the manuscript, Mr Sowden at first refused to part with his literary treasure. Then, after six months of bullying, he reluctantly exchanged it for £500 — a considerable sum, probably equivalent to five years salary for an Anglican minister. Lady Bute then locked the *Embassy Letters* away, giving thanks for the family's narrow escape. But Minerva was on Lady Mary's side.

The Butes went into shock when the *London Chronical* of 7-10 May 1763 announced that 'This Day was published the letters of the Right Honourable Lady M..y W.....y M------e!' Lady Bute, seething, put the Rev. Mr Sowden on the mat. At first he was bewildered. Then he remembered a visit from two English gentlemen — who it seemed were not, after all, gentlemen... They had wished to look at Lady Mary's letters, had engineered his being called away and disappeared with the volumes. Next day they apologetically returned them, and not until he found himself on the Bute mat did it occur to Mr Sowden that the manuscript might have been copied overnight. Lady Mary's mischievous aspect would doubtless have relished that act of literary banditry, on which depended the fulfillment of her dying wish.

The *Embassy Letters* had to be rapidly reprinted, over and over again, to meet the demands of a wildly enthusiastic public. And they were more than a popular success; the main monthly book reviews were almost deliriously admiring and from Smollett, Gibbon, Dr Johnson and Voltaire came undiluted praise. But this response did nothing to console Lady Bute, a primly tedious woman in whom the paternal genes had always been disastrously dominant. She had never been able to learn from her mother, who at the age of twenty wrote to Anne Wortley:

I believe more follies are committed out of complaisance to the world than in following our own inclinations... I am amazed to see that people of good sense in other things can make their happiness consist in the opinion of others...

Posterity can be unwittingly cruel. The author of Lady Mary's notice, in *Chambers Biographical Dictionary* quotes Horace Walpole on his meeting in Florence with 'an old, foul, tawdry, painted, plastered personage'. This loutishness tells us more about the young Walpole than about the fifty-one-year-old Lady Mary. He loathed his stepmother, Maria Skerrett, whose pre-marital relationship with Papa Walpole Lady Mary had aided and abetted; so Horace's hatred for the 'plastered personage' predated their first meeting. To have been libelled in Pope's poetry and Horace Walpole's letters was extraordinary bad luck: accusations which would otherwise have been forgotten within weeks became part of the mainstream of English literature. Lady Mary's journals, had they survived, would probably have done likewise, thus counterbalancing (even if they were occasionally *risqué* by Bute standards) the misrepresentations of vindictive contemporaries. Unfortunately Lady Bute was too blinkered to see that her censorship would boomerang. In 1794, not long before her death, she burned the detailed journal kept by Lady Mary for half a century (1712-62). Only one of her daughters had been permitted to read it and she remained forever silent about Rémond, Algarotti, Palazzi and other contentious matters. As an act of vandalism this outdid even John Murray's burning of Byron's unread *Memoirs* at the insistence of Hobhouse and the poet's sister; Byron's family had more reason that Lady Mary's to fear 'shocking revelations'. Ironically, Byron had deplored the neurotic attitude to Lady Mary's writings dis-

played by three generations of her 'proud and foolish family'. He himself much admired 'the charming Mary Montagu', not only for her charm but for the brilliance and versatility of her literary talent.

It would be too glib to assert that Lady Mary had all her life 'longed for literary fame'. True, she felt an urge to put pen to paper as soon as she could form her letters and at the age of seventy she began an idiosyncratic history of her own time, 'to divert my solitary hours'. (Her long, lively and perceptive essay on George I's court is now regarded as a valuable historical document.) Obviously she *needed* to be creative with words, to relive her experiences and impressions on paper, to share her own emotions with others through her writings; but all this is a more complicated impulse than the desire for literary fame though that desire may be part of it. Writing well is hard work and Lady Mary would not have anonymously written so much so excellently had fame been her only spur. Yet one wishes the *Embassy Letters* could have been published during her lifetime; their reception would have confirmed her own view of her talent and compensated for other disappointments and frustrations. In 1726 she had written to Lady Mar:

The last pleasure that fell in my way was Madame de Sévigné's letters; very pretty they are, but I assert without the least vanity that mine will be full as entertaining forty years hence. I advise you therefore to put none of 'em to the use of waste paper'.

Lady Mary would have been gratified by Voltaire's opinion (spread throughout Europe in the *Gazette Litteraire de l'Europe*) that her letters were 'far superior' to Madame de Sévigné's because written 'not only for her own nation but for all nations who wish to be instructed'. And, he might have added, who wish to be amused.

Dervla Murphy

Lady Mary Wortley Montagu in Turkish Dress (painting attributed to Charles Philips)

The spring and early summer of 1716 were filled with preparations for the journey to Constantinople. Since Wortley was expecting to be away for at least five years, the domestic arrangements, which he left in Lady Mary's hands, were considerable. She appointed a chaplain, one William Crosse, who had already served as chaplain to the English settlement in Constantinople in 1712, and a surgeon, Charles Maitland. Another important post was

that of nurse to the Wortleys' three-year-old son Edward; despite all the dangers and rigours of the forthcoming journey, Lady Mary was determined not to leave him behind. She chose the sister of her servant Matthew Northall, someone she must already have judged would be a reliable and loving companion for the boy, and soon persuaded her to travel down from Yorkshire so that child and nurse could get to know one another before the journey began. Lady Mary had hoped to persuade Sarah Chiswell, her childhood friend from Nottingham, to join the party as her own companion, and must have been disappointed when Sarah's fearful relatives prevented her from accepting the invitation.

There were possessions to attend to as well. Lady Mary had twenty suits of livery made for the servants, and no doubt ordered clothes for herself and her husband, medical supplies and equipment, and the inevitable books: everything she and her entourage could possibly require for such a long stay abroad. The lavish presents that a newly arrived ambassador customarily gave to the Sultan and his officials also had to be procured; parsimonious as ever, Wortley negotiated a £500 payment from the Levant Company to cover both these and his travelling expenses.

Once the leave-takings were over — Pope was particularly effusive, claiming that he valued no woman more than Lady Mary — and the commissions had been received (Jane Smith asked for lace to be sent from the Continent, and Lady Bristol wanted exotic eastern stuffs), the Ambassador's party set forth from London on 1 August 1716. Offered a choice of routes, Wortley had for once decided against saving money. Although either a direct sea voyage to Constantinople or an overland journey to Marseilles and then a sea passage would have enabled him to make a profit on his expenses, he decided to travel via Vienna; the opportunity of an audience with the Emperor Charles VI would, he anticipated, assist his peace-making efforts, especially since he carried a letter to the Emperor from the English King George I. After a difficult crossing from Gravesend on the Thames estuary — a two-day calm was followed by a violent storm — the party landed in Holland, hired horses and immediately set out south towards Vienna. Progress was quick at first, not least because all the heavy baggage had been sent ahead to Turkey by sea, but between Nijmegen and Cologne there were unexpected delays, and at Ratisbon the Ambassador had to wait several days while Lady Mary recovered from a heavy cold.

Even in these first few weeks of her journey, Lady Mary found all her high expectations of travel fulfilled. She took a lively, if sometimes rather censorious, interest in everything and everyone. While the cleanliness of the streets and people of Rotterdam was approved, and Nijmegen was judged to enjoy 'one of the finest prospects in the world', the statues of the saints and the relics encountered in the Roman Catholic churches of southern Germany were dismissed as vulgar farce — Lady Mary confessed to coveting a pearl necklace decorating an image of Saint Ursula — and the intrigues of the princely court at Ratisbon as petty quarrelling.

In Vienna, which she reached on 3 September, there was rich material for Lady Mary's pen. While her husband was deep in political negotiations (he was received by the Emperor the day following their arrival), she had ample time to explore the city, to attend the opera and dine with 'several of the first people of quality', and, following her reception at Court, to attend all its ceremonies and festivities. But her audience with the Empress Elisabeth had to wait until the correct gown was made — it was, she wrote, 'a dress very inconvenient, but which certainly shows the neck and shape to great advantage'. Lady Mary's letters record many of the foibles of Court life: the obsession with rank, for instance, and the delicacy with which affairs of the heart were managed. As was to be the case in Turkey, she dwelt at length on matters of marital fidelity. In Vienna, she wrote to Lady Rich on 20 September, it was 'the established custom for every Lady to have two husbands, one that bears the name, and another that performs the duties'. When, attending an assembly one evening, a young count made the most polite and tactful of overtures to Lady Mary, she declined gravely, refusing even his offer to approach on her behalf anyone else she preferred. What thoughts, one wonders, did she confine to her Journal that night — for by now, after four years of marriage, her husband's true nature, his self-centredness and meagre passions, must have been apparent to her.

By November, Wortley might have been expected to press on east in order to take advantage of an unexpected opportunity for diplomacy. Following his army's defeat by the Imperial forces under Prince Eugene of Savoy at Peterwaradin in August, Sultan Ahmed III had agreed to allow the English to mediate, and the Pasha of Belgrade had sent a message urging Wortley to set out for Turkey immediately. Instead, Wortley left Vienna on 13 November for the English court at Hanover, where he received further instructions and credentials from the King. It was an eventful journey which Wortley and Lady Mary almost failed to complete; crossing the Bohemian mountains, the coach almost plunged off the path into the River Elbe below as the postillions dozed in their seats. At least when they reached Leipzig, Lady Mary was able to buy liveries for her pages, and material for herself, at rather less than half their price in Vienna.

Lady Mary's brief stay in Hanover must have been a pleasant interlude in her constant journeying: many Court friends and acquaintances had joined the King at his German capital, and at dinner at the King's table she was served oranges, lemons and pineapples ripened in nearby hothouses. Soon Wortley and Lady Mary were underway once again, travelling over Christmas to reach Vienna on 27 December. Before they set out once more on 16 January 1717, Lady Mary had time to enjoy the Viennese carnival with its balls and performances of Italian comedy. She looked forward to her journey across the Hungarian plain to Peterwaradin and Belgrade with trepidation; she feared 'being froze to death, buried in the snow, and taken by the Tartars', she told Pope, and wished that Wortley would delay until the Danube had thawed and they could travel by boat.

The journey was nothing like as unpleasant as she had feared, and through the expedient of fixing their coaches on sleighs the party made rapid progress over the deep snow. Buda was reached after five days, then, after the crossing of the Danube, Esseck (modern Osijek) and finally Peterwaradin, a fortress town on the very edge of the Imperial lands. Here Wortley awaited word from the Pasha that they might cross into Ottoman territory. A strong escort of 200 Imperial troops accompanied them to the border at a tiny village named Betsko, where the new Ambassador was met by an even stronger force of Janissaries (soldiers), who escorted them to Belgrade.

Belgrade gave Lady Mary her first taste of the East she had so longed to see. Her initial impressions were largely favourable, even though she felt uneasy in a town so subject to 'insolent soldiery'; while nominally ruled by a Pasha, the city was in fact controlled by Janissaries. Always susceptible to men of breeding and culture, she was greatly entertained by Ahmed Bey Effendi, the scholar with whom they were lodged; he read Arabic verse to her, she in return helped him to master the Roman alphabet, and together they supped, drank wine and conversed about religion and what was soon to become a favourite topic of Lady Mary's, the true position of women in Ottoman society. But Wortley and Lady Mary were both eager to continue their journey, and immediately permission arrived from the Sultan they set out for Adrianople.

To Lady Mar[1]— *Rotterdam 3 August 1716*[2]

I flatter myself (dear sister) that I shall give you some pleasure in letting you know that I am safely past the sea, though we had the ill fortune of a storm. We were persuaded by the captain of our yacht to set out in a calm, and he pretended that there was nothing so easy as to tide it over, but after two days slowly moving, the wind blew so hard that none of the sailors could keep their feet, and we were all Sunday night tossed very handsomely. I never saw a man more frightened than the captain. For my part I have been so lucky neither to suffer from fear or sea sickness, though I confess I was so impatient to see myself once more upon dry land, that I would not stay till the yacht could get to Rotterdam, but went in the long boat to Hellevoetsluis where we hired voitures to carry us to the Brill.

I was charmed with the neatness of this little town, but my arrival at Rotterdam presented me a new scene of pleasure. All the streets are paved with broad stones, and before the meanest artificers' doors, seats of various coloured marbles, and so neatly kept that I'll assure you I walked almost all over the town yesterday, incognito, in my slippers without receiving one spot of dirt, and you may see the Dutch maids washing the pavement of the street with more application than ours do our bedchambers. The town seems so full of people with such busy faces, all in motion, that I can hardly fancy that it is not some celebrated fair, but I see 'tis every day the same. 'Tis certain no town can be more advantageously situated for commerce. Here are seven large canals on which the merchant ships come up to the very doors of their houses. The shops and warehouses are of a suprising neatness and magnificence, filled with an incredible quantity of fine merchandise, and so much cheaper than what we see in England, I have much ado to persuade myself I am still so near it. Here is neither dirt nor beggary to be seen. One is not shocked with those loathsome cripples so common in London, nor teased with the importunities of idle fellows and wenches that choose to be nasty and lazy. The common servants and little shop women here are more nicely clean than most of our ladies, and the great variety of neat dresses (every woman dressing her head after her own fashion) is an additional pleasure in seeing the town.

You see hitherto, dear sister, I make no complaints, and if I continue to like travelling as well as I do at present, I shall not repent my project. It will go a great

---

1. Lady Mary's sister; she had remained in London after her husband, a leader of the Jacobite rebellion of 1715, fled to France.

2. All dates are Old Style. The date that Lady Mary wrote here is only approximately accurate, as is the case with many of the Embassy letters.

way in making me satisfied with it if it affords me opportunities of entertaining you, but it is not from Holland that you must expect a disinterested offer. I can write enough in the style of Rotterdam to tell you plainly, in one word, I expect returns of all the London news. You see I have already learnt to make a good bargain, and that it is not for nothing I will so much as tell you that I am your affectionate sister.

To Miss Jane Smith[1] — *Hague 5 August 1716*

I make haste to tell you, dear madam, that after all the dreadful fatigues you threatened me with, I am hitherto very well pleased with my journey. We take care to make such short stages every day, I rather fancy myself upon parties of pleasure than upon the road, and sure nothing can be more agreeable than travelling in Holland. The whole country appears a large garden, the roads all well paved, shaded on each side with rows of trees and bordered with large canals full of boats passing and repassing. Every twenty paces gives you the prospect of some villa and every four hours a large town, so surprisingly neat, I am sure you would be charmed with them. The place I am now at is certainly one of the finest villages in the world. Here are several squares finely built, and (what I think a particular beauty) set with large trees. The Voorhout is at the same time the Hyde Park and the Mall of the people of quality, for they take the air in it both on foot and in coaches. There are shops for wafers, cool liquors, etc. I have been to see several of the most celebrated gardens, but I will not tease you with their descriptions.

I dare swear you think my letter already long enough, but I must not conclude without begging your pardon for not obeying your commands in sending the lace you ordered me. Upon my word, I can yet find none that is not dearer than you may buy it in London. If you want any Indian goods, here are great variety of penn'orths, and I shall follow your orders with great pleasure and exactness, being, dear madam, etc.

1. Almost certainly daughter of John Smith, former Speaker of the House of Commons; an early friend of Lady Mary's and since 1715 a Maid of Honour to the Princess of Wales.

To Miss Sarah Chiswell[1] — *Nijmegen 13 August 1716*

I am extremely sorry, my dear Sarah, that your fears of disobliging your relations and their fears for your health and safety has hindered me the happiness of your company, and you the pleasure of a diverting journey. I receive some degree of mortification from every agreeable novelty or pleasing prospect by the reflection of your having so unluckily missed the same pleasure, which I know it would have given you. If you were with me in this town you would be ready to expect to receive visits from your Nottingham friends. No two places were ever more resembling; one has but to give the Maese[2] the name of the Trent and there is no distinguishing the prospects: the houses, like those of Nottingham, built one above another and intermixed in the same manner with trees and gardens. The tower they call Julius Caesar's has the same situation with Nottingham Castle, and I can't help fancying I see from it the Trent field, Adboulton, etc., places so well known to us. 'Tis true the fortifications make a considerable difference. All the learned in the art of war bestow great commendations on them. For my part, that know nothing of the matter, I shall content myself with telling you 'tis a very pretty walk on the ramparts, on which there is a tower very deservedly called the Belvedere, where people go to drink coffee, tea, etc., and enjoy one of the finest prospects in the world. The public walks have no great beauty but the thick shades of the trees, but I must not forget to take notice of the bridge, which appeared very surprising to me. 'Tis large enough to hold hundreds of men with horses and carriages. They give the value of an English two pence to get upon it and then away they go, bridge and all, to the other side of the river, with so slow a motion one is hardly sensible of any at all.

I was yesterday at the French church and stared very much at their manner of service. The parson claps on a broad brimmed hat in the first place, which gave him entirely the air of what de'e call him,[3] in Bartholomew Fair, which he kept up by extraordinary antic gestures and talking much such stuff as t'other preached to the puppets. However, the congregation seemed to receive it with great devotion, and I was informed by some of his flock that he is a person of particular fame among 'em. I believe you are by this time as much tired of my account of him as I was with his sermon, but I'm sure your brother[4] will excuse a digression in favour of the Church of England. You know, speaking disrespectfully of Calvinists is the

1. A childhood friend of Lady Mary's from Nottingham.

2. Nijmegen stands on the River Waal, not on the Maas.

3. Zeal-of-the-Land Busy in Ben Jonson's play.

4. Probably brother-in-law, Humphrey Perkins, rector of Holme Pierrepont.

same thing as speaking honourably of the Church.

Adieu, my dear Sarah. Always remember me and be assured I can never forget you.

To Lady — *Cologne 16 August 1716*

If my Lady _____ could have any notion of the fatigues that I have suffered these last two days, I am sure she would own it a great proof of regard that I now sit down to write to her. We hired horses from Nijmegen hither, not having the convenience of the post, and found but very indifferent accommodation at Reinburg, our first stage, but that was nothing to what I suffered yesterday. We were in hopes to reach Cologne. Our horses tired at Stamel three hours from it, where I was forced to pass the night in my clothes in a room not at all better than a hovel, for though I have my own bed, I had no mind to undress where the wind came in from a thousand places. We left this wretched lodging at day break and about six this morning came safe here, where I got immediately into bed and slept so well for three hours that I found myself perfectly recovered and have had spirits enough to go see all that is curious in the town, that is to say, the churches, for here is nothing else worth seeing, though it is a very large town, but most part of it old built.

The Jesuits' church is the neatest, which was showed me in a very complaisant manner by a handsome young Jesuit, who, not knowing who I was, took a liberty in his compliments and railleries which very much diverted me. Having never before seen anything of that nature, I could not enough admire the magnificence of the altars, the rich images of the saints (all massy silver) and the enchassures of the relics, though I could not help murmuring in my heart at the profusion of pearls, diamonds and rubies bestowed on the adornment of rotten teeth, dirty rags, etc. I own that I had wickedness enough to covet St Ursula's pearl necklace, though perhaps it was no wickedness at all, an image not being certainly one's neighbour; but I went yet farther and wished even she herself converted into dressing plate, and a great St Christopher I imagined would have looked very well in a cistern. These were my pious reflections, though I was very well satisfied to see, piled up to the honour of our nation, the skulls of the 11,000 virgins. I have seen some hundreds of relics here of no less consequence, but I will not imitate the common style of travellers so far as to give you a list of 'em, being persuaded that you have no manner of curiosity for the titles given to jaw bones and bits of worm-eaten wood.

Adieu. I am just going to supper where I shall drink your health in an admirable sort of Lorraine wine, which I am sure is the same you call Burgundy in London.

To Lady Bristol[1] — *Nuremberg 22 August 1716*

After five days of travelling post I am sure I could sit down to write on no other occasion but to tell my dear Lady Bristol that I have not forgot her obliging command of sending her some account of my travels. I have already past a large part of Germany. I have seen all that is remarkable in Cologne, Frankfurt, Wurzburg, and this place, and 'tis impossible not to observe the difference between the free towns and those under the government of absolute princes 'as all the little sovereigns of Germany are'. In the first there appears an air of commerce and plenty. The streets are well built and full of people neatly and plainly dressed, the shops loaded with merchandise, and the commonalty clean and cheerful. In the other, a sort of shabby finery, a number of dirty people of quality tawdered out, narrow nasty streets out of repair, wretchedly thin of inhabitants, and above half of the common sort asking alms. I can't help fancying one under the figure of a handsome, clean, Dutch citizen's wife and the other like a poor town lady of pleasure, painted and ribboned out in her head-dress, with tarnished silver laced shoes, and a ragged under-petticoat, a miserable mixture of vice and poverty.

They have sumptuary laws in this town which distinguish their rank by their dress and prevent that excess which ruins so many other cities and has a more agreeable effect to the eye of a stranger than our fashions. I think after the Archbishop of Cambrai[2] having declared for them, I need not be ashamed to own that I wish these laws were in force in other parts of the world. When one considers impartially the merit of a rich suit of clothes in most places, the respect and the smiles of favour that it procures, not to speak of the envy and the sighs that it

1. Elizabeth, wife of John Hervey, first Earl of Bristol.

2. The Archbishop, François Fénelon, had denounced luxury in two works published in 1687 and 1699.

occasions (which is very often the principal charm to the wearer), one is forced to confess that there is need of an uncommon understanding to resist the temptation of pleasing friends and mortifying rivals, and that it is natural to young people to fall into a folly which betrays them to that want of money which is the source of a thousand basenesses. What numbers of men have begun the world with generous inclinations that have afterwards been the instruments of bringing misery on a whole people! led by a vain expense into debts that they could clear no other way but by the forfeit of their honour, and which they would never have contracted if the respect the many pay to habits was fixed by law only to a particular colour or cut of plain cloth! These reflections draw after them others that are too melancholy.

I will make haste to put 'em out of your head by the farce of relics with which I have been entertained in all the Romish churches. The Lutherans are not quite free from those follies. I have seen here in the principal church a large piece of the Cross set in jewels, and the point of a spear which they told me very gravely was the same that pierced the side of our Saviour. But I was particularly diverted in a little Roman Catholic church which is permitted here, where the professors of that religion are not very rich and consequently cannot adorn their images in so rich a manner as their neighbours, but not to be quite destitute of all finery they have dressed up an image of our Saviour over the altar in a full-bottomed wig, very well powdered. I imagine I see your ladyship stare at this article, of which you very much doubt the veracity, but upon my word I have not yet made use of the privilege of a traveller, and my whole account is writ with the same plain sincerity of heart with which I assure you that I am, my dear madam, your ladyship's etc.

To Miss Anne Thistlethwayte[1] — *Ratisbon 30 August 1716*

I had the pleasure of receiving yours but the day before I left London. I give you a thousand thanks for your good wishes, and have such an opinion of their efficacy I am persuaded that I owe 'in part' to them the luck of having proceeded so far in my long journey without any ill accident, for I do not reckon it any being stopped a few days in this town by a cold, since it has not only given me an opportunity of seeing

1. A friend who lived near West Dean, Wiltshire.

all that is curious in it, but of making some acquaintance with the ladies, who have all been to see me with great civility, particularly Madame 'von Wrisberg', the wife of our King's envoy from Hanover. She has carried me to all the assemblies and I have been magnificently entertained at her house, which is one of the finest here. You know that all the nobility of this place are envoys from different states. Here are a great number of them, and they might pass their time agreeably enough if they were less delicate on the point of ceremony. But instead of joining in the design of making the town as pleasant to one another as they can and improving their little societies, they amuse themselves no other way than with perpetual quarrels, which they take care to eternize by leaving them to their successors, and an envoy to Ratisbon receives regularly half a dozen quarrels amongst the perquisites of his employment.

You may be sure the ladies are not wanting on their side in cherishing and improving these important piques, which divide the town almost into as many parties as there are families, and they choose rather to suffer the mortification of sitting almost alone on their assembly nights than to recede one jot from their pretensions. I have not been here above a week and yet I have heard from almost every one of 'em the whole history of their wrongs and dreadful complaints of the injustice of their neighbours in hopes to draw me to their party, but I think it very prudent to remain neuter, though if I was to stay amongst them there would be no possibility of continuing so, their quarrels running so high they will not be civil to those that visit their adversaries. The foundation of these everlasting disputes turns entirely upon place and the title of Excellency, which they all pretend to, and what is very hard, will give it to nobody. For my part, I could not forbear advising them (for public good) to give the title of Excellency to everybody, which would include the receiving it from everybody, but the very mention of such a dishonourable peace was received with as much indignation as Mrs Blackacre did the notion of a reference,[2] and I begun to think myself ill natured to offer to take from 'em, in a town where there is so few diversions, so entertaining an amusement. I know that my peaceable disposition already gives me a very ill figure, and that 'tis publicly whispered as a piece of impertinent pride in me that I have hitherto been saucily civil to everybody as if I thought nobody good enough to quarrel with. I should be obliged to change my behaviour if I did not intend to pursue my journey in a few days.

I have been to see the churches here and had the permission of touching the

2. In William Wycherley's *The Plain Dealer* (1677), Mrs Blackacre scorns a 'reference' — that a dispute be settled by a Master in Chancery.

relics, which was never suffered in places where I was not known. I had by this privilege the opportunity of making an observation, which I don't doubt might have been made in all the other churches, that the emeralds and rubies that they show round their relics and images are most of them false, though they tell you that many of the crosses and Madonnas set round with them stones have been the gifts of the emperors and other great princes, and I don't doubt but they were at first jewels of value, but the good fathers have found it convenient to apply them to other uses and the people are just as well satisfied with bits of glass. Amongst these relics they showed me a prodigious claw set in gold, which they called the claw of a griffin, and I could not forbear asking the reverend priest that showed it, whether the griffin was a saint. This question almost put him beside his gravity, but he answered, they only kept it as a curiosity. But I was very much scandalized at a large silver image of the Trinity where the Father is represented under the figure of a decrepit old man with a beard down to his knees and a triple crown on his head, holding in his arms the Son fixed on the Cross, and the Holy Ghost in the shape of a dove hovering over him.

Madame [von Wrisberg] is come this minute to call me to the assembly and forces me to tell you very abruptly that I am ever yours.

To Lady Mar — *Vienna 8 September 1716*

I am now (my dear sister) safely arrived at Vienna and I thank God have not at all suffered in my health nor (what is dearer to me) in that of my child by all our fatigues. We travelled by water from Ratisbon, a journey perfectly agreeable, down the Danube in one of those little vessels that they very properly call wooden houses, having in them all the conveniencies of a palace; stoves in the chambers, kitchens, etc. They are rowed by twelve men each, and move with an incredible swiftness that in the same day you have the pleasure of a vast variety of prospects, and within a few hours' space of time one has the different diversion of seeing a populous city adorned with magnificent palaces, and the most romantic solitudes which appear distant from the commerce of mankind, the banks of the Danube being charmingly diversified with woods, rocks, mountains covered with vines, fields of corn, large cities, and ruins of ancient castles. I saw the great towns of Passau and Linz, famous for the retreat of the Imperial court when Vienna was besieged.

This town, which has the honour of being the Emperor's residence[1], did not at all answer my ideas of it, being much less than I expected to find it. The streets are very close and so narrow one cannot observe the fine fronts of the palaces, though many of them very well deserve observation, being truly magnificent, all built of fine white stone and excessive high. The town being so much too little for the number of the people that desire to live in it, the builders seem to have projected to repair that misfortune by clapping one town on the top of another, most of the houses being of five and some of them six stories. You may easily imagine that the streets being so narrow, the upper rooms are extreme dark, and what is an inconvenience much more intolerable in my opinion, there is no house that has so few as five or six families in it. The apartments of the greatest ladies and even of the ministers of state are divided but by a partition from that of a tailor or a shoemaker, and I know nobody that has above two floors in any house, one for their own use and one higher for their servants. Those that have houses of their own let out the rest of them to whoever will take 'em; thus the great stairs (which are all of stone) are as common and as dirty as the street. 'Tis true when you have once travelled through them, nothing can be more surprisingly magnificent than the apartments. They are commonly a suite of eight or ten large rooms, all inlaid, the doors and windows richly carved and gilt, and the furniture such as is seldom seen in the palaces of sovereign princes in other countries: the hangings the finest tapestry of Brussels, prodigious large looking glasses in silver frames, fine Japan tables, the beds, chairs, canopies and window curtains of the richest Genoa damask or velvet, almost covered with gold lace or embroidery — the whole made gay by pictures and vast jars of Japan china, and almost in every room large lustres of rock crystal.

I have already had the honour of being invited to dinner by several of the first people of quality, and I must do them the justice to say the good taste and magnificence of their tables very well answers to that of their furniture. I have been more than once entertained with fifty dishes of meat, all served in silver and well dressed, the dessert proportionable, served in the finest china; but the variety and richness of their wines is what appears the most surprising. The constant way is to lay a list of their names upon the plates of the guests along with the napkins, and I

1. In 1683, when the Turkish army reached the walls of Vienna, Emperor Leopold and his court fled until the Turks were driven back by the King of Poland's army.

have counted several times to the number of eighteen different sorts, all exquisite in their kinds. I was yesterday at Count Schönborn's, the vice-chancellor's garden, where I was invited to dinner, and I must own that I never saw a place so perfectly delightful as the *faubourgs* of Vienna. It is very large and almost wholly composed of delicious palaces; and if the Emperor found it proper to permit the gates of the town to be open that the *faubourgs* might be joined to it, he would have one of the largest and best built cities of Europe. Count Schönborn's villa is one of the most magnificent, the furniture all rich brocades, so well fancied and fitted up, nothing can look more gay and splendid, not to speak of a gallery full of rarities of coral, mother of pearl, etc., and throughout the whole house a profusion of gilding, carving, fine paintings, the most beautiful porcelain, statues of alabaster and ivory, and vast orange and lemon trees in gilt pots. The dinner was perfectly fine and well ordered and made still more agreeable by the good humour of the Count. I have not yet been at Court, being forced to stay for my gown, without which there is no waiting on the Empress, though I am not without a great impatience to see a beauty that has been the admiration of many nations. When I have had that honour I will not fail to let you know my real thoughts, always taking a particular pleasure in communicating them to my dear sister.

2. Friedrich Karl, Count von Schönborn, had a reputation for affability and magnificence. His palace was the centre of Viennese social life and he himself the arbiter of its elegance.

To Alexander Pope[1] — *Vienna 14 September 1716*

Perhaps you'll laugh at me for thanking you very gravely for all the obliging concern you express for me. 'Tis certain that I may, if I please, take the fine things you say to me for wit and raillery, and it may be it would be taking them right, but I never in my life was half so well disposed to believe you in earnest, and that distance which makes the continuation of your friendship improbable has very much increased my faith for it, and I find that I have (as well as the rest of my sex), whatever face I set on't, a strong disposition to believe in miracles. Don't fancy, however, that I am infected by the air of these popish countries, though I have so far wandered from the discipline of the Church of England to have been last Sunday at the opera, which was performed in the garden of the Favorita, and I was so much pleased with it, I have not yet repented my seeing it. Nothing of that kind

1. The poet and wit and, at the time of the Embassy letters, devoted admirer of Lady Mary.

2. The present-day Theresianum.

ever was more magnificent, and I can easily believe what I am told, that the decorations and habits cost the Emperor £30,000 sterling. The stage was built over a very large canal, and at the beginning of the second act divided into two parts, discovering the water, on which there immediately came from different parts two fleets of little gilded vessels that gave the representation of a naval fight. The story of the opera is the enchantments of Alcina, which gives opportunity for a great variety of machines and changes of the scenes, which are performed with a surprising swiftness. The theatre is so large that 'tis hard to carry the eye to the end of it, and the habits in the utmost magnificence to the number of one hundred and eight. No house could hold such large decorations, but the ladies all sitting in the open air exposes them to great inconveniencies, for there is but one canopy for the Imperial family, and the first night it was represented, a shower of rain happening, the opera was broke off and the company crowded away in such confusion I was almost squeezed to death.

But if their operas are thus delightful, their comedies are in as high a degree ridiculous. They have but one playhouse, where I had the curiosity to go to a German comedy, and was very glad it happened to be the story of Amphitryon. That subject having been already handled by a Latin, French, and English poet, I was curious to see what an Austrian author would make of it. I understood enough of the language to comprehend the greatest part of it, and besides I took with me a lady that had the goodness to explain every word. The way is to take a box which holds four for yourself and company. The fixed price is a gold ducat. I thought the house very low and dark but I confess the comedy admirably recompensed that defect. I never laughed so much in my life. It begun with Jupiter's falling in love out of a peep hole in the clouds and ended with the birth of Hercules; but what was most pleasant was the use Jupiter made of his metamorphose, for you no sooner saw him under the figure of Amphitryon, but instead of flying to Alcmena with the raptures Mr Dryden puts into his mouth, he sends to Amphitryon's tailor and cheats him of a laced coat, and his banker of a bag of money, a Jew of a diamond ring, and bespeaks a great supper in his name; and the greatest part of the comedy turns upon poor Amphitryon's being tormented by these people for their debts, and Mercury uses Sosia in the same manner. But I could not easily pardon the liberty the poet has taken of larding his play with not only indecent expressions but such gross words as I don't think our mob would suffer from a mountebank, and the two Sosias very fairly let down their breeches in the direct view of the boxes, which were full of people of the first rank that seemed very well pleased with their entertainment, and they assured me this was a celebrated piece. I shall conclude my letter with this remarkable relation very well worthy the serious consideration of Mr Collier.[3] I won't trouble you with farewell compliments, which I think generally as impertinent as curtsies at leaving the room when the visit has been too long already.

3. Jeremy Collier in his *Short View of the Immorality and Profaneness of the English Stage* (1698) attacked the Restoration playwrights, Dryden among them.

To Lady Mar — *Vienna 14 September 1716*

Though I have so lately troubled you (dear sister) with a long letter, yet I will keep my promise in giving you an account of my first going to Court.

In order to attend that ceremony, I was squeezed up in a gown and adorned with a gorget and the other implements thereunto belonging: a dress very inconvenient, but which certainly shows the neck and shape to great advantage. I cannot forbear in this place giving you some description of the fashions here, which are more monstrous and contrary to all common sense and reason than 'tis possible for you to imagine. They build certain fabrics of gauze on their heads about a yard high consisting of three or four stories fortified with numberless yards of heavy riband. The foundation of this structure is a thing they call a *bourlé* which is exactly of the same shape and kind, but about four times as big, as those rolls our prudent milk maids make use of to fix their pails upon. This machine they cover with their own hair, which they mix with a great deal of false, it being a particular beauty to have their heads to go in a moderate tub. Their hair is prodigiously powdered to conceal the mixture, and set out with three or four rows of bodkins, wonderfully large, that stick two or three inches from their hair, made of diamonds, pearls, red, green and yellow stones, that it certainly requires as much art and experience to carry the load upright as to dance upon May Day with the garland. Their whalebone petticoats out-do ours by several yards' circumference and cover some acres of ground. You may easily suppose how much this extraordinary dress sets off and improves the natural ugliness with which God Almighty has been pleased to endow them all generally. Even the lovely Empress[1] herself is obliged to comply in some degree with these absurd fashions, which they

1. Elisabeth Christine, who married Charles VI in 1708; she was reputed one of the most beautiful and charming women of her time.

would not quit for all the world.

I had a private audience (according to ceremony) of half an hour and then all the other ladies were permitted to come make their Court. I was perfectly charmed with the Empress. I cannot, however, tell you that her features are regular. Her eyes are not large but have a lively look full of sweetness, her complexion the finest I ever saw, her nose and forehead well made, but her mouth has ten thousand charms that touch the soul. When she smiles 'tis with a beauty and sweetness that forces adoration. She has a vast quantity of fine fair hair, but then her person! One must speak of it poetically to do it rigid justice; all that the poets have said of the mien of Juno, the air of Venus, comes not up to the truth. The Graces move with her; the famous statue of Medici's[2] was not formed with more delicate proportions, nothing can be added to the beauty of her neck and hands. Till I saw them I did not believe there were any in nature so perfect; and I was almost sorry that my rank here did not permit me to kiss them, but they are kissed sufficiently, for everybody that waits on her pays that homage at their entrance and when they take leave. When the Ladies were come in, she sat down to Quinze.[3] I could not play at a game I had never seen before, and she ordered me a seat at her right hand and had the goodness to talk to me very much with that grace so natural to her. I expected every moment when the men were to come in to pay their Court, but this drawing room is very different from that of England. No man enters it but the old Grand Master, who comes in to advertise the Empress of the approach of the Emperor.[4] His Imperial Majesty did me the honour of speaking to me in a very obliging manner, but he never speaks to any of the other ladies and the whole passes with a gravity and air of ceremony that has something very formal in it. The Empress Amalie, Dowager of the late Emperor Joseph, came this evening to wait on the reigning Empress, followed by the Archduchesses, her daughters, who are very agreeable young Princesses.[5] Their Imperial Majesties rise and go to meet her at the door of the room, after which she is seated in an arm chair next the Empress, and in the same manner at supper, and there the men have the permission of paying their Court. The Archduchesses sit on chairs with backs without arms. The table is entirely served and all the dishes set on by the Empress's Maids of honour, which are twelve young ladies of the first quality. They have no salary but their chambers at Court where they live in a sort of confinement, not being suffered to go to the assemblies or public places in town except in compliment to the wedding of a sister maid, whom the Empress always presents

2. The Venus di Medici, which Lady Mary saw many years later in Florence.

3. A card game.

4. Charles VI, who had succeeded his brother Joseph I in 1711.

5. Wilhelmine Amalie, widow of Joseph I; her daughters were Maria Josefa and Marie Amalie.

with her picture set in diamonds. The three first of them are called ladies of the key, and wear gold keys by their sides, but what I find most pleasant is the custom which obliges them as long as they live after they have left the Empress's service to make her some present every year on the day of her feast. Her majesty is served by no married woman but the Grand Maitresse, who is generally a widow of the first quality, always very old, and is at the same time groom of the stole and mother of the maids. The dressers are not all in the figure they pretend to in England, being looked upon no otherwise than as downright chamber maids.

I had audience the next day of the Empress Mother,[6] a Princess of great virtue and goodnesse, but who piques herself so much on a violent devotion, she is per-petually performing extraordinary acts of penance without having ever done anything to deserve them. She has the same number of maids of honour, whom she suffers to go in colours, but she herself never quits her mourning, and sure nothing can be more dismal than the mournings here, even for a brother. There is not the least bit of linen to be seen: all-black crape instead of it, the neck, ears and side of the face covered with a plaited piece of the same stuff; and the face that peeps out in the midst of it looks as if it were pilloried. The widows wear over and above a crape forehead cloth, and in this solemn weed go to all the public places of diversion without scruple.

The next day I was to wait on the Empress Amalie, who is now at her palace of retirement half a mile from the town. I had there the pleasure of seeing a diversion wholly new to me, but which is the common amusement of this Court. The Empress herself was seated on a little throne at the end of a fine alley in her garden, and on each side of her ranged two parties of her ladies of honour with other young ladies of quality, headed by the two young Archduchesses, all dressed in their hair, full of jewels, with fine light guns in their hands, and at proper distances were placed three oval pictures which were the marks to be shot at. The first was that of a Cupid filling a bumper of Burgundy, and the motto, 'tis easy to be valiant here; the second, a Fortune holding a garland in hand, the motto, for her whom fortune favours; the third was a sword with a laurel wreath on the point, the motto, here is no shame to the vanquished. Near the Empress was a gilded trophy wreathed with flowers and made of little crooks on which were hung rich Turkish handkerchiefs, tippets, ribands, laces etc., for the small prizes. The Empress gave the first with her own hand, which was a fine ruby ring set round

6. Eleonore Magdalene, widow of Leopold I.

with diamonds, in a gold snuff box. There was the second a little Cupid set with brilliants, and besides these a set of fine china for a tea table enchased in gold, Japan trunks, fans, and many gallantries of the same nature. All the men of quality at Vienna were spectators, but only the ladies had permission to shoot, and the Archduchess Amalie carried off the first prize. I was very well pleased with having seen this entertainment, and I don't know but it might make as good a figure as the prize shooting in the Aeneid if I could write as well as Virgil. This is the favourite pleasure of the Emperor, and there is rarely a week without some feast of this kind, which makes the young ladies skilful enough to defend a fort, and they laughed very much to see me afraid to handle a gun.

My dear sister, you will easily pardon an abrupt conclusion. I believe by this time you are ready to fear I would never conclude at all.

To Lady Rich[1] — *Vienna 20 September 1716*

I am extremely pleased, but not at all surprised, at the long delightful letter you have had the goodness to send me. I know that you cannot think of an absent friend even in the midst of a Court, and that you love to oblige where you can have no view of a return, and I expect from you that you should love me and think of me when you don't see me.

I have compassion for the mortifications that you tell me befall our little friend, and I pity her much more since I know that they are only owing to the barbarous customs of our country. Upon my word, if she was here she would have no other fault but being something too young for the fashion, and she has nothing to do but to transplant hither about seven years hence to be again a young and blooming beauty. I can assure you that wrinkles or a small stoop in the shoulders, nay, grey hair itself, is no objection to the making new conquests. I know you can't easily figure to yourself a young fellow of five and twenty ogling my Lady Suffolk with passion, or pressing to lead the Countess of Oxford from an opera, but such are the sights I see every day, and I don't perceive anybody surprised at 'em but myself. A woman till five and thirty is only looked upon as a raw girl and can possibly make no noise in the world till about forty. I don't know what your Lady-

1. Elizabeth, wife of Sir Robert Rich; she was vain and frivolous.

ship may think of this matter, but 'tis a considerable comfort to me to know there is upon earth such a paradise for old women, and I am content to be insignificant at present in the design of returning when I am fit to appear nowhere else.

I cannot help lamenting upon this occasion the pitiful case of so many good English ladies long since retired to prudery and ratafia, whom, if their stars had luckily conducted them hither, would still shine in the first rank of beauties; and then that perplexing word reputation has quite another meaning here than what you give it at London, and getting a lover is so far from losing, that 'tis properly getting reputation, ladies being much more respected in regard to the rank of their lovers than that of their husbands. But what you'll think very odd, the two sects that divide our whole nation of petticoats are utterly unknown. Here are neither coquettes nor prudes. No woman dares appear coquette enough to encourage two lovers at a time, and I have not seen any such prudes as to pretend fidelity to their husbands, who are certainly the best natured set of people in the world, and they look upon their wives' gallants as favourably as men do upon their deputies that take the troublesome part of their business off of their hands, though they have not the less to do, for they are generally deputies in another place themselves. In one word, 'tis the established custom for every lady to have two husbands, one that bears the name, and another that performs the duties; and these engagements are so well known, that it would be a downright affront and publicly resented if you invited a woman of quality to dinner without at the same time inviting her two attendants of lover and husband, between whom she always sits in state with great gravity. These sub-marriages generally last twenty years together, and the lady often commands the poor lover's estate even to the utter ruin of his family, though they are as seldom begun by any passion as other matches. But a man makes but an ill figure that is not in some commerce of this nature, and a woman looks out for a lover as soon as she's married as part of her equipage, without which she could not be genteel; and the first article of the treaty is establishing the pension, which remains to the lady though the gallant should prove inconstant, and this chargeable point of honour I look upon as the real foundation of so many wonderful instances of constancy. I really know several women of the first quality whose pensions are as well known as their annual rents, and yet nobody esteems them the less. On the contrary, their discretion would be called in question if they should be suspected to be mistresses for nothing, and a great part of their emulation consists in trying who shall get most; and having no intrigue at all is so far a disgrace that

I'll assure you a lady who is very much my friend here told me but yesterday how much I was obliged to her for justifying my conduct in a conversation on my subject, where it was publicly asserted that I could not possibly have comon sense that had been about town above a fortnight and had made no steps towards commencing an *amour*. My friend pleaded for me that my stay was uncertain and she believed that was the cause of my seeming stupidity, and this was all she could find to say in my justification.

But one of the pleasantest adventures I ever met in my life was last night and which will give you a just idea after what delicate manner the *belles passions* are managed in this country. I was at the assembly of the Countess of _____ and the young Count of _____ led me down the stairs, and he asked me how long I intended to stay here. I made answer that my stay depended on the Emperor and it was not in my power to determine it. 'Well, Madame,' said he, 'whether your time here is to be long or short, I think you ought to pass it agreeably, and to that end you must engage in a little affair of the heart.' — 'My heart,' answered I gravely enough, 'does not engage very easily, and I have no design of parting with it.' — 'I see, Madame,' said he, sighing, 'by the ill nature of that answer that I am not to hope for it, which is a great mortification to me that am charmed with you; but, however, I am still devoted to your service, and since I am not worthy of entertaining you myself, do me the honour of letting me know who you like best amongst us, and I'll engage to manage the affair entirely to your satisfaction.' — You may judge in what manner I should have received this compliment in my own country, but I was well enough acquainted with the way of this to know that he really intended me an obligation, and thanked him with a grave curtsy for his zeal to serve me and only assured him that I had no occasion to make use of it. Thus you see, my dear, gallantry and good breeding are as different in different climates as morality and religion. Who have the rightest notions of both we shall never know till the Day of Judgement, for which great day of *éclaircissement* I own there is very little impatience in your, etc.

To Mrs T———— 1 — *Vienna 26 September 1716*

I never was more agreeably surprised than by your obliging letter. 'Tis a particular mark of my esteem that I tell you so, and I can assure you that if I loved you one grain less than I do, I should have been very sorry to see it, as diverting as it is. The mortal aversion I have to writing makes me tremble at the thought of a new correspondent, and I believe I disobliged no less than a dozen of my London acquaintance by refusing to hear from them, though I did verily think they intended to send me very entertaining letters; but I had rather lose the pleasure of reading several witty things than be forced to write many stupid ones. Yet in spite of these considerations, I am charmed with this proof of your friendship and beg a continuation of the same goodness, though I fear the dullness of this will make you immediately repent of it.

It is not from Austria that one can write with vivacity, and I am already infected with the phlegm of the country. Even their amours and their quarrels are carried on with a surprising temper, and they are never lively but upon points of ceremony. There, I own, they show all their passions; and 'tis not long since two coaches meeting in a narrow street at night, the ladies in them, not being able to adjust the ceremonial of which should go back, sat there with equal gallantry till two in the morning, and were both so fully determined to die upon the spot rather than yield in a point of that importance that the street would never have been cleared till their deaths if the Emperor had not sent his guards to part 'em; and even then they refused to stir till the expedient was found out of taking them both out in chairs exactly at the same moment, after which it was with some difficulty the pass was decided between the two coachmen, no less tenacious of their rank than the ladies. Nay, this passion is so omnipotent in the breasts of the women that even their husbands never die but they are ready to break their hearts because that fatal hour puts an end to their rank, no widows having any place at Vienna.

The men are not much less touched with this point of honour, and they do not only scorn to marry but to make love to any woman of a family not as illustrious as their own, and the pedigree is much more considered by 'em than either the complexion or features of their mistresses. Happy are the she's that can number amongst their ancestors Counts of the Empire. They have neither occasion for beauty, money or good conduct to get them lovers and husbands. 'Tis true, as to money, 'tis seldom any advantage to the man they marry. The laws of Austria confine a woman's portion not to exceed 2,000 florins, about £200 English, and whatever they have beside remains in their own possession and disposal. Thus here are many ladies much richer than their husbands, who are however obliged to allow them pin money agreeable to their quality, and I attribute to this considerable branch of prerogative the liberty that they take upon other occasions.

I am sure you, that know my laziness and extreme indifference on this subject, will pity me entangled amongst all these ceremonies, which are wonderful burdensome to me, though I am the envy of the whole town, having, by their own customs, the *pas* before them all. But they revenge upon the poor envoys this great respect showed to ambassadors, using them with a contempt that (with all my indifference) I should be very uneasy to suffer. Upon days of ceremony they have no entrance at Court, and on other days must content themselves with walking after every soul and being the very last taken notice of — but I must write a volume to let you know all the ceremonies, and I have already said too much on so dull a subject, which, however, employs the whole care of the people here. I need not, after this, tell you how agreeably the time slides away with me. You know as well as I do the taste of your, etc.

To Lady X ﹏﹏﹏ — *Vienna 1 October 1716*

You desire me, madam, to send you some acount of the customs here and at the same time a description of Vienna. I am always willing to obey your commands, but I must upon this occasion desire you to take the will for the deed. If I should undertake to tell you all the particulars in which the manner here differs from ours, I must write a whole quire of the dullest stuff that ever was read or printed without being read.

Their dress agrees with the French or English in no one article but wearing petticoats, and they have many fashions peculiar to themselves, as that 'tis indecent for a widow ever to wear green or rose colour, but all the other gayest colours at her own discretion. The assemblies here are the only regular diversion, the operas being always at Court and commonly on some particular occasion. Madame Rabutin[1] has the assembly constantly every night at her house and the other ladies whenever they have a fancy to display the magnificence of their apartments or oblige a friend by complimenting them on the day of their saint; they declare that on such a day the assembly shall be at their house in honour of the feast of the Count or Countess such a one. These days are called days of gala, and all the friends or relations of the lady whose saint it is, are obliged to appear in their best clothes and all their jewels. The mistress of the house takes no particular notice of anybody, nor returns anybody's visit, and whoever pleases may go without the formality of being presented. The company are entertained with ice in several forms, winter and summer. Afterwards they divide into parties of ombre, piquet or conversation, all games of hazard being forbid. I saw t'other day the gala for Count Althann, the Emperor's favourite, and never in my life saw so many fine clothes ill fancied. They embroider the richest gold stuffs, and provided they can make their clothes expensive enough, that is all the taste they show in them. On other days the general dress is a scarf and what you please under it.

But now I am speaking of Vienna I am sure you expect I should say something of the convents. They are of all sorts and sizes, but I am best pleased with that of St Lawrence, where the ease and neatness they seem to live with appears to me much more edifying than those stricter orders where perpetual penance and nastiness must breed discontent and wretchedness. The nuns are all of quality; I think there is to the number of fifty. They have each of them a little cell perfectly clean, the walls covered with pictures, more or less fine according to their quality. A long white stone gallery runs by all of 'em, furnished with the pictures of exemplary sisters; the chapel extreme neat and richly adorned. But I could not forbear laughing at their showing me a wooden head of our Saviour which they assured me spoke during the siege of Vienna, and as proof of it, bid me remark his mouth which had been open ever since. Nothing can be more becoming than the dress of these nuns. It is a fine white camlet, the sleeves turned up with fine white calico, and their head dress and [[2]] the same, only a small veil of black crape that falls behind. They have a lower sort of serving nuns that wait on them as their chamber maids. They receive all visits of women and play at ombre in their chambers with permission of the Abbess, which is very easy to be obtained. I never saw an old woman so good natured. She is near four-score and yet shows very little sign of decay, being still lively and cheerful. She caressed me as if I had been her daughter,

1. Dorothea Elisabeth, daughter of the Duke of Holstein and wife of Count von Rabutin.

2. The ms has a blank space here.

giving me some pretty things of her own work and sweetmeats in abundance. The grate is not one of the most rigid. It is not very hard to put a head through and I don't doubt but a man a little more slender than ordinary might squeeze in his whole person. The young Count of Salm came to the grate while I was there, and the Abbess gave him her hand to kiss.

But I was surprised to find here the only beautiful young woman I have seen at Vienna, and not only beautiful but genteel, witty and agreeable, of a great family, and who had been the admiration of the town. I could not forbear showing my surprise at seeing a nun like her. She made me a thousand obliging compliments and desired me to come often. It will be an infinite pleasure to me (said she sighing) to see you, but I avoid with the greatest care seeing any of my former acquaintance, and whenever they come to our convent I lock myself in my cell. — I observed tears come into her eyes, which touched me extremely, and I began to talk to her in that strain of tender pity she inspired me with, but she would not own to me that she is not perfectly happy. I have since endeavoured to learn the real

cause of her retirement without being able to get any account but that everybody was surprised at it and nobody guessed the reason. I have been several times to see her, but it gives me too much melancholy to see so agreeable a young creature buried alive, and I am not surprised that nuns have so often inspired violent passions, the pity one naturally feels for them when they seem worthy of another destiny making an easy way for yet more tender sentiments; and I never in my life had so little charity for the Roman Catholic religion as since I see the misery it occasions so many poor unhappy women, and the gross superstition of the common people who are, some or other of 'em, day and night offering bits of candle to the wooden figures that are set up almost in every street. The processions I see very often are a pageantry as offensive and apparently contradictory to all common sense as the pagoda of China. God knows whether it be the womanly spirit of contradiction that works in me, but there never before was so much zeal against popery in the heart of, dear madam, etc.

Views of the 'Novi Ambulacri', a pleasure drive planted with 400 trees, and of the palace of the Prince of Schwarzenberg from Saloman Kleiner's *Views in Vienna*. Lady Mary was impressed with the parks and palaces of Vienna.

19th-century view of Leipzig, which Lady Mary described as 'the neatest [town] I have seen in Germany' (letter of 21 November 1716 to Lady Mar).

To Lady Mar — *Leipzig 21 November 1716*

I believe (dear sister) you will easily forgive my not writing to you from Dresden as I promised, when I tell you that I never went out of my chaise from Prague to that place. You may imagine how heartily I was tired with twenty-four hours post travelling without sleep or refreshment (for I can never sleep in a coach however fatigued). We passed by moonshine the frightful precipices that divide Bohemia from Saxony, at the bottom of which runs the River Elbe, but I cannot say that I had reason to fear drowning in it, being perfectly convinced that in case of a tumble it was utterly impossible to come alive to the bottom. In many places the road is so narrow that I could not discern an inch of space between the wheels and the precipice; yet I was so good a wife not to wake Mr Wortley, who was fast asleep by my side, to make him share in my fears, since the danger was unavoidable, till I perceived, by the bright light of the moon, our postilions nodding on horseback while the horses were on a full gallop, and I thought it very convenient to call out to desire 'em to look where they were going. My calling waked Mr Wortley and he was much more surprised than myself at the situation we were in, and assured me that he had passed the Alps five times in different places without ever having done a road so dangerous.[1] I have been told since, 'tis common to find the bodies of travellers in the Elbe, but thank God that was not our destiny and we came safe to Dresden, so much tired with fear and fatigue it was not possible for me to compose myself to write. After passing these dreadful rocks, Dresden appeared to me a wonderful agreeable situation in a fine large plain on the banks of the Elbe. I was very glad to stay there a day to rest myself.

The town is the neatest I have seen in Germany. Most of the houses are new built, the Elector's palace very handsome, and his repository full of curiosities of different kinds with a collection of medals very much esteemed. Sir [Richard Vernon], our King's envoy, came to see me here, and Madame de L[orme], whom I knew in London when her husband was minister to the King of Poland there. She offered me all things in her power to entertain me and brought some ladies with her whom she presented to me. The Saxon ladies resemble the Austrian no more than the Chinese those of London. They are very genteely dressed after the French and English modes, and have generally pretty faces, but the most determined *minaudières* in the whole world. They would think it a mortal sin against

1. Wortley had made the Grand Tour from 1700 to 1703.

65

good breeding if they either spoke or moved in a natural manner. They all affect a little soft lisp and a pretty pit-pat step, which female frailties ought, however, to be forgiven 'em in favour of their civility and good nature to strangers, which I have a great deal of reason to praise.

The Countess of Cosel[2] is kept prisoner in a melancholy castle some leagues from hence, and I cannot forbear telling you what I have heard of her, because it seems to me very extraordinary, though I foresee I shall swell my letter to the size of a packet. She was mistress to the King of Poland (Elector of Saxony) with so absolute a dominion over him that never any lady had had so much power in that Court. They tell a pleasant story of His Majesty's first declaration of love, which he made in a visit to her, bringing in one hand a bag of 100,000 crowns, and in the other a horseshoe, which he snapped in sunder before her face, leaving her to draw consequences from such remarkable proofs of strength and liberality. I know not which charmed her, but she consented to leave her husband to give herself up to him entirely, being divorced publicly in such a manner as (by their law) permits either party to marry again. God knows whether it was at this time or in some other fond fit, but 'tis certain the King had the weakness to make her a formal contract of marriage, which though it could signify nothing during the life of the Queen, pleased her so well that she could not be contented without telling all people she saw of it and giving herself the airs of a queen.

Men endure everything while they are in love, but when the excess of passion was cooled by long possession, His Majesty begun to reflect on the ill consequences of leaving such a paper in her hands, and desired to have it restored to him. She rather chose to endure all the most violent effects of his anger than give it up; and though she is one of the richest and most avaricious ladies of her country she has refused the offer of the continuation of a large pension and the security of a vast sum of money she has amassed, and has at last provoked the King to confine her person where she endures all the terrors of a strait imprisonment and remains still inflexible either to threats or promises, though her violent passion has brought her into fits, which 'tis supposed will soon put an end to her life. I cannot forbear having some compassion for a woman that suffers for a point of honour, however mistaken, especially in a country where points of honour are not over scrupulously observed amongst ladies.

I could have wished Mr Wortley's business had permitted a longer stay at Dresden. Perhaps I am partial to a town where they profess the Protestant

2. In 1700 Anna Constanze von Brockdorf, who was Countess von Hoym, became mistress to Augustus the Strong, who created her Countess von Cosel in 1706. She died in 1765, aged 85.

religion, but everything seemed to me with quite another air of politeness than I have found in other places. Leipzig, where I am at present, is a town very considerable for its trade, and I take this opportunity of buying pages' liveries, gold stuffs for myself, etc., all things of that kind being at least double the price at Vienna, partly because of the excessive customs and partly the want of genius and industry in the people, who make no one sort of thing there, and the ladies are obliged to send even for their shoes out of Saxony. The fair here is one of the most considerable in Germany, and the resport of all the people of quality as well as the merchants. This is a fortified town, but I avoid ever mentioning fortifications, being sensible that I know not how to speak of 'em. I am the more easy under my ignorance when I reflect that I am sure you'll willingly forgive the omission, for if I made you the most exact description of all the ravelins and bastions I see in my travels, I dare swear you would ask me — what is a ravelin? and what is a bastion?

Adieu, my dear sister.

To Lady Bristol — *Hanover 25 November 1716*

I received your Ladyship's but the day before I left Vienna, though by the date I ought to have had it much sooner, but nothing was ever worse regulated than the post in most parts of Germany. I can assure you the pacquet at Prague was tied behind my chaise and in that manner conveyed to Dresden. The secrets of half the country were at my mercy if I had any curiosity for 'em. I would not longer delay my thanks for yours, though the number of my acquaintance here and my duty of attending at Court leaves me hardly any time to dispose of. I am extremely pleased that I can tell you without either flattery or partiality that our young Prince[1] has all the accomplishments that 'tis possible to have at his age, with an air of sprightliness and understanding, and somethng so very engaging and easy in his behaviour, that he needs not the advantage of his rank to appear charming. I had the honour of a long conversation with him last night before the King came in. His governor retired on purpose (as he told me afterwards) that I might make some judgment of his genius by hearing him speak without constraint, and I was surprised at the quickness and politeness that appeared in everything he said, joined

1. Frederick Louis, eldest son of the Prince of Wales.

to a person perfectly agreeable and the fine fair hair of the Princess?[2]

This town is neither large nor handsome, but the palace capable of holding a greater Court than that of St James's, and the King has had the goodness to appoint us a lodging in one part of it, without which we should be very ill accommodated; for the vast number of English crowds the town so much, 'tis very good luck to be able to get one sorry room in a miserable tavern. I dined today with the Portuguese Ambassador, who thinks himself very happy to have two wretched parlours in an inn.

I have now made the tour of Germany and cannot help observing a considerable difference between travelling here and in England. One sees none of those fine seats of noblemen that are so common amongst us, nor anything like a country gentleman's house, though they have many situations perfectly fine; but the whole people are divided into absolute sovereignties, where all the riches and magnificence are at Court, or communities of merchants, such as Nuremberg and Frankfurt, where they live always in town for the convenience of trade. The King's company of French Comedians play here every night. They are very well dressed and some of them not ill actors. His Majesty dines and sups constantly in public. The Court is very numerous and his affability and goodness makes it one of the most agreeable places in the world too, dear madam, your Ladyship's etc.

2. His mother, the Princess of Wales.

To Lady Rich — *Hanover 1 December 1716*

I am very glad, my dear Lady R[ich], that you have been so well pleased, as you tell me, at the report of my returning to England, though, like other pleasures, I can assure you it has no real foundation. I hope you know me enough to take my word against any report concerning myself. 'Tis true, as to distance of place, I am much nearer London than I was some weeks ago, but as to the thoughts of a return, I never was farther off in my life. I own I could, with great joy, indulge the pleasing hopes of seeing you and the very few others that share my esteem, but while Mr [Wortley] is determined to proceed in his design, I am determined to follow him. — I am running on upon my own affairs; that is to say, I am going to write very dully as most people do when they write of themselves.

I will make haste to change the disagreeable subject by telling you that I am now got into the region of beauty. All the women here have literally rosy cheeks, snowy foreheads and bosoms, jet eyebrows, and scarlet lips, to which they generally add coal black hair. These perfections never leave them till the hour of their death and have a very fine effect by candlelight, but I could wish they were handsome with a little more variety. They resemble one another as much as Mrs Salmon's court of Great Britain,[1] and are in as much danger of melting away by too near approaching the fire, which they for that reason carefully avoid, though 'tis now such excessive cold weather, that I believe they suffer extremely by that piece of self denial. The snow is already very deep and people begin to slide about in their *traineaus*. This is a favourite diversion all over Germany. They are little machines fixed upon a sledge that hold a lady and a gent[leman] and are drawn by one horse. The Gentleman has the honour of driving and they move with a prodigious swiftness. The lady, the horse and the *traineau* are all as fine as they can be made, and when there are many of 'em together, 'tis a very agreeable show. At Vienna, where all pieces of magnificence are carried to excess, there are sometimes *traineaus* that cost 5 or £600 English.

The Duke of Wolfenbüttel is now at this Court. You know he is nearly related to our King, and uncle to the reigning Empress, who is (I believe) the most beautiful Queen upon earth. She is now with child, which is all the consolation of the Imperial Court for the loss of the Archduke. I took my leave of her the day before I left Vienna, and she began to speak to me with so much grief and tenderness of the death of that young Prince, I had much ado to withhold my tears. You know that I am not at all partial to people for the titles, but I own that I love that charming Princess (if I may use so familiar and expression) and if I did not, I should have been very much moved at the tragical end of an only son born after being so long desired and at length killed by want of good management, weaning him in the beginning of the winter.[2]

Adieu, my dear Lady R[ich]. Continue to write to me, and believe none of your goodness is lost upon Your's etc.

1. Mrs Salmon owned a waxwork exhibition in Fleet Street.

2. Archduke Leopold, born in April 1716, had died on 4 November. The future Empress Maria Theresa was born in May 1717.

To Lady Mar — *Blankenburg 17 December 1716*

I received yours (dear sister) the very day I left Hanover. You may easily imagine I was then in too great a hurry to answer it, but you see I take the first opportunity of doing myself that pleasure. I came here the fifteenth very late at night, after a terrible journey in the worst roads and weather that ever poor travellers suffered. I have taken this little fatigue merely to oblige the reigning Empress and carry a message from Her Imperial Majesty to the Duchess of Blankenburg, her mother, who is a princess of great address and good breeding, and may be still called a fine woman. It was so late when I came to this town, I did not think it proper to disturb the Duke and Duchess with the news of my arrival and took up my quarters in a miserable inn; but as soon as I had sent my compliment to their Highnesses, they immediately sent me their own coach and six horses, which had, however, enough to do to draw us up the very high hill on which the castle is situated. The Duchess is extremely obliging to me and this little Court is not without its diversions. The Duke tallies at basset[1] every night; and the Duchess tells me that she is so well pleased with my company, I should find it very difficult to steal time to write if she was not now at church, where I cannot wait on her, not understanding the language enough to pay my devotions in it.

You will not forgive me if I do not say something of Hanover. I cannot tell you that the town is either large or magnificent. The opera house, which was built by the late Elector,[2] is much finer than that of Vienna. I was very sorry the ill weather did not permit me to see Herrenhausen in all its beauty, but in spite of the snow I thought the gardens very fine. I was particularly surprised at the vast number of orange trees, much larger than any I have ever seen in England, though this climate is certainly colder. But I had more reason to wonder that night at the King's table. There was brought to him from a gentleman of this country two large baskets full of ripe oranges and lemons of different sorts, many of which were quite new to me, and what I thought worth all the rest, two ripe ananas, which to my taste are a fruit perfectly delicious. You know they are naturally the growth of Brazil, and I could not imagine how they could come there but by enchantment. Upon inquiry I learnt that they have brought their stoves to such perfection, they lengthen the summer as long as they please, giving to every plant the degree of heat it would receive from the sun in its native soil. The effect is very near the

1. Plays cards.

2. Built inside the palace, 1688-89, by Ernst August I, it was one of the largest and handsomest theatres of the time.

same. I am surprised we do not practise in England so useful an invention. This reflection naturally leads me to consider our obstinacy in shaking with cold six months in the year rather than make use of stoves, which are certainly one of the greatest conveniences of life; and so far from spoiling the form of a room, they add very much to the magnificence of it when they are painted and gilt as at Vienna, or at Dresden where they are often in the shapes of china jars, statues, or fine cabinets, so naturally represented they are not to be distinguished. If ever I return, in defiance to the fashion you shall certainly see one in the chamber of, dear sister, etc.

I will write often, since you desire it, but I must beg you to be a little more particular in yours. You fancy me at forty miles distance and forget that after so long an absence I can't understand hints.

To Lady M — *Vienna 1 January 1717*

I have just received here at Vienna your Ladyship's compliment on my return to England, sent me from Hanover. You see, madam, all things that are asserted with confidence are not absolutely true and that you have no sort of reason to complain of me for making my designed return a mystery to you when you say all the world are informed of it. You may tell all the world in my name that they are never so well informed of my affairs as I am myself, and that I am very positive I am at this time at Vienna, where the carnival is begun and all sort of diversions in perpetual practice except that of masquing, which is never permitted during a war with the Turks. The balls are in public places, where the men pay a gold ducat at entrance, but the ladies nothing. I am told that these houses get sometimes a thousand ducats on a night. They are very magnificently furnished, and the music good if they had not that detestable custom of mixing hunting horns with it that almost deafen the company, but that noise is so agreeable here they never make a consort without 'em. The ball always concludes with English country dances to the number of thirty or forty couple, and so ill danced that there is very little pleasure in 'em. They know but half a dozen, and they have danced them over and over this fifty year. I would fain have taught them some new ones, but I found it would be some months' labour to make them comprehend 'em.

Last night there was an Italian comedy acted at Court. The scenes were pretty, but the comedy itself such intolerable low farce without either wit or humour, that I was surprised how all the Court could sit there attentively for four hours together. No women are suffered to act on the stage, and the men dressed like 'em were such awkward figures they very much added to the ridicule of the spectacle. What completed the diversion was the excessive cold, which was so great I thought I should have died there. It is now the very extremity of the winter here. The Danube is entirely frozen, and the weather not to be supported without stoves and furs, but, however, the air is so clear almost everybody is well, and colds not half so common as in England, and I am persuaded there cannot be a purer air, nor more wholesome than that of Vienna. The plenty and excellence of all sort of provisions is greater here than in any place I was ever in, and 'tis not very expensive to keep a splendid table. 'Tis really a pleasure to pass through the markets and see the abundance of what we should think rarities of fowls and venisons that are daily brought in from Hungary and Bohemia. They want nothing but shell fish, and are so fond of oysters they have 'em sent from Venice and eat 'em very greedily, stink or not stink.

Thus I obey your commands, madam, in giving you an account of Vienna, though I know you will not be satisfied with it. You chide me for my laziness in not telling you a thousand agreeable and surprising things that you say you are sure I have seen and heard. Upon my word, madam, 'tis my regard to truth and not laziness that I do not entertain you with as many prodigies as other travellers use to divert their readers with. I might easily pick up wonders in every town I pass through, or tell you a long series of Popish miracles, but I cannot fancy that there is anything new in letting you know that priests can lie and the mob believe all over the world. Then, as for news that you are so inquisitive about, how can it be entertaining to you that don't know the people, that the Prince of _____ has forsaken the Countess of _____ ? or that the Princess such a one has an intrigue with Count such a one? Would you have me write novelties like the Countess of D'Alnoy?[1] and is it not better to tell you a plain truth, that I am, etc.

1. Marie Catherine d'Aulnoy, author of historical romances and fairy tales.

To Lady Mar — *Vienna 16 January 1717*

I am now, dear sister, to take leave of you for a long time and of Vienna for ever, designing tomorrow to begin my journey through Hungary in spite of the excessive cold and deep snows which are enough to damp a greater courage that I am mistress of, but my principle of passive obedience carries me through everything. I have had my audiences of leave of the Empresses. His Imperial Majesty was pleased to be present when I waited on the reigning Empress, and after a very obliging conversation both their Imperial Majesties invited me to take Vienna in my road back, but I have no thoughts of enduring over again so great a fatigue.

I delivered a Letter to the Empress from the Duchess of Blankenburg. I stayed but a few days at that Court, though her Highness pressed me very much to stay, and when I left her engaged me to write to her. I wrote you a long letter from thence which I hope you received, though you don't mention it, but I believe I forgot to tell you one curiosity in all the German Courts, which I cannot forbear taking notice of. All the Princes keep favourite dwarfs. The Emperor and Empress have two of these little monsters as ugly as devils, especially the female, but all bedaubed with diamonds and stands at Her Majesty's elbow in all public places. The Duke of Wolfenbüttel has one and the Duchess of Blankenburg is not without hers, but indeed the most proportionable I ever saw. I am told the King of Denmark has so far improved upon this fashion that his dwarf is his chief minister. I can assign no reason for their fondness for these pieces of deformity but the opinion that all absolute Princes have that 'tis below them to converse with the rest of mankind; and not to be quite alone they are forced to seek their companions amongst the refuse of human nature, these creatures being the only part of their Court privileged to talk freely to 'em.

I am at present confined to my chamber by a sore throat, and am really glad of the excuse to avoid seeing people that I love well enough to be very much mortified when I think I am going to part with them for ever. 'Tis true the Austrians are not commonly the most polite people in the world or the most agreeable, but Vienna is inhabited by all nations, and I had formed to myself a little society of such as were perfectly to my own taste, and though the number was not very great, I could never pick up in any other place such a number of reasonable, agreeable people. We were almost always together, and you know I have ever been of opinion that a chosen conversation composed of a few that one esteems is the greatest happiness of life. Here are some Spaniards of both sexes that have all the vivacity and generosity of sentiments anciently ascribed to the nation, and could I believe the whole Kingdom were like them, I should wish nothing more than to end my days there.

The ladies of my acquaintance have so much goodness for me, they cry whenever they see me, since I am determined to undertake this journey, and indeed I am not very easy when I reflect on what I am going to suffer. Almost every body I see frights me with some new difficulty. Prince Eugene[1] has been so good to say all things he could to persuade me to stay till the Danube is thawed that I may have the conveniency of going by water, assuring me that the houses in Hungary are such as are no defence against the weather and that I shall be obliged to travel three or four days between Buda and Esseck without finding any house at all, through desert plains covered with snow, where the cold is so violent many have been killed by it. I own these terrors have made a very deep impression on my mind because I believe he tells me things truly as they are, and nobody can be better informed of them. Now I have named that great man I am sure you expect I should say something particular of him, having the advantage of seeing him very often, but I am as unwilling to speak of him at Vienna as I should be to talk of Hercules in the Court of Omphale if I had seen him there. I don't know what comfort people find in considering the weaknesses of great men because it brings them nearer to their own level, but 'tis always a mortification to me to observe that there is no perfection in humanity. The young Prince of Portugal[2] is the admiration of the whole Court. He is handsome and polite with a great vivacity. All the officers tell wonders of his gallantry the last campaign. He is lodged at Court with all the honours due to his rank.

Adieu, dear sister. This is the last account you will have from me of Vienna. If I survive my journey you shall hear from me again. I can say with great truth in the words of Moneses, I have long learnt to hold myself at nothing,[3] but when I think of the fatigue my poor infant must suffer, I have all a mother's fondness in my eyes and all her tender passions in my heart.

P.S. I have written a letter to my Lady _____ that I believe she won't like, and upon cooler reflection, I think I had done better to have let it alone, but I was downright peevish at all her questions and her ridiculous imagination that I have certainly seen abundance of wonders that I keep to myself out of mere malice. She

1. Prince Eugene of Savoy, the famous Austrian general and victor over the Turkish army at Peterwaradin.

2. Dom Manuel of Braganza, brother of the King of Portugal, who had joined the Austrian army against his brother's orders and had fought bravely at Peterwardadin.

3. Prince Moneses says this in Nicholas Rowe's play *Tamerlane*

is angry that I won't lie like other travellers. I verily believe she expects I should tell her of the Anthropophagi and men whose heads grow below their shoulders. However, pray say something to pacify her.

To Alexander Pope — *Vienna 16 January 1717*

I have not time to answer your letter, being in all the hurry of preparing for my journey, but I think I ought to bid adieu to my friends with the same solemnity as if I was going to mount a breach, at least if I am to believe the information of the people here, who denounce all sorts of terrors to me; and indeed the weather is at present such as very few ever set out in. I am threatened at the same time with being froze to death, buried in the snow, and taken by the Tartars who ravage that part of Hungary I am to pass. 'Tis true we shall have a considerable escort, so that possibly I may be diverted with a new scene by finding myself in the midst of a battle. How my adventures will conclude I leave entirely to Providence; if comically, you shall hear of 'em.

Pray be so good to tell Mr _____[1] I have received his letter. Make him my adieus. If I live I will answer it. The same compliment to my Lady R[ich].

1. Probably the dramatist William Congreve, an intimate friend of Pope's, and a friend of Lady Mary's since her girlhood. Lady Mary eventually answered him on 1st April.

To Lady Mar — *Peterwaradin 30 January 1717*

At length (dear sister) I am safely arrived with all my family in good health at Peterwaradin,[1] having suffered little from the rigour of the season (against which we were well provided by furs) and found everywhere (by the care of sending before) such tolerable accommodation, I can hardly forbear laughing when I recollect all the frightful ideas that were given me of this journey, which were wholly owing to the tenderness of my Vienna friends and their desire of keeping me with 'em for this winter. Perhaps it will not be disagreeable to give you a short journal of my journey, being through a country entirely unknown to you, and very little passed even by the Hungarians themselves who generally choose to take the

1. Present-day Petrovaradin, in Yugoslavia.

convenience of going down the Danube. We have had the blessing of being favoured by finer weather than is common at this time of the year, though the snow was so deep we were obliged to have our coaches fixed upon *traineaus*, which move so swift and so easily 'tis by far the most agreeable manner of travelling post.

We came to Raab[2] the second day from Vienna on the 17 instant where Mr Wortley, sending word of our arrival to the Governor, we had the best house in the town provided for us, the garrison put under arms, a guard ordered at our door, and all other honours paid to us, the Governor and officers immediately waiting on Mr Wortley to know if there was anything to be done for his service. The Bishop of Temesvar came to visit us with great civility, earnestly pressing us to dine with him the next day, which we refusing, as being resolved to pursue our journey, he sent us several baskets of winter fruit and a great variety of fine Hungarian wines with a young hind just killed. This is a prelate of great power in this country, of the ancient family of Nadasti, so considerable for many ages in this Kingdom. He is a very polite, agreeable, cheerful old man, wearing the Hungarian habit, with a venerable white beard down to this girdle.

Raab is a strong town, well garrisoned and fortified, and was a long time the frontier town between the Turkish and German Empires. It has its name from the River Rab, on which it is situated just on its meeting with the Danube in an open champagne country. It was first taken by the Turks under the command of Pasha Sinan in the reign of Sultan Amurath the Third, 1594. The Governor, being supposed to have betrayed it, was afterwards beheaded by the Emperor's command. The Counts of Schwarzenberg and Palffy retook it by surprise 1598, since which time it has remained in the hands of the Germans, though the Turks once more attempted to gain it by stratagem, 1642. The cathedral is large and well built, which is all that I saw remarkable in the town.

Leaving Comora on the other side the river, we went the 18th to Nosmuhl, a small village where, however, we made shift to find tolerable accommodation. We continued two days travelling between this place and Buda, through the finest plains in the world, as even as if they were paved, and extreme fruitful, but for the most part desert and uncultivated, laid waste by the long war between the Turk and Emperor, and the more cruel civil war occasioned by the barbarous persecution of the protestant religion by the Emperor Leopold. That Prince has left behind him the character of an extraordinary piety and was naturally of a mild merciful temper, but putting his conscience into the hands of a Jesuit, he was more

2. Present-day Gyor, in Hungary.

cruel and treacherous to his poor Hungarian subjects than ever the Turk has been to the Christians, breaking without scruple his coronation oath and his faith solemnly given in many public treaties. Indeed, nothing can be more melancholy than travelling through Hungary, reflecting on the former flourishing state of that Kingdom and seeing such a noble spot of earth almost uninhabited.

This is also the present circumstances of Buda (where we arrived very early the 22nd), once the royal seat of the Hungarian Kings, where their palace was reckoned one of the most beautiful buildings of the age, now wholly destroyed, no part of the town having been repaired since the last siege but the fortifications and the castle, which is the present residence of the governor, General Ragule, an officer of great merit. He came immediately to see us and carried us in his coach to his house, where I was received by his lady with all possible civility and magnificently entertained. This city is situated upon a little hill on the south side of the Danube,[3] the castle being much higher than the town, from whence the prospect is very noble. Without the walls lie a vast number of little houses, or rather huts, that they call the Rascian [Serbian] Town, being altogether inhabited by that people. The Governor assured me it would furnish 12,000 fighting men. These towns look very odd; their houses stand in rows, many thousands of them so close together they appear at a little distance like odd fashioned thatched tents. They consist, every one of them, of one hovel above and another under ground; these are their summer and winter apartments.

Buda was first taken by Süleyman the Magnificent, 1526, and lost the following year to Ferdinand I, King of Bohemia. Süleyman regained it, 1529, by the treachery of the garrison, and voluntarily gave it into the hand of King John of Hungary, afer whose death, his son being an infant, Ferdinand laid siege to it, and the Queen Mother was forced to call Süleyman to her aid, who raised the siege but left a Turkish garrison in the town and commanded her to remove her court from thence, which she was forced to submit to, 1541. It resisted afterwards the sieges laid to it by the Marquis of Brandenburg, 1542; the Count of Schwarzenberg, 1598; General Rüssworm, 1602; and of the Duke of Lorraine, commander of the Emperor's forces, 1684, to whom it yielded, 1686, after an obstinate defence, Abd-al-Rahman Pasha, the Governor, being killed fighting in the breach with a Roman bravery. The loss of this town was so important and so much resented by the Turks, it occasioned the deposing of their Emperor Mehmet the Fourth the year following.

3. In fact Buda is on the west bank of the Danube.

We did not proceed on our journey till the 23rd, passing through Adam and Fodowar, both considerable towns when in the hands of the Turks. They are now quite ruined; only the remains of some Turkish towers show something of what they have been. This part of the country is very much overgrown with wood, and so little frequented 'tis incredible what vast numbers of wild fowl we saw, who often live here to a good old age

And, undisturb'd by guns, in quiet sleep.

We came the 25th to Mohatch[4] and were showed the field near it where Lewis, the young King of Hungary, lost his army and his life, being drowned in a ditch, trying to fly from Balybeus, the General of Süleyman the Magnificent. This battle opened the first passage for the Turks into the heart of Hungary. I don't name to you the little villages of which I can say nothing remarkable, but I'll assure you I have always found a warm stove and great plenty, particularly of wild boar, venison, and all kind of gibier. The few people that inhabit Hungary live easily enough. They have no money, but the woods and plains afford them provision in great abundance. They were ordered to give us all things necessary, even what horses we pleased to demand, gratis, but Mr Wortley would not oppress the poor country people by making use of this order, and always paid them the full worth of what we had from 'em. They were so surprised at this unexpected generosity, which they are very little used to, they always pressed upon us at parting a dozen of fat pheasants or something of that sort, for a present. Their dress is very primitive, being only a plain sheep's skin without other dressing than being dried in the sun, and a cap and boots of the same stuff. You may imagine this lasts them for many winters, and thus they have very little occasion for money.

The 26th we passed over the frozen Danube with all our equipage and carriages. We met on the other side General Veterani, who invited us with great civility to pass the night at a little castle of his a few miles off, assuring us we should have a very hard day's journey to reach Esseck, which we found but too true, the woods being scarce passable, and very dangerous from the vast quantity of wolves that herd in them. We came, however, safe though late to Esseck,[5] where we stayed a day to dispatch a courier with letters to the Pasha of Belgrade, and I took the opportunity of seeing the town, which is not very large but fair built and well forti-fied. This was a town of great trade, very rich and populous when in the hands of the Turks. It is situated on the Drave, which runs into the Danube. The bridge was esteemed one of the most extraordinary in the world, being 8,000 paces long and

4. Present-day Mohacs, in Hungary.

5. Present-day Osijek, in Yugoslavia.

all built of oak, which was burnt and the city laid in ashes by Count Leslie, 1685, but again repaired and fortified by the Turks, who however abandoned it, 1687, and General Dünewalt took possession of it for the Emperor, in whose hands it has remained ever since, and is esteemed one of the bulwarks of Hungary.

The 28th we went to Bocowar,[6] a very large Rascian Town, all built after the manner I have described to you. We were met there by Colonel _____, who would not suffer us to go any where but to his quarters, where I found his wife, a very agreeable Hungarian lady, and his niece and daughter, two pretty young women, crowded in three or four Rascian houses cast into one and made as neat and convenient as those places were capable of being made. The Hungarian ladies are much handsomer than those of Austria. All the Vienna beauties are of that country; they are generally very fair and well shaped. Their dress I think extreme becoming. This lady was in a gown of scarlet velvet, lined and faced with sables, made exact to her shape and the skirt falling to her feet. The sleeves are straight to their arms and the stays buttoned before with two rows of little buttons of gold, pearl or diamonds. On their heads they wear a cap embroidered with a tassel of gold that hangs low on one side, lined with sable or some other fine fur. They gave us a handsome dinner, and I thought their conversation very polite and agreeable. They would accompany us part of our way.

The 29th we arrived here, where we were met by the Commandant at the head of all the officers of the garrison. We are lodged in the best apartment of the Governor's house and entertained in a very splendid manner by the Emperor's order. We wait here till all points are adjusted concerning our reception on the Turkish frontiers. Mr Wortley's courier, which he sent from Esseck, returned this morning with the Pasha's answer in a purse of scarlet satin, which the interpreter here has translated. 'Tis to promise him to be honourably received, and desires him to appoint where he would be met by the Turkish convoy. He has dispatched the courier back naming Betsko, a village in the midway between Peterwaradin and Belgrade. We shall stay here till we receive the answer. Thus, dear sister, I have given you a very particular and, I'm afraid you'll think, a tedious account of this part of my travels. It was not an affectation of showing my reading that has made me tell you some little scraps of the history of the towns I passed through. I have always avoided anything of that kind when I spoke of places which I believed you knew the story of as well as myself, but Hungary being a part of the world that I believe quite new to you, I thought you might read with some pleasure an

6. Present-day Vukovar, in Yugoslavia.

account of it which I have been very solicitous to get from the best hands. However, if you don't like it, 'tis in your power to forbear reading it. I am, dear sister, etc.

I am promised to have this letter carefully sent to Vienna.

To Alexander Pope — *Belgrade 12 February 1717*

I did verily intend to write you a long letter from Peterwaradin[1], where I expected to stay three or four days, but the Pasha here was in such haste to see us, he dispatched our courier back (which Mr Wortley had sent to know the time he would send the convoy to meet us) without suffering him to pull off his boots. My letters were not thought important enough to stop our journey, and we left Peterwaradin the next day, being waited on by the chief officers of the garrison and a considerable convoy of Germans and Rascians. The Emperor has several regiments of these people, but to say truth, they are rather plunderers than soldiers, having no pay and being obliged to furnish their own arms and horses. They rather look like vagabond gipsies or stout beggars than regular troops. I can't forbear speaking a word of this race of creatures, who are very numerous all over Hungary. They have a Patriarch of their own at Grand Cairo and are really of the Greek church, but their extreme ignorance gives their priests occasion to impose several new notions upon 'em. These fellows, letting their hair and beards grow inviolate, make exactly the figure of the Indian brahmins. They are heirs general to all the money of the laity, for which in return they give 'em formal passports signed and sealed for heaven, and the wives and children only inherit the houses and cattle. In most other points they follow the Greek rites.

This little digression has interrupted my telling you we passed over the fields of Carlowitz, where the last great victory was obtained by Prince Eugene over the Turks. The marks of that glorious bloody day are yet recent, the field being strewed with the skulls and carcases of unburied men, horses and camels. I could not look without horror on such numbers of mangled human bodies, and reflect on the injustice of war, that makes murder not only necessary but meritorious. Nothing seems to me a plainer proof of the irrationality of mankind (whatever

1. Prince Eugene had routed an Ottoman attack on Peterwaradin in August 1716. Under the terms of the peace of Karlowitz (1699), Peterwaradin, formerly in Ottoman hands, was ceded to the Austrian Empire.

19th-century view of Belgrade by W.H. Bartlett. When Lady Mary stayed in the city, it was still part of the Ottoman Empire.

fine claims we pretend to reason) than the rage with which they contest for a small spot of ground, when such vast parts of fruitful earth lie quite uninhabited. 'Tis true, custom has now made it unavoidable, but can there be a greater demonstration of want of reason than a custom being firmly established so plainly contrary to the interest of man in general? I am a good deal inclined to believe Mr Hobbs that the state of nature is a state of war,[2] but thence I conclude humane nature not rational, if the word reason means common sense, as I suppose it does. I have a great many admirable arguments to support this reflection, but I won't trouble you with 'em but return in a plain style to the history of my travels.

We were met at Betsko (a village in the midway between Belgrade and Peterwaradin) by an aga of the janissaries with a body of Turks exceeding the Germans by one hundred men, though the Pasha had engaged to send exactly the same number. You may judge by this of their fears. I am really persuaded that they hardly thought the odds of one hundred men set them even with the Germans.

2. A paraphrase from Thomas Hobbes' *Leviathan*.

Portrait of Sheik-ul-Islam the Mufti of Constantinople after Jean-Baptiste Vanmour. The Mufti was the head of both the religious functionaries and the judicary.

3. Süleyman captured Belgrade in 1521. Maxmilian II, the Elector of Bavaria, took the town in 1688, Köprülüzade Mustafa Pasha recaptured it in 1690, while in August 1717, a few months after Lady Mary's visit, it fell to the Austrians again.

4. The Sultan, Ahmet III.

5. A Kadi was a civil judge, a Mufti a jurisconsult (an expert on law and custom who acted as adviser to the Kadi).

However, I was very uneasy till they were parted, fearing some quarrel might arise notwithstanding the parole given.

We came late to Belgrade, the deep snows making the ascent to it very difficult. It seems a strong city, fortified on the east side by the Danube and on the south by the River Save, and was formerly the barrier of Hungary. It was first taken by Süleyman the Magnificent and since by the Emperor's forces led by the Elector of Bavaria,[3] who held it only two year, it being retaken by the Grand Vizier,[4] and is now fortified with the utmost care and skill the Turks are capable of, and strengthened by a very numerous garrison of their bravest janissaries commanded by a Pasha Seraskier (i.e. General). This last expression is not very just, for to say truth the Seraskier is commanded by the janissaries, who have an absolute authority here, not much unlike a rebellion, which you may judge of by the following story, which at the same time will give you an idea of the admirable intelligence of the Governor of Peterwaradin, though so few hours distant.

We were told by him at Peterwaradin that the garrison and inhabitants of Belgrade were so weary of the war, they had killed their Pasha about two months ago in a mutiny because he had suffered himself to be prevailed upon by a bribe of five purses (£500 sterling) to give permission to the Tartars to ravage the German frontiers. We were very well pleased to hear of such favourable dispositions in the people, but when we came hither we found the Governor had been ill informed, and this the real truth of the story. The late Pasha fell under the displeasure of his soldiers for no other reason but restraining their incursions on the Germans. They took it into their heads from that mildness, he was of intelligence with the enemy, and sent such information to the Grand Signor at Adrianople, but redress not coming quick from thence, they assembled themselves in a tumultuous manner and by force dragged their Pasha before the Kadi and Mufti,[5] and there demanded justice in a mutinous way; one crying out, why he protected the infidels? another, why he squeezed them of their money? that easily guessing their purpose, he calmly replied to them that they asked him too many questions; he had but one life, which must answer for all. They immediately fell upon him with their scimitars (without waiting the sentence of their heads of the law) and in a few moments cut him in pieces. The present Pasha has not dared to punish the murder. On the contrary, he affected to applaud the actors of it as brave fellows that knew how to do themselves justice. He takes all pretences of throwing money amongst the garrison and suffers them to make little excursions into Hungary, where they burn some poor Rascian houses. You may imagine I cannot be very easy in a town which is really under the government of an insolent soldiery. We expected to be immediately dismissed after a night's lodging here, but the Pasha detains us till he receives orders from Adrianople, which may possibly be a month a coming.

In the meantime we are lodged in one of the best houses, belonging to a very considerable man amongst 'em, and have a whole chamber of janissaries to guard us. My only diversion is the conversation of our host, Achmet-Beg, a title something like that of Count in Germany. His father was a great Pasha and he has been educated in the most polite eastern learning, being perfectly skilled in the Arabic and Persian languages, and is an extraordinary scribe, which they call Effendi. This accomplishment makes way to the greatest preferments, but he has had the good sense to prefer an easy, quiet, secure life to all the dangerous honours of the Porte.[6] He sups with us every night and drinks wine very freely. You cannot imagine how much he is delighted with the liberty of conversing with me. He has explained to me many pieces of Arabian poetry, which I observed are in numbers not unlike ours, generally alternate verse, and of a very musical sound. Their expressions of love are very passionate and lively. I am so much pleased with them, I really believe I should learn to read Arabic if I was to stay here a few months. He has a very good library of their books of all kinds and, as he tells me, spends the greatest part of his life there. I pass for a great scholar with him by relating to him some of the Persian Tales, which I find are genuine. At first he believed I understood Persian. I have frequent disputes with him concerning the difference of our customs, particularly the confinements of women. He assures me there is nothing at all in it; only, says he, we have the advantage that when our wives cheat us, no body knows it. He has wit and is more polite than many Christian men of quality. I am very much entertained with him. He has had the curiosity to make one of our servants set him an alphabet of our letters and can already write a good Roman hand; but these amusements do not hinder my wishing heartily to be out of this place, though the weather is colder than I believed it ever was anywhere but in Greenland. We have a very large stove constantly kept hot and yet the windows of the room are frozen on the inside. God knows when I may have an opportunity of sending this letter, but I have writ it in the discharge of my own conscience, and you cannot now reproach me that one of yours can make ten of mine.

Portrait by an anonymous Greek artist of a rifleman *tüsekci.*

6. The Porte was the title given in the west to the Sultan's Court.

Road over the Balkan Mountain
by Luigi Mayer. On her
journey from Belgrade to Sofia
and Philippopolis Lady Mary
travelled through terrain
similar to the mountains
shown here.

84

View of the central room of a male bathhouse showing the massage slab done by an anonymous Greek artist. Lady Mary visited the female baths in both Adrianople and Constantinople: 'it [the bathhouse] is built of stone in the shape of a dome with no windows but in the roof, which give light enough' (letter of 1 April 1717 to Lady —-).

To The Princess of Wales[1] — *Adrianople 1 April[2] 1717*

I have now, madam, passed a journey that has not been undertaken by any Christian since the time of the Greek Emperors,[3] and I shall not regret all the fatigues I have suffered in it if it gives me an opportunity of amusing your Royal Highness by an account of places utterly unknown amongst us, the Emperor's ambassadors and those few English that have come hither, always going on the Danube to Nicopolis,[4] but that river was now frozen, and Mr Wortley so zealous for the service of His Majesty he would not defer his journey to wait for the conveniency of that passage.[5] We crossed the deserts of Serbia almost quite overgrown with wood, though a country naturally fertile and the inhabitants industrious, but the oppression of the peasants is so great they are forced to abandon their houses and neglect their tillage, all they have being a prey to the janissaries whenever they please to seize upon it. We have a guard of five hundred of 'em, and I was almost in tears every day to see their insolencies in the poor villages through which we passed.

After seven days travelling through thick woods we came to Nis, once the Capital of Serbia, situate in a fine plain on the River Nissava, in a very good air, and so fruitful a soil that the great plenty is hardly credible. I was certainly assured that the quantity of wine last vintage was so prodigious they were forced to dig holes in the earth to put it in, not having vessels enough in the town to hold it. The happiness of this plenty is scarce perceived by the oppressed people. I saw here a new occasion for my compassion, the wretches that had provided twenty wagons for our baggage from Belgrade hither for a certain hire, being all sent back without payment, some of their horses lamed and others killed without any satisfaction made for 'em. The poor fellows came round the house weeping and tearing their hair and beards in the most pitiful manner without getting anything but drubs from the insolent soldiers. I cannot express to your Royal Highness how much I was moved at this scene. I would have paid them the money out of my own pocket with all my heart, but it had been only giving so much to the Aga, who would have taken it from them without any remorse.

After four days' journey from this place over the mountains we came to Sophia, situated in a large beautiful plain on the River Isca, surrounded with distant mountains. 'Tis hardly possible to see a more agreeable landscape. The

1. Caroline of Ansbach, wife of the future George II.

2. Lady Mary dated so many letters 1st April because they were dispatched that day in two packets, one of which went by land, the other by sea.

3. Lady Mary exaggerates; the overland journey had been undertaken as early as the 16th century.

4. Present-day Edirne.

5. Wortley gave a different account. By the time he could depart from Belgrade, the Danube had thawed, but the Pasha refused him an escort without express orders, and rather than stay any longer he set out by land.

city itself is very large and extremely populous. Here are hot baths, very famous for their medicinal virtues. Four days journey from hence we arrived at Philippopolis,[6] after having passed the ridges between the mountains of Haemus and Rhodope, which are always covered with snow. This town is situated on a rising ground near the River Hebrus and is almost wholly inhabited by Greeks. Here are still some ancient Christian churches. They have a bishop, and several of the richest Greeks live here, but they are forced to conceal their wealth with great care, the appearance of poverty (which includes part of its inconveniencies) being all their security against feeling it in earnest. The country from hence to Adrianople is the finest in the world. Vines grow wild on all the hills, and the perpetual spring they enjoy makes everything look gay and flourishing, but this climate, as happy as it seems, can never be preferred to England with all its snows and frosts, while we are blessed with an easy government under a King who makes his own happiness consist in the liberty of his people, and chooses rather to be looked upon as their father than their master. This theme would carry me very far, and I am sensible that I have already tired out your Royal Highness's patience, but my letter is in your hands, and you may make it as short as you please by throwing it into the fire when you are weary of reading it.

I am, madam, with the greatest respect, etc.

6. Present-day Plovdiv, in Bulgaria.

IN TURKEY

Accompanied by an escort of 500 Janissaries, Wortley and his party reached Adrianople (modern Edirne) on 13 March by way of Sofia and Philippopolis. Lady Mary's two-month stay here, in elegant lodgings provided by the Sultan in one of his palaces, gave her every opportunity to explore the city and to become acquainted with Ottoman society. The enthusiasm of her letters from Adrianople, the zestful curiosity they display, make evident Lady

A prince or nobleman riding with an escort of spahis (horsemen); view by an anonymous Greek artist. A group of janissaries accompanied Lady Mary and the French ambassador's wife when they explored Adrianople; 'they [the janissaries] are very zealous and faithful where they serve, and look upon it as their business to fight for you upon all occasions' (Letter of 1 April 1717 to Lady Bristol, see pages 104-106.)

Portrait by an anonymous
Greek artist of a Palace scribe.

*View of the throne room in the
Sultan's Palace, the Topkapi
Saray,* by an anonymous
Greek artist. The Sultan
generally received viziers and
ambassadors here; the throne
is on the right. Wortley was
received in April 1717, not in
Constantinople but in
Adrianople; Lady Mary, who
as a woman was of course
unable to be present, does not
describe the occasion.

Mary's rapture with all she saw. In Sofia, she had already penetrated the hot baths (the *hammam*), travelling incognito in a hired coach, and had marvelled at their furnishings and, more especially, at the fact that the 200 women present were all 'in the state of nature, that is, in plain English, stark naked, without any beauty or defect concealed'. So pressing was their invitation to Lady Mary to join them that she was able to decline only by showing them her stays, into which, she reported, they were convinced that her husband had locked her. (Lady Mary's visits to the baths in Adrianople and later in Constantinople provided the inspiration for Ingres' painting *Le Bain Turc* 1862 with its throng of naked women embracing.) In Adrianople, which had served as the Ottoman capital until 1453 and was still much visited by the Sultan and his court, she watched the Sultan pass by in procession to the Mosque, dined with the Lady of the Grand Vizier (the Sultan's Chief Minister) and, dressed in her Turkish costume, visited the Selimiye Mosque. The dinner was rather dull — her host turned out to be a respectable middle-aged lady 'entirely given up to devotion' and Lady Mary was evidently becoming a little tired of Turkish cooking — but the evening was saved by an invitation to go on to visit the Lady of the Kahya, the second minister. Lady Mary was entranced with Fatima — she could find no imperfection in her features, she was 'so struck with admiration that I could not for some time speak to her' — and with the rich furnishings and sensual atmosphere of her *harem*; the two parted with every expression of friendship, and indeed did meet again in Constantinople.

Such meetings, and the discussions she had had with Ahmed Bey in Belgrade about the customs of Islam, led Lady Mary to develop one of her favourite themes: the freedom enjoyed by Turkish women (or at least those of high rank) in comparison with their counterparts in England. Almost inevitably, Lady Mary viewed this freedom primarily in sexual terms: the strict rules requiring women to remain veiled at all times gives them 'entire liberty of following their inclinations without danger of discovery....'Tis impossible for the most jealous husband to know his wife when he meets her....You may easily imagine the number of faithful wives very small in a country where they have nothing to fear from their lovers' indiscretion.' A Turkish woman, Lady Mary found, also preserves her financial independence; while married, she retains control of her own money, and should her husband divorce her he is obliged to continue to maintain her. Can one perhaps detect, in these passages, some element of wistfulness, some kicking against the fetters of her own marriage?

What Lady Mary's Turkish letters, both those from Adrianople and those composed during her fourteen-month stay in Constantinople, lack is any insight into the political and military situation, which is scarcely even discussed. Visits to *harems* and mosques, and rambles around Adrianople and Constantinople, could be arranged. Meetings with high court ladies were permitted; as well as Fatima and the Grand Vizier's lady, Lady Mary also made the acquaintance of Sultana Hafise, the widow of Mustafa II whom the present Sultan, Ahmed III, had deposed in 1703. But the Sultan himself and his officials she saw only at a distance, usually in procession, while the whole realm of politics and court intrigue and diplomatic negotiation was entirely closed to her. How frustrating Lady Mary (whose years spent in English Court circles had enabled her to develop some shrewd political instincts) found this situation her letters do not reveal. Nor can we be certain how much Wortley told her about the progress of his negotiations with the

Sultan, or how far she was able to bring her influence to bear on him in private.

What we do know is that Wortley made his task, for which he would not have been ideally suited at the best of times, more difficult still by his rapidly growing Turkophilia and his apparent unwillingness to recognize the weakness of the Ottoman military position. The peace proposal he despatched to Vienna from Adrianople after more than a month's negotiations with the Grand Vizier was ill received there. The Turks, he suggested, would agree to a cease-fire if Temesvar, which they had lost to Austria the previous year, were restored to them. From the Austrian point of view, there was little logic about this proposal. While the Turks had reached the city gates of Vienna little more than thirty years before, since then they had been beaten back, and now most of Hungary was in Imperial hands. Prince Eugene had defeated an army twice the size of his at Peterwaradin in 1716, and even now was planning to beseige Belgrade before the Turks could bring in troops from Asia. Wortley's argument for his plan — that failure to agree on peace terms would lead to the deposition of Ahmed III by a less peaceable Sultan more willing to use his Empire's great wealth to prolong the war — failed to impress either the Austrian Emperor or Abraham Stanyan, the English ambassador in Vienna, who was already intriguing to have Wortley replaced.

Events soon swept past Wortley. Vienna simply made no response to his plan, in August the Turks were defeated in Belgrade, and in September the English government announced that it was replacing Wortley with Stanyan, who was to be assisted in his negotiations by Sir Robert Sutton, Wortley's predecessor in Constantinople. Word of his recall did not reach Wortley for some time — in early autumn he had set out for the Grand Vizier's military camp near Sofia, where he remained until the following May — and when it did he redoubled his efforts to devise peace terms acceptable to both sides; if only he could achieve peace before his successor arrived in Turkey, both the diplomatic and financial fruits of success would then be his.

He failed, and must have alienated his friends in government with his naïve and rather pathetic appeals to be allowed to remain in office. Stanyan arrived in Adrianople in May 1718, the Wortleys left Constantinople for home in July, and in the autumn the Treaty of Passarowitz was signed, by which the Turks ceded to Austria a slab of territory in Hungary, Serbia and Wallachia.

But all this lay ahead as Wortley and Lady Mary left Adrianople for Constantinople towards the end of May 1717. They took a palace in Pera, the hilltop suburb on the north bank of the Golden Horn where foreigners were lodged. Here, and also at their summer villa in the woods at Belgrade Village close to the Black Sea, Lady Mary fell into a pleasant routine. In the country days were passed, she recounted to Pope on 17 June, in reading, writing, studying the Turkish language and listening to music. In the city, there were visits to the old quarter of Constantinople on the far side of the Golden Horn, where, properly veiled and dressed, Lady Mary rambled through streets and markets, visited the baths once again, saw as much of the Seraglio as was permitted, examined mosques and monasteries, in one of which she observed the 'devotions of the dervishes, which are as whimsical as any in Rome', and took boat excursions up the 'canal' (the Bosphorous). As persistent as ever, she made at least three applications for permission, eventually granted, to visit the Santa Sophia mosque.

Two other events marked Lady Mary's stay in Constantinople. The first was the birth of her daughter, in late January; she was named Mary after her mother. Charles

Caravanserai at Borgas by Luigi Mayer. There was a network of *caravanserais*, secure resting-places where travellers could spend the night, throughout the Turkish Empire; the government provided food and accommodation free in order to encourage trade. The small cells where travellers slept are ranged around a central courtyard with a fountain. This caravanserai was on the road from Constantinople to Adrianople, the former Ottoman capital where the Sultan and his court still spent much time.

Street scene in Pera, the European quarter of Constantinople, outside the French embassy, done by an anonymous Greek artist. A patrol of watchmen carrying clubs is passing. The Wortleys lodged in Pera, and Lady Mary became friendly with the wife of the French ambassador, who had arrived in Constantinople a few months before her.

Portrait by an anonymous Greek artist of a senior janissary officer in full outfit. In her letter of 1 April 1717 to Lady Bristol (see page 104), Lady Mary described the guard of janissaries in ceremonial uniform that escorted the Sultan to the mosque in Adrianople.

Maitland, the surgeon whom Lady Mary had engaged in England, and also the eminent Constantinople physician Emanuel Timoni, attended her. Wortley himself was away from Constantinople, attending the Grand Vizier near Sofia. Lady Mary was struck with the easy acceptance of childbirth in Turkey — pregnant women 'see all company the day of their delivery and at the fortnight's end return visits, set out in their jewels and new clothes' — but was less certain that she approved of the habit of large families and the constant child-bearing women underwent. A couple of months later, the same doctors were involved in a courageous and potentially risky experiment initiated by Lady Mary. It was in Adrianople that she had first observed the practice of innoculating young children against smallpox, and in Constantinople she continued her investigations, eventually deciding to have her son Edward 'engrafted'. (The technique developed in England by Edward Jenner towards the end of the 18th century used the cowpox virus, while in Turkey innoculation was performed, at much greater risk, with the smallpox virus). Dr Timoni, a Fellow of the Royal Society who had described the process in the Society's *Transactions* in 1714, was no doubt on hand to give advice. An old Greek woman was found to perform the innoculation, but she so distressed the child that Charles Maitland stepped in and administered the injection himself. (On his return to England, Maitland was to find himself swept up in Lady Mary's enthusiastic advocacy of innoculation, and he came out of retirement to take part in the experimental innoculations she arranged.) The boy suffered no ill effects.

This must have been a good time to live in Constantinople. True, many of the problems that led to the gradual decline of the Ottoman Empire were already manifesting themselves: inflation and economic difficulties; increasing social distress; the declining ability of the Sultans, which in turn lessened the authority of the central government in the face of powerful provincial rulers; and the weakening of the administrative system, which was now opening high office to people with the money to purchase it rather than on merit. But, given the closed and secretive nature of Ottoman society, none of this would have come to Lady Mary's notice. On a more superficial level, life was easy. The Sultan was devoted to extravagance and luxury raher than to war, or even to the arts of government and administration. His two grand passions (aside from those of the flesh) were parties and tulips. According to one authority, he 'had so many offspring that, with the celebration of the children's births, the sons' circumcisions, and the daughters' marriages, there was a holiday atmosphere in the Saray [the *harem*] throughout his reign'; for one such celebration, where the feast was prepared by 1500 cooks and the guests were entertained by jugglers and no fewer than 2000 musicians, he himself designed 18-foot 'sugar gardens', extravagant concoctions installed in tents for the guests to nibble. So great was his mania for tulips — bulbs were imported by the thousand for the *harem* gardens, and each April a magnificent tulip fête was staged there — that the latter part of his reign is commonly known as the Tulip Period, *Läle Devri*.

Some of this was still in the future when Lady Mary and her husband reluctantly left Constantinople in midsummer 1718; Passarowitz enabled the Sultan to turn his whole attention from the cares of war to those of frivolity. But the memories of her stay in this magical city at the gateway to Asia, filled with people of every race and religion, its markets laden with goods from the exotic, unknown East, were to remain with Lady Mary for the rest of her life.

To Lady ＿＿＿ — *Adrianople 1 April 1717*

I an now got into a new world where everything I see appears to me a change of scene, and I write to your Ladyship with some content of mind, hoping at least that you will find the charm of novelty in my letters and no longer reproach me that I tell you nothing extraordinary. I won't trouble you with a relation of our tedious journey, but I must not omit what I saw remarkable at Sophia, one of the most beautiful towns in the Turkish Empire and famous for its hot baths that are resorted to both for diversion and health. I stopped here one day on purpose to see them. Designing to go incognito, I hired a Turkish coach. These *voitures* are not at all like ours, but much more convenient for the country, the heat being so great that glasses would be very troublesome. They are made a good deal in the manner of the Dutch coaches, having wooden lattices painted and gilded, the inside being painted with baskets and nosegays of flowers, intermixed commonly with little poetical mottoes. They are covered all over with scarlet cloth, lined with silk and very often richly embroidered and fringed. This covering entirely hides the persons in them, but may be thrown back at pleasure and the ladies peep through the lattices. They hold four people very conveniently, seated on cushions, but not raised.

In one of these covered wagons I went to the *bagnio* about ten o'clock. It was already full of women. It is built of stone in the shape of a dome with no windows but in the roof, which gives light enough. There was five of these domes joined together, the outmost being less than the rest and serving only as a hall where the porteress stood at the door. Ladies of quality generally give this woman the value of a crown or ten shillings, and I did not forget that ceremony. The next room is a very large one, paved with marble, and all round it raised two sofas of marble, one above another. There were four fountains of cold water in this room, falling first into marble basins and then running on the floor in little channels made for that purpose, which carried the streams into the next room, something less than this, with the same sort of marble sofas, but so hot with steams of sulphur proceeding from the baths joining to it, 'twas impossible to stay there with one's clothes on. The two other domes were the hot baths, one of which had cocks of cold water turning into it to temper it to what degree of warmth the bathers have a mind to.

I was in my travelling habit, which is a riding dress, and certainly appeared

View of a coffee house by an anonymous Greek artist. Coffee houses were generally patronized by men alone; here wealthy merchants can be seen relaxing. Lady Mary describes the baths as 'the women's coffee-house, where all the news of the town is told, scandal invented, etc'.

very extraordinary to them, yet there was not one of 'em that showed the least surprise or impertinent curiosity, but received me with all the obliging civility possible. I know no European court where the ladies would have behaved themselves in so polite a manner to a stranger. I believe in the whole there were two hundred women and yet none of those disdainful smiles or satiric whispers that never fail in our assemblies when anybody appears that is not dressed exactly in fashion. They repeated over and over to me 'Uzelle, pek uzelle,[1] which is nothing but, 'Charming, very charming'. The first sofas were covered with cushions and rich carpets, on which sat the ladies, and on the second their slaves behind 'em, but without any distinction of rank by their dress, all being in the state of nature, that is in plain English, stark naked, without any beauty or defect concealed, yet there was not the least wanton smile or immodest gesture amongst 'em. They walked and moved with the same majestic grace which Milton describes of our General Mother.[2] There were many amongst them as exactly proportioned as ever any goddess was drawn by the pencil of Guido or Titian, and most of their skins shiningly white, only adorned by their beautiful hair divided into many tresses hanging on their shoulders, braided either with pearl or riband, perfectly representing the figures of the Graces.

I was here convinced of the truth of a reflection that I had often made, that if 'twas the fashion to go naked the face would be hardly observed. I perceived that the ladies with the finest skins and most delicate shapes had the greatest share of my admiration, though their faces were sometimes less beautiful than those of their companions. To tell you the truth, I had wickedness enough to wish secretly that Mr Jervas[3] could have been there invisible. I fancy it would have very much improved his art to see so many fine women naked in different postures, some in conversation, some working, others drinking coffee or sherbet, and many negligently lying on their cushions while their slaves (generally pretty girls of seventeen or eighteen) were employed in braiding their hair in several pretty manners. In short, 'tis the women's coffee-house, where all the news of the town is told, scandal invented, etc. They generally take this diversion once a week, and stay there at least four or five hours without getting cold by immediate coming out of the hot bath into the cool room, which was very surprising to me. The lady that seemed the most considerable amongst them entreated me to sit by her and would fain have undressed me for the bath. I excused myself with some difficulty, they

1. Lady Mary seems to have misheard slightly. The ladies were probably saying 'Güzel, pek güzel'.

2. Book iv of *Paradise Lost.*

3. Chárles Jervas, portrait painter and friend of the London wits.

being all so earnest in persuading me. I was at last forced to open my skirt and show them my stays, which satisfied 'em very well, for I saw they believed I was so locked up in that machine that it was not in my own power to open it, which contrivance they attributed to my husband. I was charmed with their civility and beauty and should have been very glad to pass more time with them, but Mr Wortley resolving to pursue his journey the next morning early I was in haste to see the ruins of Justinian's church, which did not afford me so agreeable a prospect as I had left, being little more than a heap of stones.

Adieu, madam. I am sure I have now entertained you with an account of such a sight as you never saw in your life and what no book of travels could inform you of. 'Tis no less than death for a man to be found in one of these places.

To The Abbé Conti[1] — *Adrianople 1 April 1717*

You see that I am very exact in keeping the promise you engaged me to make, but I know not whether your curiosity will be satisfied with the accounts I shall give you, though I can assure you that the desire I have to oblige you to the utmost of my power has made me very diligent in my enquiries and observations. 'Tis certain we have but very imperfect relations of the manners and religion of these people, this part of the world being seldom visited but by merchants who mind little but their own affairs, or travellers who make too short a stay to be able to report any thing exactly of their own knowledge. The Turks are too proud to converse familiarly with merchants, etc., who can only pick up some confused informations which are generally false, and they can give no better an account of the ways here than a French refugee lodging in a garret in Greek Street[2] could write of the Court of England. The journey we have made from Belgrade hither by land cannot possibly be passed by any out of a public character. The desert woods of Serbia are the common refuge of thieves who rob in a company, that we had need of all our guards to secure us, and the villages so poor that only force could extort from them necessary provisions. Indeed, the janissaries had no mercy on their poverty, killing all the poultry and sheep they could find without asking who they belonged to, while the wretched owners durst not put in their claim for fear of being beaten. Lambs just fallen, geese and turkeys big with egg: all massacred

1. The Italian savant, philosopher and poet, whom Lady Mary had met in London in 1715. He visited England again from March 1717 to March 1718.

2. After the revocation of the Edict of Nantes (1685), many French Protestants fled to England. Greek Street is in Soho, where many of them settled.

without distinction. I fancied I heard the complaints of Moelibeus for the hope of his flock.[3] When the Pashas travel 'tis yet worse. Those oppressors are not content with eating all that is to be eaten belonging to the peasants; after they have crammed themselves and their numerous retinue, they have impudence to exact what they call teeth-money, a contribution for the use of their teeth, worn with doing them the honour of devouring their meat. This is a literal known truth, however extravagant it seems, and such is the natural corruption of a military government, their religion not allowing of this barbarity no more than ours does.

I had the advantage of lodging three weeks at Belgrade with a principal effendi, that is to say, a scholar. This set of men are equally capable of preferments in the law or the church, those sciences being cast into one, a lawyer and a priest being the same word. They are the only men really considerable in the Empire; all the profitable employments and church revenues are in their hands. The Grand Signior, though general heir to his people, never presumes to touch their lands or money, which goes in an uninterrupted succession to their children. 'Tis true they lose this privilege by accepting a place at Court or the title of Pasha, but there are few examples of such fools amongst 'em. You may easily judge the power of these men who have engrossed all the learning and almost all the wealth of the Empire. 'Tis they that are the real authors, though the soldiers are the actors of revolutions. They deposed the late Sultan Mustafa, and their power is so well known 'tis the Emperor's interest to flatter them. This is a long digression.

I was going to tell you that an intimate daily conversation with the effendi Achmet Beg gave me opportunity of knowing their religion and morals in a more particular manner than perhaps any Christian ever did. I explained to him the difference between the religion of England and Rome, and he was pleased to hear there were Christians that did not worship images or adore the Virgin Mary. The ridicule of transubstantiation appeared very strong to him. Upon comparing our creeds together, I am convinced that if our friend Dr Clarke[4] had free liberty of preaching here, it would be very easy to persuade the generality to Christianity, whose notions are already little different from his. Mr Whiston[5] would make a very good apostle here. I don't doubt but his zeal will be much fired if you communicate this account to him, but tell him he must first have the gift of tongues before he could possibly be of any use.

Muhammadanism is divided into as many sects as Christianity, and the first institution as much neglected and obscured by interpretations. I cannot here

Subaltern officer of the janissaries from *The Costume of Turkey* by William Miller.

3. In Virgil's first *Eclogue.*

4. Dr Samuel Clarke, a mild deist and controversialist who remained in the Church.

5. William Whiston, an intimate friend of Dr Clarke, and even more unorthodox in his views.

Portrait of the Janissary-Aga, or commander of the janissaries, after Jean-Baptiste Vanmour.

forbear reflecting on the natural inclination of mankind to make mysteries and novelties. The Zeidi, Kadari, Jabari,[6] etc. put me in mind of the Catholic, Lutheran, Calvinist, etc., and are equally zealous against one another. But the most prevailing opinion, if you search into the secret of the effendis, is plain Deism, but this is kept from the people, who are amused with a thousand different notions according to the different interests of their preachers. There are very few amongst them (Achmet Beg denied there were any) so absurd as to set up for wit by declaring they believe no God at all. Sir Paul Rycaut[7] is mistaken (as he commonly is) in calling the sect Muserin (i.e. the secret with us) Atheists, they being deists, and their impiety consists in making a jest of their Prophet. Achmet Beg did not own to me that he was of this opinion, but made no scruple of deviating from some part of law by drinking wine with the same freedom we did. When I asked him how he came to allow himself that liberty, he made answer, all the creatures of God were good and designed for the use of man; however, that the prohibition of wine was a very wise maxim and meant for the common people, being the source of all disorders amongst them, but that the Prophet never designed to confine those that knew how to use it with moderation; however, scandal ought to be avoided, and that he never drank it in public. This is the general way of thinking amongst them, and very few forbear drinking wine that are able to afford it.

He assured me that if I understood Arabic I should be very well pleased with reading the Koran, which is so far from the nonsense we charge it with, tis the purest morality delivered in the very best language. I have since heard impartial Christians speak of it in the same manner, and I don't doubt but all our translations are from copies got from the Greek priests, who would not fail to falsify it with the extremity of malice. No body of men ever were more ignorant and more corrupt, yet they differ so little from the Romish Church, I confess there is nothing gives me a greater abhorrence of the cruelty of your clergy than the barbarous persecutions of 'em whenever they have been their masters, for no other reason than not acknowledging the Pope. The dissenting in that one article has got them the titles of heretics, schismatics, and what is worse, the same treatment. I found at Philippopolis a sect of Christians that call themselves Paulines.[8] They show an old church where they say St Paul preached, and he is the favourite saint after the same manner as St Peter is at Rome; neither do they forget to give him the same preference over the rest of the apostles.

6. The three sects of Islam to which Lady Mary refers are Al-Zaidıyra, Kadarıya and Djabarıya.

7. Paul Rycaut, secretary to the Turkish Embassy of the Earl of Winchilsea from 1661 for about six years and author of *The Present State of the Ottoman Empire* (1668), several chapters of which deal with Islamic sects.

8. A dualistic, heretical sect many of whom lived in Philippopolis. They were maltreated by the Muslims and despised by the Greek Orthodox.

But of all the religions I have seen, the Arnounts seem to me the most particular. They are natives of Arnountlick, the ancient Macedonia, and still retain something of the courage and hardiness, though they have lost the name of Macedonians, being the best militia in the Turkish Empire and the only check upon the janissaries. They are foot soldiers. We had a guard of them, relieved in every considerable town we passed. They are all clothed and armed at their own expense, generally lusty young fellows, dressed in clean white coarse cloth, carrying guns of a prodigious length, which they run with on their shoulders as if they did not feel the weight of 'em, the leader singing a sort of rude tune, not unpleasant, and the rest making up the chorus. These people, living between Christians and Muhammadans and not being skilled in controversy, declare that they are utterly unable to judge which religion is best; but to be certain of not entirely rejecting the truth, they very prudently follow both, and go to the mosque on Fridays and the church on Sundays, saying for their excuse, that at the day of judgement they are sure of protection from the true prophet, but which that is they are not able to determine in this world. I believe there is no other race of mankind have so modest an opinion of their own capacity. These are the remarks I have made on the diversity of religions I have seen. I don't ask your pardon for the liberty I have taken in speaking of the Roman. I know you equally condemn the quackery of all churches as much as you revere the sacred truths in which we both agree.

You will expect I should say something to you of the antiquities of this country, but there are few remains of ancient Greece. We passed near the piece of an arch which is commonly called Trajan's Gate, as supposing he made it to shut up the passage over the mountains between Sophia and Philippopolis, but I rather believe it the remains of some triumphal arch (though I could not see any inscription), for if that passage had been shut up there are many others that would serve for the march of an army; and notwithstanding the story of Baldwin, Earl of Flanders, being overthrown in these straits after he had won Constantinople,[10] I don't fancy the road is now made (with great industry) as commodious as possible for the march of the Turkish army. There is not one ditch or puddle between this place and Belgrade that has not a large strong bridge of planks built over it, but the precipices were not so terrible as I had heard them represented.

At the foot of these mountains we lay at the little village of Kiskoi, wholly inhabited by Christians, as all the peasants of Bulgaria are. Their houses are

Portraits by an anonymous Greek artist of the *Sheyh ul Islam*, the dignitary responsible for canon law and education, and the *Reis Effendi*, the senior minister responsible for foreign affairs. The *Sheyh ul Islam* came next to the Grand Vizier in precedence.

9. Arnavutluk was the Ottoman Turkish name for Albania.

10. Baldwin I (d.1205), Count of Flanders, Emperor of Constantinople (1204), was overthrown by a Greek revolt in Thrace.

View of a funeral procession
after Jean-Baptiste Vanmour.

nothing but little huts raised of dirt baked in the sun, and they leave them and fly into the mountains some months before the march of the Turkish army, who would else entirely ruin them by driving away their whole flocks.

This precaution secures them in a sort of plenty, for such vast tracts of land lying in common they have liberty of sowing what they please, and are generally very industrious husbandmen. I drank here several sorts of delicious wine. The women dress themselves in a great variety of coloured glass beads, and are not ugly but of tawny complexions. I have now told you all that is worth telling you (and perhaps more) relating to my journey. When I am at Constantinople I'll try to pick up some curiosities and then you shall hear again from, etc.

To Lady Bristol — *Adrianople 1 April 1717*

As I never can forget the smallest of your Ladyship's commands, my first business here has been to inquire after the stuffs you ordered me to look for, without being able to find what you would like. The difference of the dress here and at London is so great, the same sort of things are not proper for caftans and *manteaus*. However, I will not give over my search, but renew it again at Constantinople, though I have reason to believe there is nothing finer than what is to be found here, being the present residence of the Court.

The Grand Signior's eldest daughter was married some few days before I came, and upon that occasion the Turkish ladies display all their magnificence. The bride was conducted to her husband's house in very great splendour. She is widow of the late Vizier who was killed at Peterwaradin, though that ought rather to be called a contract than a marriage, not having ever lived with him. However, the greatest part of his wealth is hers. He had the permission of visiting her in the Seraglio and, being one of the handsomest men in the Empire, had very much engaged her affections. When she saw this second husband, who is at least fifty, she could not forbear bursting into tears. He is a man of merit and the declared favourite of the Sultan, which they call Mosaip,[1] but that is not enough to make him pleasing in the eyes of a girl of thirteen.[2]

1. The Musahib was a gentleman and companion of the Sultan.

2. Princess Fatima married Ibrahim Pasha on 20 February 1717, more than a month before Lady Mary's arrival. He was in fact about the same age as her first husband, Ali Pasha, killed the previous year.

The government here is entirely in the hands of the army, and the Grand Signior with all his absolute power as much a slave as any of his subjects, and trembles at a janissary's frown. Here is, indeed, a much greater appearance of subjection than amongst us. A minister of state is not spoke to but upon the knee. Should a reflection on his conduct be dropped in a coffee-house (for they have spies everywhere) the house would be razed to the ground and perhaps the whole company put to the torture. No huzzaing mobs, senseless pamphlets and tavern disputes about politics:

A consequential ill that freedom draws,
A bad effect but from a noble cause,

none of our harmless calling names; but when a minister here displeases the people, in three hours' time he is dragged even from his master's arms. They cut off his hands, head and feet, and throw them before the palace gate with all the respect in the world, while that Sultan (to whom they all profess an unlimited adoration) sits trembling in his apartment, and dare neither defend nor revenge his favourite. This is the blessed condition of the most absolute monarch upon earth, who owns no law but his will. I cannot help wishing (in the loyalty of my heart) that the Parliament would send hither a shipload of your passive obedient men that they might see arbitrary government in its clearest strongest light,[3] where 'tis hard to judge whether the prince, people or ministers are most miserable. I could make many reflections on this subject, but I know, madam, your own good sense has already furnished you with better than I am capable of.

I went yesterday with the French Ambassadress[4] to see the Grand Signior in his passage to the Mosque. He was preceded by a numerous guard of janissaries with vast white feathers on their heads, *spahis* and *bostangees*, these are the foot and horse guard; and the royal gardeners, which are a very considerable body of men, dressed in different habits of fine, lively colours that at a distance they appeared like a parterre of tulips; after them, the Aga of the janissaries in a robe of purple velvet lined with silver tissue, his horse led by two slaves richly dressed; next him the Kuzlir Aga[5] (your ladyship knows this is the chief guardian of the Seraglio ladies) in a deep yellow cloth (which suited very well to his black face) lined with sables; and last His Sublimity himself in green lined with the fur of a black Muscovite fox, which is supposed worth 1,000 sterling, mounted on a fine horse

3. The High Anglican Tories believed in passive obedience to authority.

4. A daughter of the Duc de Biron, she had married the Marquis de Bonnac in 1715, and arrived in Adrianople in January 1717.

5. Lady Mary's Turkish is somewhat inaccurate. The correct name for these guards are *sipahis* and *bostancis*, while the chief guardian of the Seraglio ladies is the Kizlar ağa.

with furniture embroidered with jewels. Six more horses richly furnished were led after him, and two of his principal courtiers bore, one his gold and the other his silver coffee pot, on a staff. Another carried a silver stool on his head for him to sit on. It would be too tedious to tell your ladyship the various dresses and turbans (by which their rank is distinguished) but they were all extreme rich and gay to the number of some thousands, that perhaps there cannot be seen a more beautiful procession. The Sultan appeared to us a handsome man of about forty, with a very graceful air but something severe in his countenance, his eyes very full and black. He happened to stop under the window where we stood and (I suppose being told who we were) looked upon us very attentively that we had full leisure to consider him, and the French Ambassadress agreed with me as to his good mien.

I see that lady very often. She is young and her conversation would be a great relief to me if I could persuade her to live without those forms and ceremonies that make life formal and tiresome, but she is so delighted with her guards, her twenty-four footmen, gentleman ushers, etc., that she would rather die than make me a visit without 'em, not to reckon a coach full of attending damsels yclep'd maids of honour. What vexes me is that as long as she will visit with this troublesome equipage I am obliged to do the same. However, our mutual interest makes us much together. I went with her t'other day all round the town in an open gilt chariot with our joint train of attendants, preceded by our guards, who might have summoned the people to see what they never had seen, nor ever would see again, two young Christian Ambassadresses never yet having been in this country at the same time nor, I believe, ever will again. Your ladyship may easily imagine that we drew a vast crowd of spectators, but all silent as death. If any of them had taken the liberties of our mob upon any strange sight, our janissaries had made no scruple of falling on 'em with their scimitars without danger of so doing, being above law. Yet these people have some good qualities. They are very zealous and faithful where they serve, and look upon it as their business to fight for you upon all occasions, of which I had a very pleasant instance in a village on this side of Philippopolis, where we were met by our domestic guard. I happened to bespeak pigeons for my supper, upon which one of my janissaries went immediately to the cadi (the chief civil officer of the town) and ordered him to send in some dozens. The poor man answered that he had already sent about but could get none. My janissary, in the height of his zeal for my service, immediately locked him up prisoner in his room, telling him he deserved death for his impudence in offering to excuse his not

View of a marriage procession
after Jean-Baptiste Vanmour.
The bride is walking under a
canopy, accompanied by
clowns and musicians.

obeying my command, but out of respect to me he would not punish him but by my order, and accordingly came very gravely to me to ask what should be done to him, adding by way of compliment that, if I pleased, he would bring me his head. This may give some idea of the unlimited power of these fellows, who are all sworn brothers and bound to revenge the injuries done to one another, whether at Cairo, Aleppo, or any part of the world; and this inviolable league makes them so power-ful, the greatest man at the Court never speaks to them but in a flattering tone, and in Asia any man that is rich is forced to enroll himself a janissary to secure his estate. — But I have already said enough and I dare swear, dear madam, that by this time 'tis a very comfortable reflection to you that there is no possibility of your receiving such a tedious letter but once in six months. 'Tis that consideration has given me the assurance to entertain you so long and will, I hope, plead the excuse of, dear madam, etc.

To Lady Mar — *Adrianople April 1 1717*

I wish to God (dear sister) that you was as regular in letting me have the pleasure of knowing what passes on your side of the globe as I am careful in endeavouring to amuse you by the account of all I see that I think you care to hear of. You content yourself with telling me over and over that the town is very dull. It may possibly be dull to you when every day does not present you with something new, but for me that am in arrear at least two months' news, all that seems very stale with you would be fresh and sweet here; pray let me into more particulars. I will try to awaken your gratitude by giving you a full and true relation of the novelties of this place, none of which would surprise you more than a sight of my person as I am now in my Turkish habit, though I believe you would be of my opinion that 'tis admirably becoming. I intend to send you my picture; in the meantime accept of it here.

The first piece of my dress is a pair of drawers, very full, that reach to my shoes and conceal the legs more modestly than your petticoats. They are of a thin, rose-colour damask brocaded with silver flowers, my shoes of white kid leather embroidered with gold. Over this hangs my smock of a fine white silk gauze edged with embroidery. This smock has wide sleeves hanging half-way down the arm and is closed at the neck with a diamond button, but the shape and colour of the bosom very well to be distinguished through it. The *antery* is a waistcoat made close to the shape, of white and gold damask, with very long sleeves falling back and fringed with deep gold fringe, and should have diamond or pearl buttons. My *caftan* of the same stuff with my drawers is a robe exactly fitted to my shape and reaching to my feet, with very long straight falling sleeves. Over this is the girdle of about four fingers broad, which all that can afford have entirely of diamonds or other precious stones. Those that will not be at the expense have it of exquisite embroidery on satin, but it must be fastened before with a clasp of diamonds. The *curdee* is a loose robe they throw off or put on according to the weather, being of a rich brocade (mine is green and gold) either lined with ermine or sables; the sleeves reach very little below the shoulders. The head-dress is composed of a cap called *talpack*, which is in winter of fine velvet embroidered with pearls or diamonds and in summer of a light, shining silver stuff. This is fixed on one side of the head, hanging a little way down with a gold tassel and bound on either with a circle of diamonds (as I have seen several) or a rich embroidered handkerchief. On the other side of the head the hair is laid flat, and here the ladies are at liberty to show their fancies, some putting flowers, others a plume of heron's feathers, and in short what they please, but the most general fashion is a large bouquet of jewels made like natural flowers, that is the buds of pearl, the roses of different coloured rubies, the jasmines of diamonds, jonquils of topazes, etc., so well set and enamelled 'tis hard to imagine anything of that kind so beautiful. The hair hangs at its full length behind, divided into tresses braided with pearl or riband, which is always in great quantity.

I never saw in my life so many fine heads of hair. I have counted one hundred and ten of these tresses of one lady's, all natural; but it must be owned that every beauty is more common here than with us. 'Tis surprising to see a young woman that is not very handsome. They have naturally the most beautiful complexions in the world and generally large black eyes. I can assure you with great truth that the Court of England (though I believe it the fairest in Christendom) cannot show so many beauties as are under our protection here. They generally shape their eyebrows, and the Greeks and Turks have a custom of putting round their eyes on the inside a black tincture that, at a distance or by candlelight, adds very much to the

Portrait of a veiled Turkish woman by an anonymous Greek artist. Lady Mary maintained that the veils and *ferigee*, or long cloak, worn by Turkish women paradoxically allowed them 'more liberty than we have ... You may guess how effectually this [the *ferigée*] disguises them, that there is no distinguishing the great lady from her slave, and 'tis impossible for the most jealous husband to know his wife when he meets her, and no man dare either touch or follow a woman in the street.'

Asme Sultane, the Sultan's Sister, in her State Araba by Thomas Allom. Women were allowed to go outdoors so long as they remained veiled: 'no woman of what rank soever [is] permitted to go in the streets without two muslins, one that covers her face all but her eyes and another that hides the whole dress of her head and hangs half-way down her back'.

blackness of them. I fancy many of our ladies would be overjoyed to know this secret, but 'tis too visible by day. They dye their nails rose colour; I own I cannot enough accustom myself to this fashion to find any beauty in it.

As to their morality or good conduct, I can say like Harlequin, ''Tis just as 'tis with you'; and the Turkish ladies don't commit one sin the less for not being Christians. Now I am a little acquainted with their ways, I cannot forbear admiring either the exemplary discretion or extreme stupidity of all the writers that have given accounts of 'em. 'Tis very easy to see they have more liberty than we have, no woman of what rank soever being permitted to go in the streets without two muslins, one that covers her face all but her eyes and another that hides the whole dress of her head and hangs half-way down her back; and their shapes are wholly concealed by a thing they call a *ferigée,*[1] which no woman of any sort appears without. This has strait sleeves that reach to their fingers' ends and it laps all round 'em, not unlike a riding hood. In winter 'tis of cloth, and in summer, plain stuff or silk. You may guess how effectually this disguises them, that there is no distinguishing the great lady from her slave, and 'tis impossible for the most jealous husband to know his wife when he meets her, and no man dare either touch or follow a woman in the street.

This perpetual masquerade gives them entire liberty of following their inclinations without danger of discovery. The most usual method of intrigue is to send an appointment to the lover to meet the lady at a Jew's shop, which are as notoriously convenient as our Indian houses, and yet even those that don't make that use of 'em do not scruple to go to buy penn'orths and tumble over rich goods, which are chiefly to be found amongst that sort of people. The great ladies seldom let their gallants know who they are, and 'tis so difficult to find it out that they can very seldom guess at her name they have corresponded with above half a year together. You may easily imagine the number of faithful wives very small in a country where they have nothing to fear from their lovers' indiscretion, since we see so many that have the courage to expose themselves to that in this world and all the threatened punishment of the next, which is never preached to the Turkish damsels. Neither have they much to apprehend from the resentment of their husbands, those ladies that are rich having all their money in their own hands, which they take with 'em upon a divorce with an addition which he is obliged to give 'em. Upon the whole, I look upon the Turkish women as the only free people in the empire. The very Divan pays a respect to 'em, and the Grand Signior

1. The correct names for the various items of Lady Mary's costume are *entari, kaftan, cüppe, kalpak* and *ferace.*

himself, when a Pasha is executed, never violates the privileges of the harem (or women's apartment) which remains unsearched entire to the widow. They are queens of their slaves, which the husband has no permission so much as to look upon, except it be an old woman or two that his lady chooses. 'Tis true their law permits them four wives, but there is no instance of a man of quality that makes use of this liberty, or of a woman of rank that would suffer it. When a husband happens to be inconstant (as those things will happen) he keeps his mistress in a house apart and visits her as privately as he can, just as 'tis with you. Amongst all the great men here I only know the *defterdar* (i.e. treasurer) that keeps a number of she slaves for his own use (that is, on his own side of the house, for a slave once given to serve a lady is entirely at her disposal), and he is spoke of as a libertine, or what we should call a rake, and his wife won't see him, though she continues to live in his house.

Thus you see, dear sister, the manners of mankind do not differ so widely as our voyage writers would make us believe. Perhaps it would be more entertaining to add a few surprising customs of my own invention, but nothing seems to me so agreeable as truth, and I believe nothing so acceptable to you. I conclude with repeating the great truth of my being, dear sister, etc.

To Alexander Pope — *Adrianople 1 April 1717*

I dare say you expect at least something very new in this letter after I have gone a journey not undertaken by any Christian of some hundred years. The most remarkable accident that happened to me was my being very near overturned into the Hebrus; and if I had much regard for the glories that one's name enjoys after death I should certainly be sorry for having missed the romantic conclusion of swimming down the same river in which the musical head of Orpheus repeated verses so many ages since.

———— Caput a cervice revulsum,
Gurgite cum medio portans Oeagrius Hebrus
Volveret, Euridicen vox ipsa, et frigida lingua,
Ah! Miseram Euridicen! anima fugiente vocabat,
Euridicen toto referebant flumine ripae.[1]

Who knows but some of your bright wits might have found it a subject affording many poetical turns, and have told the world in a heroic elegy that

As equal were our Souls, so equal were our fates?

Musician from *The Costume of Turkey* by William Miller.

I despair of ever having so many fine things said of me as so extraordinary a death would have given occasion for.[2]

I am at this present writing in a house situated on the banks of the Hebrus, which runs under my chamber window. My garden is full of tall cypress trees, upon the branches of which several couple of true turtles are saying soft things to one another from morning till night. How naturally do boughs and vows come into my head at this minute! And must not you confess to my praise that 'tis more than an ordinary discretion that can resist the wicked suggestions of poetry in a place where truth for once furnishes all the ideas of pastoral? The summer is already far advanced in this part of the world, and for some miles round Adrianople the whole ground is laid out in gardens, and the banks of the river set with rows of fruit trees, under which all the most considerable Turks divert themselves every evening; not with walking, that is not one of their pleasures, but a set party of 'em choose out a green spot where the shade is very thick, and there they spread a carpet on which they sit drinking their coffee and generally attended by some slave with a fine voice or that plays on some instrument. Every twenty paces you may see one of these little companies listening to the dashing of the river, and this taste is so universal that the very gardeners are not without it. I have often seen them and their children sitting on the banks and playing on a rural instrument perfectly answering the description of the ancient fistula, being composed of unequal reeds, with a simple but agreeable softness in the sound. Mr Addison might here make the experiment he speaks of in his travels, there not being one instrument of music among the Greek or Roman statues that is not to be found in the hands of the people of this country. The young lads generally divert them-

1. '...[while] Oeagrian Hebrus swept and rolled in mid-current that head, plucked from its [marble] neck, the bare voice and death-cold tongue, with fleeting breath, called Eurydice — ah, hapless Eurydice! "Eurydice" the banks re-echoed, all adown the stream' (Virgil, *Georgics*).

2. These ideas helped to inspire Pope with sentiments that went into his 'Elegy to the Memory of an Unfortunate Lady'.

selves with making garlands for their favourite lambs, which I have often seen painted and adorned with flowers, lying at their feet while they sung or played. It is not that they ever read romances, but these are the ancient amusements here, and as natural to them as cudgel playing and football to our British swains, the softness and warmth of the climate forbidding all rough exercises, which were never so much as heard of amongst 'em, and naturally inspiring a laziness and aversion to labour, which the great plenty indulges. These gardeners are the only happy race of country people in Turkey. They furnish all the city with fruit and herbs, and seem to live very easily. They are most of 'em Greeks and have little houses in the midst of their gardens where their wives and daughters take a liberty not permitted in the town: I mean, to go unveiled. These wenches are very neat and handsome, and pass their time at their looms under the shade of their trees. I no longer look upon Theocritus as a romantic writer; he has only given a plain image of the way of life amongst the peasants of his country, which before oppression had reduced them to want, were I suppose all employed as the better sort of 'em are now. I don't doubt had he been born a Briton his idylliums had been filled with descriptions of thrashing and churning, both which are unknown here, the corn being all trod out by oxen, and butter (I speak it with sorrow) unheard of.

I read over your Homer[3] here with an infinite pleasure, and find several little passages explained that I did not before entirely comprehend the beauty of, many of the customs and much of the dress then in fashion being yet retained; and I don't wonder to find more remains here of an age so distant than is to be found in any other country, the Turks not taking that pains to introduce their own manners as has been generally practised by other nations that imagine themselves more polite. It would be too tedious to you to point out all the passages that relate to the present customs, but I can assure you that the Princesses and great ladies pass their time at their looms embroidering veils and robes, surrounded by their maids, which are always very numerous, in the same manner as we find Andromache and Helen described. The description of the belt of Menelaus exactly resembles those that are now worn by the great men, fastened before with broad golden clasps and embroidered round with rich work. The snowy veil that Helen throws over her face is still fashionable; and I never see (as I do very often) half a dozen old Pashas with their reverend beards sitting basking in the sun, but I recollect good King Priam and his councellors. Their manner of dancing is certainly the same that

3. The second volume of Pope's translation of the *Iliad*.

Portrait of a Tchinguis, or Turkish dancer after Jean-Baptiste Vanmour. Professional dancers were generally gipsies.

Diana is sung to have danced by Eurotas. The great lady still leads the dance and is followed by a troop of young girls who imitate her steps, and if she sings, make up the chorus. The tunes are extreme gay and lively, yet with something in 'em wonderful soft. The steps are varied according to the pleasure of her that leads the dance, but always in exact time and infinitely more agreeable than any of our dances, at least in my opinion. I sometimes make one in the train, but am not skilful enough to lead. These are Grecian dances, the Turkish being very different.

I should have told you in the first place that the eastern manners give a great light into many scripture passages that appear odd to us, their phrases being commonly what we should call scripture language. The vulgar Turk is very different from what is spoke at Court or amongst the people of figure, who always mix so much Arabic and Persian in their discourse that it may very well be called another language; and 'tis as ridiculous to make use of the expressions commonly used, in speaking to a great man or a lady, as it would be to talk broad Yorkshire or Somersetshire in the drawing-room. Besides this distinction they have what they call the sublime, that is a style proper for poetry, and which is the exact scripture style. I believe you would be pleased to see a genuine example of this, and I am very glad I have it in my power to satisfy your curiosity by sending you a faithful copy of the Verses that Ibrahim Pasha, the reigning favourite, has made for the young Princess, his contracted wife, whom he is not yet permitted to visit without witnesses, though she is gone home to his house. He is a man of wit and learning, but whether or no he is capable of writing good verse himself, you may be sure that on such an occasion he would not want the assistance of the best poets in the Empire. Thus the verses may be looked upon as a sample of their finest poetry, and I don't doubt you'll be of my mind that it is most wonderfully resembling the Song of Solomon, which was also addressed to a royal bride.

Turkish verses addressed to the Sultana,
eldest daughter of Sultan Achmet 3rd.
Stanza 1st

1 The nightingale now wanders in the vines,
  Her passion is to seek roses.
2 I went down to admire the beauty of the vines,

The sweetness of your charms has ravished my soul.
3 Your eyes are black and lovely
    But wild and disdainful as those of a stag.

Stanza 2nd

1 The wished possession is delayed from day to day,
    The cruel Sultan Achmed will not permit me to see those
    cheeks more vermillion than roses.
2 I dare not snatch one of your kisses,
    The sweetness of your charms has ravished my soul.
3 Your eyes are black and lovely
    But wild and disdainful as those of a stag.

Stanza 3rd

1 The wretched Pasha Ibrahim sighs in these verses,
    One dart from your eyes has pierced through my heart.
2 Ah, when will the hour of possession arrive?
    Must I yet wait a long time?
    The sweetness of your charms has ravished my soul.
3 Ah Sultana stag-eyed, an angel amongst angels,
    I desire and my desire remains unsatisfied.
    Can you take delight to prey upon my heart?

Stanza 4th

1 My cries pierce the heavens,
    My eyes are without sleep;
    Turn to me, Sultana, let me gaze on thy beauty.
2 Adieu, I go down to the grave;
    If you call me I return.
    My heart is hot as sulphur; sigh and it will flame.
3 Crown of my life, fair light of my eyes, my Sultana,
    my Princess,

I rub my face against the earth, I am drowned in scalding
tears — I rave!
Have you no compassion? Will you not turn to look upon me?

I have taken abundance of pains to get these verses in a literal translation, and if you were acquainted with my interpreters, I might spare myself the trouble of assuring you that they have received no poetical touches from their hands. In my opinion (allowing for the inevitable faults of a prose translation into a language so very different) there is a good deal of beauty in them. The epithet of stag-eyed (though the sound is not very agreeable in English) pleases me extremely, and is, I think, a very lively image of the fire and indifference in his mistress's eyes. Monsieur Boileau[5] has very justly observed, we are never to judge of the elevation of an expression in an ancient author by the sound it carries with us, which may be extremely fine with them, at the same time it looks low or uncouth to us. You are so well acquainted with Homer, you cannot but have observed the same thing, and you must have the same indulgence for all oriental poetry. The repetitions at the end of the two first stanzas are meant for a sort of chorus and agreeable to the ancient manner of writing. The music of the verses apparently changes in the third stanza where the burden is altered, and I think he very artfully seems more passionate at the conclusion as 'tis natural for people to warm themselves by their own discourse, especially on a subject where the heart is concerned, and is far more touching than our modern custom of concluding a song of passion with a turn which is inconsistent with it. The verse is a description of the season of the year, all the country being now full of nightingales, whose *amours* with roses is an Arabian fable[6] as well known here as any part of Ovid amongst us, and is much the same thing as if an English poem should begin by saying: Now Philomela sings — Or what if I turned the whole into the style of English poetry to see how 'twould look?

Stanza 1

Now Philomel renews her tender strain,
Indulging all the night her pleasing pain.
I sought the groves to hear the wanton sing,
There saw a face more beauteous than the spring.

5. Nicholas Boileau, known as Despréaux, a French poet and critic whose writings Pope studied.

6. In Persian and Turkish poetry, the nightingale its consumed with unrequited love for the rose; hence its unceasing song.

Your large stag's eyes where thousand glories play,
As bright, as lively, but as wild as they.

2

In vain I'm promised such a heavenly prize,
Ah, cruel Sultan who delays my joys!
While piercing charms transfix my amorous heart
I dare not snatch one kiss to ease the smart.
Those eyes like, etc.

3

Your wretched lover in these lines complains,
From those dear beauties rise his killing pains.
When will the hour of wished-for bliss arrive?
Must I wait longer? Can I wait and live?
Ah, bright Sultana? Maid divinely fair!
Can you unpitying see the pain I bear?

4

The heavens relenting hear my piercing cries,
I loath the light and sleep forsakes my eyes.
Turn thee, Sultana, ere thy lover dyes.
Sinking to earth, I sigh the last Adieu -
Call me, my Goddess, and my life renew.
My Queen! my angel! my fond heart's desire,
I rave — my bosom burns with heavenly fire.
Pity that passion which thy charms inspire.

I have taken the liberty in the second verse of following what I suppose is the true sense of the author, though not literally expressed. By saying he went down to admire the beauty of the vines and her charms ravished his soul, I understand by this a poetical fiction of having first seen her in a garden where he was admiring the beauty of the spring; but I could not forbear retaining the comparison of her eyes to those of a stag, though perhaps the novelty of it may give it a burlesque sound in our language. I cannot determine upon the whole how well I have succeeded in the translation. Neither do I think our English proper to express such violence of passion, which is very seldom felt amongst us; and we want those compound words which are very frequent and strong in the Turkish language. — You see I am pretty far gone in oriental learning, and to say truth I study very hard. I wish my studies may give me occasion of entertaining your curiosity, which will be the utmost advantage hoped from it by, etc.

To Sarah Chiswell — *Adrianople 1 April 1717*

In my opinion, dear Sarah, I ought rather to quarrel with you for not answering my Nijmegen letter of August till December, than to excuse my not writing again till now. I am sure there is on my side a very good excuse for silence, having gone such tiresome land journeys, though I don't find the conclusion of 'em so bad as you seem to imagine. I am very easy here and not in the solitude you fancy me; the great quantity of Greek, French, English and Italians that are under our protection make their court to me from morning till night, and I'll assure you are many of 'em very fine ladies, for there is no possibility for a Christian to live easily under this government but by the protection of an ambassador, and the richer they are the greater their danger.

Those dreadful stories you have heard of the plague have very little foundation in truth. I own I have much ado to reconcile myself to the sound of a word which has always given me such terrible ideas, though I am convinced there is little more in it than a fever, as a proof of which we passed through two or three towns most violently infected. In the very next house where we lay, in one of 'em, two persons died of it. Luckily for me I was so well deceived that I knew nothing of the matter, and I was made believe that our second cook who fell ill there had only a great cold. However, we left our doctor to take care of him, and yesterday they both arrived here in good health and I am now let into the secret that he has had the plague. There are many that 'scape of it, neither is the air ever infected. I am persuaded it would be as easy to root it out here as out of Italy and France, but it does so little mischief, they are not very solicitous about it and are content to suffer this distemper instead of our variety, which they are utterly unacquainted with.

Apropos of distempers, I am going to tell you a thing that I am sure will make you wish yourself here. The smallpox, so fatal and so general amongst us, is here entirely harmless by the invention of engrafting (which is the term they give it). There is a set of old women who make it their business to perform the operation. Every autumn, in the month of September, when the great heat is abated, people send to one another to know if any of their family has a mind to have the smallpox. They make parties for this purpose, and when they are met (commonly fifteen or sixteen together) the old woman comes with a nutshell full of the matter of the best sort of smallpox and asks what veins you please to have opened. She immediately rips open that you offer to her with a large needle (which gives you no more pain than a common scratch) and puts into the vein as much venom as can lie upon the head of her needle, and after binds up the little wound with a hollow bit of shell, and in this manner opens four or five veins. The Grecians have commonly the superstition of opening one in the middle of the forehead, in each arm, and on the breast to mark the sign of the cross, but this has a very ill effect, all these wounds leaving little scars, and is not done by those that are not superstitious, who choose to have them in the legs or that part of the arm that is concealed. The children or young patients play together all the rest of the day and are in perfect health till the eighth. Then the fever begins to seize 'em and they keep their beds two days, very seldom three. They have very rarely above twenty or thirty in their faces, which never mark, and in eight days' time they are as well as before their illness. Where they are wounded there remains running sores during the distemper, which I don't doubt is a great relief to it. Every year thousands undergo this operation, and the French ambassador says pleasantly that they take the smallpox here by way of diversion as they take the waters in other countries. There is no example of anyone that has died in it, and you may believe I am very well satisfied on the safety of the experiment since I intend to try it on my dear little son. I am patriot enough to take pains to bring this useful invention into fashion in England, and I should not fail to write to some of our doctors very particularly about it if I knew any one of 'em that I thought had virtue enough to destroy such a considerable branch of their revenue for the good of mankind, but that distemper is too beneficial to them not to expose to all their resentment the hardy wight that should undertake to put an end to it. Perhaps if I live to return I may, however, have courage to war with 'em. Upon this occasion, admire the heroism in the heart of your friend, etc.

To Miss Anne Thistlethwayte — *Adrianople 1 April 1717*

I can now tell dear Mrs Thistlethwayte that I am safely arrived at the end of my very long journey. I will not tire you with the account of the many fatigues I have suffered. You would rather hear something of what I see here, and a letter out of Turkey that has nothing extraordinary in it would be as great a disappointment as my visitors will receive at London if I return thither without any rarities to show them. What shall I tell you of? You never saw camels in your life and perhaps the description of them will appear new to you. I can assure you the first sight of 'em was very much so to me, and though I have seen hundreds of pictures of those animals, I never saw any that was resembling enough to give me a true idea of 'em. I am going to make a bold observation, and possibly a false one, because nobody has ever made it before me, but I do take them to be of the stag-kind; their legs bodies and necks are exactly shaped like them and their colour very near the same. 'Tis true they are much larger, being a great deal higher than a horse, and so swift that after the defeat of Peterwaradin, they far out-ran the swiftest horses and brought the first news of the loss of the battle to Belgrade. They are never thoroughly tamed. The drivers take care to tie them one to another with strong ropes, fifty in a string, led by an ass on which the driver rides. I have seen three hundred in one caravan. They carry the third part more than any horse, but 'tis a particular art to load them because of the bunch on their backs. They seem to me very ugly creatures, their heads being ill formed and disproportioned to their bodies. They carry all the burdens, and the beasts destined to the plough are buffaloes,[1] an animal you are also unacquainted with. They are larger and more clumsy than an ox. They have short black horns close to their heads, which grow turning backwards. They say this horn looks very beautiful when 'tis well polished. They are all black with very short hair on their hides and extreme little white eyes that make them look like devils. The country people dye their tails and

1. These were water-buffaloes, not the North American buffalo.

the hair of their foreheads red by way of ornament. Horses are not put here to any laborious work, nor are they at all fit for it. They are beautiful and full of spirit, but generally little and not so strong as the breed of colder countries, very gentle with all their vivacity, swift and sure footed. I have a little white favourite that I would not part with on any terms. He prances under me with so much fire you would think that I had a great deal of courage to dare mount him, yet I'll assure you I never rid a horse in my life so much at my command.[2] My side saddle is the first was ever seen in this part of the world and gazed at with as much wonder as the ship of Columbus was in America. Here are some birds held in a sort of religious reverence and for that reason multiply prodigiously: turtles on the account of their innocence, and storks because they are supposed to make every winter the pilgrimage to Mecca. To say truth, they are the happiest subjects under the Turkish government, and are so sensible of their privileges they walk the streets without fear and generally build in the low parts of houses. Happy are those that are so distinguished; the vulgar Turks are perfectly persuaded that they will not be that year either attacked by fire or pestilence. I have the happiness of one of their sacred nests just under my chamber window.

Now I am talking of my chamber I remember the description of the houses here would be as new to you as any of the birds or beasts. I suppose you have read in most of our accounts of Turkey that their houses are the most miserable pieces of building in the world. I can speak very learnedly on that subject, having been in so many of 'em, and I assure you 'tis no such thing. We are now lodged in a palace belonging to the Grand Signior. I really think the manner of building here very agreeable and proper for the country. 'Tis true they are not at all solicitous to beautify the outsides of their houses, and they are generally built of wood, which I own is the cause of many inconveniences, but this is not to be charged on the ill taste of the people but the oppression of the government. Every house upon the death of its master is at the Grand Signior's disposal, and therefore no man cares to make a great expense which he is not sure his family will be the better for. All their design is to build a house commodious and that will last their lives, and are very indifferent if it falls down the year after. Every house, great and small, is divided into two distinct parts which only join together by a narrow passage. The first house has a large court before it and open galleries all round it, which is to me a thing very agreeable. This gallery leads to all the chambers, which are commonly large and with two rows of windows, the first being of painted glass. They

2. Lady Mary was an enthusiastic rider all her life. When she left Constantinople a year later, four of the Ambassador's horses — probably Arabians, like the ones she describes here — were put on the ship.

The Odalisque or Favourite of the Constantinople Harem Thomas Allom. This scene, one of the *harem* of a wealthy Turk, is almost certainly largely imaginative, since men were forbidden to enter the *har em* hence the value of the descriptions provided by Lady Mary, who makes the point that the 'common voyage-writers... are very fond of speaking of what they don't know'.

seldom build above two stories, each of which has such galleries. The stairs are broad and not often above thirty steps. This is the house belonging to the lord and the adjoining one is called the Harem, that is, the lady's apartment, for the name of Seraglio is peculiar to the Grand Signior's. It has also a gallery running round it towards the garden to which all the windows are turned, and the same number of chambers as the other, but more gay and splendid both in painting and furniture. The second row of windows are very low, with grates like those of convents.

The rooms are all spread with Persian carpets and raised at one end of 'em (my chamber is raised at both ends) about two foot. This is the sofa and is laid with a richer sort of carpet, and all round it a sort of couch raised half a foot, covered with rich silk according to the fancy or magnificence of the owner. Mine is of scarlet cloth with a gold fringe. Round this are placed, standing against the wall, two rows of cushions, the first very large and the next little ones, and here the Turks display their greatest magnificence. They are generally brocade or embroidery of gold wire upon satin. Nothing can look more gay and splendid. These seats are so convenient and easy I shall never endure chairs as long as I live. The rooms are low, which I think no fault, the ceiling always of wood, generally inlaid, or painted and gilded. They use no hangings, the rooms being all wainscoted with cedar set off with silver nails or painted with flowers which open in many places with folding doors and serve for cabinets, I think more conveniently than ours. Between the windows are little arches to set pots of perfume or baskets of flowers, but what pleases me best is the fashion of having marble fountains in the lower part of the room which throws up several spouts of water, giving at the same time an agreeable coolness and a pleasant dashing sound falling from one basin to another. Some of these fountains are very magnificent. Each house has a bagnio, which is generally two or three little rooms leaded on the top, paved with marble, with basins, cocks of water and all conveniencies for either hot or cold baths. You will perhaps be surprised at an account so different from what you have been entertained with by the common voyager-writers who are very fond of speaking of what they don't know. It must be under a very particular character or on some extraordinary occasion when a Christian is admitted into the house of a man of quality, and their harems are always forbidden ground. Thus they can only speak of the outside, which makes no great appearance; and the women's apartments are all built backward, removed from sight, and have no other prospect than the gardens, which are enclosed with very high walls. There is none of our parterres in them but they are planted with high trees, which give an agreeable shade and, to my fancy, a pleasing view. In the midst of the garden is the kiosk, that is, a large room, commonly beautified with fine fountain in the midst of it. It is raised nine or ten steps and enclosed with gilded lattices, round which vines, jasmines and honeysuckles twining make a sort of green wall. Large trees are planted round this place, which is the scene of their greatest pleasures, and where the ladies spend most of their hours, employed by their music or embroidery. In the public gardens there are public kiosks where people go that are not so well accommodated at home, and drink their coffee, sherbet, etc. Neither are they ignorant of a more durable manner of building. Their mosques are all of free stone, and the public hans or inns extremely magnificent, many of 'em taking up a large square, built round with shops under stone arches, where poor artificers are lodged gratis. They have always a mosque joining them, and the body of the han is a most noble hall, capable of holding three or four hundred persons, the court extreme spacious, and cloisters round it that give it the air of our colleges. I own I think these foundations a more reasonable piece of charity than the founding of convents. — I think I have now told you a great deal for once. If you don't like my choice of subjects, tell me what you would have me write upon. There is nobody more desirous to entertain you than, Dear Mrs Thistlethwayte, etc.

To Lady Mar — *Adrianople 18 April 1717*

I write to you (dear sister) and all my other English correspondents by the last ship, and only heaven can tell when I shall have another opportunity of sending to you, but I cannot forbear writing, though perhaps my letter may lie upon my hands this two months. To confess the truth my head is full of my entertainment yesterday that 'tis absolutely necessary for my own repose to give it some vent. Without farther preface I will then begin my story.

I was invited to dine with the Grand Vizier's lady and 'twas with a great deal of pleasure I prepared myself for an entertainment which was never given before to any Christian. I thought I should very little satisfy her curiosity (which I did not

Ponte Grande by Luigi Mayer. This was a sequence of bridges over a marshy river near Adrianople built in the 16th century by Sinan, the celebrated architect of Süleyman the Magnificent.

doubt was a considerable motive to the invitation) by going in a dress she was used to see, and therefore dressed myself in the court habit of Vienna, which is much more magnificent than ours. However, I chose to go incognito to avoid any disputes about ceremony, and went in a Turkish coach only attended by my woman that held up my train and the Greek lady who was my interpretress. I was met at the Court door by her black eunuch, who helped me out of the coach with great respect and conducted me through several rooms where her she slaves, finely dressed, were ranged on each side. In the innermost, I found the lady sitting on her sofa in a sable vest. She advanced to meet me and presented me half a dozen of her friends with great civility. She seemed a very good woman, near fifty years old. I was surprized to observe so little magnificence in her house, the furniture being all very moderate, and except the habits and number of her slaves nothing about her that appeared expensive. She guessed at my thoughts and told me that she was no longer of an age to spend either her time or money in superfluities, that her whole expence was in charity and her employment in praying to God. There was no affectation in this speech; both she and her husband are entirely given up to devotion.[1] He never looks upon any other woman, and what is much more extraordinary touches no bribes, notwithstanding the example of all his predecessors. He is so scruplous in this point, he would not accept Mr Wortley's present till he had been assured over and over 'twas a settled perquisite of his place at the entrance of every ambassador.

She entertained me with all kind of civility till dinner came in, which was served one dish at a time, to a vast number, so finely dressed after their manner, which I do not think so bad as you have perhaps heard it represented. I am a very good judge of their eating, having lived three weeks in the house of an effendi at Belgrade who gave us very magnificent dinners dressed by his own cooks, which the first week pleased me extremely, but I own I then began to grow weary of it and desired my own cook might add a dish or two after our manner, but attribute this to custom. I am very much inclined to believe an Indian that had never tasted of either would prefer their cookery to ours. Their sauces are very high, all the roast very much done. They use a great deal of rich spice. The soup is served for the last dish, and they have at least as great variety of ragouts as we have. I was very sorry I could not eat of as many as the good lady would have had me, who was very earnest in serving me of everything. The treat concluded with coffee and perfumes, which is a high mark of respect. Two slaves kneeling censed my hair,

1. The Grand Vizier at this time was Arnand Halil Pasha, an Albanian, who had been in office since August 1716; he was a mild, pious man.

clothes, and handkerchief. After this ceremony she commanded her slaves to play and dance, which they did with their guitars in their hands, and she excused to me their want of skill, saying she took no care to accomplish them in that art. I returned her thanks and soon after took my leave.

I was conducted back in the same manner I entered, and would have gone straight to my own house, but the Greek lady with me earnestly solicited me to visit the Kahya's lady, saying he was the second officer in the Empire and ought to be looked upon as the first, the Grand Vizier having only the name while he exercised the authority. I had found so little in this harem that I had no mind to go to another, but her importunity prevailed with me, and I am extreme glad that I was so complaisant. All things here were with quite another air than at the Grand Vizier's, and the very house confessed the difference between an old devotee and a young beauty. It was nicely clean and magnificent. I was met at the door by two black eunuchs who led me through a long gallery between the ranks of beautiful young girls with their hair finely plaited almost hanging to their feet, all dressed in fine light damasks brocaded with silver. I was sorry that decency did not permit me to stop to consider them nearer, but that thought was lost upon my entrance to a large room, or rather pavilion, built round with gilded sashes which were most of 'em thrown up; and the trees planted near them gave an agreeable shade which hindered the sun from being troublesome, the jasmins and honey suckles that twisted round their trunks shedding a soft perfume increased by a white marble fountain playing sweet water in the lower part of the room, which fell into three or four basins with a pleasing sound. The roof was painted with all sorts of flowers falling from out of gilded baskets that seemed tumbling down.

On a sofa raised three steps and covered with fine Persian carpets sat the Kahya's lady, leaning on cushions of white satin embroidered, and at her feet sat two young girls, the eldest about twelve year old, lovely as angels, dressed perfectly rich and almost covered with jewels. But they were hardly seen near the fair Fatima (for that is her name), so much her beauty effaced everything. I have seen all that has been called lovely either in England or Germany, and must own that I never saw anything so gloriously beautiful, nor can I recollect a face that would have been taken notice of near hers. She stood up to receive me, saluting me after their fashion, putting her hand upon her heart with a sweetness full of majesty that no court breeding could ever give. She ordered cushions to be given me and took care to place me in the corner, which is the place of honour. I confess, though

Portrait by an anonymous Greek artist of the Sultan's Chief Black Eunuch. He was in charge of the women of the Palace, and sometimes also acted as Palace treasurer. Other senior officials also employed black eunuchs (see Lady Mary's description of her dinner with the Grand Vizier's Lady in this letter to Lady Mar of 18 April 1717.)

Female dancer at Constantinople from *The Costume of Turkey* by William Miller.

the Greek lady had before given me a great opinion of her beauty I was so struck with admiration that I could not for some time speak to her, being wholly taken up in gazing. That surprising harmony of features! that charming result of the whole! that exact proportion of body! that lovely bloom of complexion unsullied by art! the unutterable enchantment of her smile! But her eyes! large and black with all the soft languishment of the bleu! every turn of her face discovering some new charm! After my first surprise was over, I endeavoured by nicely examining her face to find out some imperfection, without any fruit of my search but being clearly convinced of the error of that vulgar notion, that a face perfectly regular would not be agreeable, nature having done for her with more success what Apelles[2] is said to have essayed, by a collection of the most exact features to form a perfect face; and to that a behaviour so full of grace and sweetness, such easy motions, with an air so majestic yet free from stiffness or affectation that I am persuaded could she be suddenly transported upon the most polite throne of Europe, nobody would think her other than born and bred to be a queen, though educated in a country we call barbarous. To say all in a word, our most celebrated English beauties would vanish near her.

She was dressed in a kaftan of gold brocade flowered with silver, very well fitted to her shape and showing to advantage the beauty of her bosom, only shaded by the thin gauze of her shift. Her drawers were pale pink, green and silver; her slippers white, finely embroidered; her lovely arms adorned with bracelets of diamonds and her broad girdle set round with diamonds; upon her head a rich Turkish handkerchief of pink and silver, her own fine black hair hanging a great length in various tresses, and on one side of her head some bodkins of jewels. I am afraid you will accuse me of extravagance in this description. I think I have read somewhere that women always speak in rapture when they speak of beauty, but I can't imagine why they should not be allowed to do so. I rather think it virtue to be able to admire without any mixture of desire or envy. The gravest writers have spoken with great warmth of some celebrated pictures and statues. The workmanship of heaven certainly excels all our weak imitations, and I think has a much better claim to our praise. For me, I am not ashamed to own I took more pleasure in looking on the beauteous Fatima than the finest piece of sculpture could have given me. She told me the two girls at her feet were her daughters, though she appeared too young to be their mother.

2. The most celebrated painter of Ancient Greece.

Portrait after Jean-Baptiste Vanmour of the Grand Vizier in ceremonial robes and turban. The identity of this particular Grand Vizier is not known; the job was a risky one, and at this time most post-holders did not last long in office. In Adrianople, Lady Mary dined with the Grand Vizier's lady, an occasion on which she found 'little diversion'.

Her fair maids were ranged below the sofa to the number of twenty, and put me in mind of the pictures of the ancient nymphs. I did not think all nature could have furnished such a scene of beauty. She made them a sign to play and dance. Four of them immediately began to play some soft airs on instruments between a lute and a guitar, which they accompanied with their voices while the others danced by turn. This dance was very different from what I had seen before. Nothing could be more artful or more proper to raise certain ideas, the tunes so soft, the motions so languishing, accompanied with pauses and dying eyes, half falling back and then recovering themselves in so artful a manner that I am very positive the coldest and most rigid prude upon earth could not have looked upon them without thinking of something not to be spoke of.

I suppose you may have read that the Turks have no music but what is shocking to the ears, but this account is from those who never heard any but what is played in the streets, and is just as reasonable as if a foreigner should take his ideas of the English music from the bladder and string, and marrow bones and cleavers. I can assure you that the music is extremely pathetic. 'Tis true I am inclined to prefer the Italian, but perhaps I am partial. I am acquainted with a Greek lady who sings better than Mrs Robinson,[3] and is very well skilled in both, who gives the preference to the Turkish. 'Tis certain they have very fine natural voices; these were very agreeable.

When the dance was over four fair slaves came into the room with silver censors in their hands and perfumed the air with amber, aloes wood and other rich scents. After this they served me coffee upon their knees in the finest Japan china with *soûcoupes* of silver gilt. The lovely Fatima entertained me all this time in the most polite agreeable manner, calling me often Uzelle Sultanam,[4] or the beautiful Sultana, and desiring my friendship with the best grace in the world, lamenting that she could not entertain me in my own language. When I took my leave two maids brought in a fine silver basket of embroidered hankerchiefs. She begged I would wear the richest for her sake, and gave the others to my woman and interpretress. I retired through the same ceremonies as before, and could not help fancying I had been some time in Muhammad's paradise, so much I was charmed with what I had seen. I know not how the relation of it appears to you. I wish it may give you part of my pleasure, for I would have my dear sister share in all the diversions of, etc.

3. Anastasia Robinson, *prima donna* of the London stage from 1714 to 1724.

4. The phrase should be 'Güzel Sultanum'. The 'Japan china' in which Lady Mary was served coffee was probably Chinese porcelain.

To The Abbé Conti — *Adrianople 17 May 1717*

I am going to leave Adrianople, and I would not do it without giving some account of all that is curious in it, which I have taken a great deal of pains to see. I will not trouble you with wise dissertations whether or no this is the same city that was anciently Orestesit or Oreste, which you know better than I do. It is now called from the emperor Hadrian, and was the first European seat of the Turkish Empire and has been the favourite residence of many Sultans. Mehmet the 4th, the father, and Mustafa, the brother, of the reigning Emperor, were so fond of it that they wholly abandoned Constantinople, which humour so far exasperated the janissaries, it was a considerable motive to the rebellions which deposed them. Yet this man seems to love to keep his court here. I can give no reason for this partiality. 'Tis true the situation is fine and the country all round very beautiful, but the air is extreme bad and the Seraglio itself is not free from the ill effect of it. The town is said to be eight mile in compass; I suppose they reckon in the gardens. There are some good houses in it; I mean large ones, for the architecture of their palaces never makes any great show. It is now very full of people, but they are most of them such as follow the Court or camp, and when they are removed, I am told, 'tis no populous city. The River Maritza (anciently the Hebrus) on which it is situated is dried up every summer, which contributes very much to make it unwholesome. It is now a very pleasant stream; there are two noble bridges built over it. I had the curiosity to go and see the Exchange in my Turkish dress, which is disguise sufficient, yet I own I was not very easy when I saw it crowded with janissaries, but they dare not be rude to a woman, and made way for me with as much respect as if I had been in my own figure. It is half a mile in length, the roof arched, and kept extremely neat. It holds 365 shops furnished with all sort of rich goods exposed to sale in the same manner as at the New Exchange in London,[1] but the pavement kept much neater, and the shops all so clean they seemed just new painted. Idle people of all sorts walk here for their diversion or amuse themselves with drinking coffee or sherbet, which is cried about as oranges and sweetmeats are in our playhouses.

I observed most of the rich tradesmen were Jews. That people are in incredible power in this country. They have many privileges above the natural Turks themselves, and have formed a very considerable common wealth here,

1. A bazaar on the south side of the Strand.

being judged by their own laws, and have drawn the whole trade of the Empire into their hands, partly by the firm union amongst themselves, and prevailing on the idle temper and want of industry of the Turks. Every Pasha has his Jew who is his *homme d'affaires*. He is let into all his secrets and does all his business. No bargain is made, no bribe received, no merchandise disposed of but what passes through their hands. They are the physicians, the stewards, and the interpreters of all the great men. You may judge how advantageous this is to a people who never fail to make use of the smallest advantages. They have found the secret of making themselves so necessary, they are certain of the protection of the Court whatever ministry is in power. Even the English, French and Italian merchants, who are sensible of their artifices, are however forced to trust their affairs to their negotiation, nothing of trade being managed without 'em, and the meanest amongst them is too important to be disobliged since the whole body take care of his interests with as much vigour as they would those of the most considerable of their members. They are many of 'em vastly rich, but take care to make little public show of it, though they live in their houses in the utmost luxury and magnificence. This copious subject has drawn me from my description of the Exchange founded by Ali Pasha,[2] whose name it bears. Near it is the Shershi, a street of a mile in length, full of shops of all kind of fine merchandise but excessive dear, nothing being made here. It is covered on the top with boards to keep out the rain, that merchants may meet conveniently in all weathers. The Bisisten near it is another Exchange, built upon pillars, where all sort of horse furniture is sold; glittering every where with gold, rich embroidery and jewels, it makes a very agreeable show.

From this place I went in my Turkish coach to the camp, which is to move in a few days to the frontiers. The Sultan is already gone to his tents, and all his Court. The appearance of them is indeed very magnificent. Those of the great men are rather like palaces than tents, taking up a great compass of ground and being divided into a vast number of apartments. They are all of green, and the Pashas of three tails have those ensigns of their power placed in a very conspicuous manner before their tents,[4] which are adorned on the top with gilded balls, more or less according to their different ranks. The ladies go in their coaches to see this camp as eagerly as ours did to that of Hyde Park,[5] but 'tis easy to observe that the soldiers do not begin the campaign with any great cheefulness. The war is a general grievance upon the people but particularly hard upon the tradesmen.

2. Ali Pasha, the Grand Vizier killed at the Battle of Peterwar adin in August 1716.

3. The Shershi is now Carsi and Bisisten Bedesten.

4. Pashas were of three grades, distinguished by the number of horsetails (one, two or three) which they were entitled to display as symbols of authority.

5. During the Jacobite rebellion, soldiers were encamped in Hyde Park.

Now the Grand Signior is resolved to lead his army in person, every company of 'em is obliged upon this occasion to make a present according to their ability. I took the pains of rising at six in the morning to see that ceremony, which did not however begin till eight. The Grand Signior was at the Seraglio window to see the procession, which passed through all the principal streets. It was preceded by an effendi mounted on a camel richly furnished, reading aloud the Koran, finely bound, laid upon a cushion. He was surrounded by a parcel of boys in white, singing some verses of it, followed by a man dressed in green boughs representing a clean husbandman sowing seed. After him several reapers with garlands of ears of corn, as Ceres is pictured, with scythes in their hands seeming to mow; then a little machine drawn by oxen, in which was a windmill and boys employed in grinding corn, followed by another machine drawn by buffalos carrying an oven and two more boys, one employed in kneading the bread, and another in drawing it out of the oven. These boys threw little cakes on both sides amongst the crowd, and were followed by the whole company of bakers marching on foot, two and two, in their best clothes, with cakes, loaves, pasties, and pies of all sorts on their heads; and after them two buffoons or jack puddings with their faces and clothes smeared with meal, who diverted the mob with their antic gestures. In the same manner followed all the companies of trade in their Empire, the nobler sort, such as jewellers, mercers, etc., finely mounted, and many of the pageants that represented their trades perfectly magnificent; amongst which the furriers made one of the best figures, being a very large machine set round with the skins of ermines, foxes, etc., so well stuffed the animals seemed to be alive, followed by music and dancers. I believe they were, upon the whole, at least 20,000 men, all ready to follow His Highness if he commanded them.

The rear was closed by the volunteers, who came to beg the honour of dying in his service. This part of the show seemed to me so barbarous I removed from the window upon the first appearance of it. They were all naked to the middle, their arms pierced through with arrows left sticking in 'em, others had 'em sticking in their heads, the blood trickling down their faces, and some slashed their arms with sharp knives, making the blood spout out upon those that stood near; and this is looked upon as an expression of their zeal for glory. I am told that some make use of it to advance their love, and when they are near the window where their mistress stands (all the women in town being veiled to see this spectacle) they stick another arrow for her sake, who gives some sign of approbation and encouragment to this

Domestic from *The Costume of Turkey* by William Miller.

135

galantry. The whole show lasted near eight hours, to my great sorrow, who was heartily tired, though I was in the house of the widow of the Captain Pasha (Admiral), who refreshed me with coffee, sweetmeats, sherbet, etc., with all possible civility.

I went two days after to see the Mosque of Sultan Selim the 1st, which is a building very well worth the curiosity of a traveller.[6] I was dressed in my Turkish habit and admitted without scruple, though I believe they guessed who I was, by the extreme officiousness of the door keeper to show me every part of it. It is situated very advantageously in the midst of the city and in the highest part, making a very noble show. The first court has four gates and the innermost three. They are both of them surrounded with cloisters with marble pillars of the Ionic order, finely polished and of very lively colours, the whole pavement being white marble, the roof of the cloisters being divided into several cupolas or domes, leaded, with gilt balls on the top, in the midst of each court fine fountains of white marble, before the great gate of the mosque a portico with green marble pillars.

It has five gates, the body of the Mosque being one prodigious dome. I understand so little of architecture I dare not pretend to speak of the proportions; it seemed to me very regular. This I am sure of, it is vastly high; and I thought it the noblest building I ever saw. It had two rows of marble galleries on pillars with marble balusters, the pavement marble covered with Persian carpets; and in my opinion it is a great addition to its beauty that it is not divided into pews and encumbered with forms and benches like our churches, nor the pillars (which are most of 'em red and white marble) disfigured by the little tawdry images and pictures that give the Roman Catholic churches the air of toy shops. The walls seemed to me inlaid with such very lively colours in small flowers, I could not imagine what stones had been made use of; but going nearer, I saw they were crusted with Japan china[7] which has a very beautiful effect. In the midst hung a vast lamp of silver gilt, besides which I do verily believe there was at least two thousand of a lesser size. This must look very glorious when they are all lighted, but that being at night no women are suffered to enter. Under the large lamp is a great pulpit of carved wood gilt and just by it a fountain to wash, which you know is an essential part of their devotion. In one corner is a little gallery enclosed with gilded lattices for the Grand Signior; at the upper end, a large niche very like an altar, raised two steps, covered with gold brocade, and standing before it two silver gilt candlesticks the height of a man and in them white wax candles as thick as a

6. This was the Selimiye Mosque, built for Sultan Selim II (not Selim I as Lady Mary reports) between 1569 and 1575, the most celebrated building in Adrianople.

7. Lady Mary is mistaken. The walls of the Mosque are decorated not with Japan china, or porcelain, but with gloriously coloured Iznik tiles; Turkish tiles and other Iznik productions were still an expensive rarity in Europe.

Portrait of the Ibriktar-Agassi after Jean-Baptiste Vanmour. The role of this official was to provide the Sultan with water for washing; he was often also one of the Sultan's trusted *confidants.*

Portrait of a soulak after Jean-Baptiste Vanmour. The *soulak* provided the Sultan's guard of honour on his way to Friday prayers.

man's waist. The outside of the Mosque is adorned with four towers vastly high, gilt on the top, from whence the imams call the people to prayers. I had the curiosity to go up one of them, which is contrived so artfully as to give surprise to all that see it. There is but one door, which leads to three different staircases going to the three different storeys of the tower in such a manner that three priests may ascend rounding without ever meeting each other, a contrivance very much admired. Behind the Mosque is an exchange full of shops where poor artificers are lodged gratis. I saw several dervishes at their prayers here. They are dressed in a plain piece of woollen with their arms bare and a woollen cap on their heads like a high crowned hat without brims. I went to see some other Mosques built much after the same manner, but not comparable in point of magnificence to this I have described, which is infinitely beyond any church in Germany or England. I won't talk of other countries I have not seen. The Seraglio does not seem a very magnificent palace, but the gardens very large, plentifully supplied with water, and full of trees, which is all I know of 'em, having never been in them.

I tell you nothing of the order of Mr Wortley's entry and his audience. Those things are always the same and have been so often described, I won't trouble you with the repetition. The young Prince, about eleven year old, sits near his father when he gives audience. He is a handsome boy, but probably will not immediately succeed the Sultan, there being two sons of Sultan Mustafa (his eldest brother) remaining, the eldest about twenty year old, on whom the hopes of the people are fixed.[8] This reign has been bloody and avaricious. I am apt to believe they are very impatient to see the end of it. I am, sir, your, etc.

I will write to you again from Constantinople.

8. The young prince was Süleyman; Mustafa's eldest son ruled as Sultan Mahmut I from 1730 to 1754 and was succeeded by his younger brother Osman III (1754-57); Mustafa had a third son, whom Lady Mary does not mention.

To The Abbé Conti — *Constantinople 29 May 1717*

I have had the advantage of very fine weather all my journey, and the summer being now in its beauty I enjoyed the pleasure of fine prospects; and the meadows being full of all sorts of garden flowers and sweet herbs, my berlin perfumed the air as it pressed 'em. The Grand Signior furnished us with thirty covered wagons for

Interior of part of the Sultan's Harem by A.I. Melling. This is virtually the only known representation of the *seraglio*— and, given that the rooms the visitor sees today bear little resemblance, it seems probable that this was an imaginary portrayal. Melling was employed by the Court as an architect; perhaps this is how he envisaged rebuilding this part of the palace. Lady Mary visited 'as much of the Seraglio as is to be seen' (letter of 10 April 1718), which was probably not much. *En route* from Adrianople to Constantinople she stayed in a 'little seraglio, built for the use of the Grand Signior [the Sultan] when he goes this road. I had the curiosity to view all the apartments destined for the ladies of his court ' (details opposite).

our baggage and five coaches of the country for my women. We found the road full of the great *spahis* horsemen and their equipages, coming out of Asia to the war. They always travel with tents, but I chose to lie in houses all the way. I will not trouble you with the names of the villages we passed in which there was nothing remarkable, but at Corlu we were lodged in a konak, or little seraglio, built for the use of the Grand Signior when he goes this road. I had the curiosity to view all the apartments destined for the ladies of his court. They were in the midst of a thick grove of trees, made fresh by fountains, but I was surprised to see the walls almost covered with little distiches of Turkish verse writ with pencils. I made my interpreter explain them to me and I found several of them very well turned, though I easily believed him that they lost much of their beauty in the translation. One runs literally thus in English:

> We come into this world, we lodge, and we depart;
> He never goes that's lodged within my heart.

The rest of our journey was through fine painted meadows by the side of the Sea of Marmara, the ancient Propontis. We lay the next night at Selivria, anciently a noble town. It is now a very good seaport, and neatly built enough, and has a bridge of thirty-two arches. Here is a famous ancient Greek church. I had given one of my coaches to a Greek lady who desired the convenience of travelling with me. She designed to pay her devotions and I was glad of the opportunity of going with her. I found it an ill built place, set out with the same sort of ornaments but less rich than the Roman Catholic churches. They showed me a saint's body, where I threw a piece of money, and a picture of the Virgin Mary drawn by the hand of St Luke, very little to the credit of his painting, but, however, the finest Madonna of Italy is not more famous for her miracles. The Greeks have the most monstrous taste in their pictures, which for more finery are always drawn upon a gold ground. You may imagine what a good air this has, but they have no notion either of shade or proportion. They have a Bishop here, who officiated in his purple robe, and sent me a candle almost as big as myself for a present when I was at my lodging.

We lay the next night at a town called Büyük Çekmece¹ or Great Bridge, and the night following at Küyük Çekmece, Little Bridge, in a very pleasant lodging, formerly a monastery of dervishes, having before it a large court encompassed

1. Çekmece in fact means drawbridge.

142

with marble cloisters with a good fountain in the middle. The prospect from this place and the gardens round it are the most agreeable I have seen, and shows that monks of all religions know how to choose their retirements. 'Tis now belonging to a *hoca* or schoolmaster, who teaches boys here; and asking him to show me his own apartment I was surprised to see him point to a tall cypress tree in the garden, on the top of which was a place for a bed for himself, and a little lower, one for his wife and two children, who slept there every night. I was so much diverted with the fancy I resolved to examine his nests nearer, but after going up fifty steps I found I had still fifty to go and then I must climb from branch to branch with some hazard of my neck. I thought it the best way to come down again.

We arrived the next evening at Constantinople, but I can yet tell you very little of it, all my time having been taken up with receiving visits, which are at least a very good entertainment to the eyes, the young women being all beauties and their beauty highly improved by the good taste of their dress. Our palace is in Pera, which is no more a suburb of Constantinople than Westminster is a suburb to London. All the ambassadors are lodged very near each other. One part of our house shows us the port, the city and the Seraglio, and the distant hills of Asia, perhaps altogether the most beautiful prospect in the world. A certain French author says that Constantinople is twice as large as Paris.[2] Mr Wortley is unwilling to own 'tis bigger than London, though I confess it appears to me to be so, but I don't believe 'tis so populous. The burying fields about it are certainly much larger than the whole city. 'Tis surprising what a vast deal of land is lost this way in Turkey. Sometimes I have seen burying places several miles belonging to very inconsiderable villages which were formerly great towns and retain no other mark of their ancient grandeur. On no occasion will they remove a stone that serves for a monument. Some of them are costly enough, being of very fine marble. They set up a pillar with a carved turban on the top of it to the memory of a man, and as the turbans by their different shapes show the quality or profession, 'tis in a manner putting up the arms of the deceased; besides, the pillar commonly bears a large inscription in gold letters. The ladies have a simple pillar without other ornament, except those that die unmarried, who have a rose on the top of it. The sepulchres of particular families are railed in and planted round with trees. Those of the Sultans and some great men have lamps constantly burning in them.

When I spoke of their religion I forgot to mention two particularities, one of which I had read of, but it seemed so odd to me I could not believe it. Yet 'tis

2. Jean Dumont, French historian, whose *Nouveau Voyage au Levant* (1694) was translated into English in 1696.

certainly true that when a man has divorced his wife in the most solemn manner, he can take her again upon no other terms than permitting another man to pass a night with her, and there are some examples of those that have submitted to this law rather than not have back their beloved.[3] The other point of doctrine is very extraordinary: any woman that dies unmarried is looked upon to die in a state of reprobation. To confirm this belief, they reason that the end of the creation of woman is to increase and multiply, and she is only properly employed in the works of her calling when she is bringing children or taking care of 'em, which are all the virtues that God expects from her; and indeed their way of life, which shuts them out of all public commerce, does not permit them any other. Our vulgar notion that they do not own women to have any souls is a mistake. 'Tis true they say they are not of so elevated a kind and therefore must not hope to be admitted into the paradise appointed for the men, who are to be entertained by celestial beauties; but there is a place of happiness destined for souls of the inferior order, where all good women are to be in eternal bliss. Many of 'em are very superstitious and will not remain widows ten days for fear of dying in the reprobate state of a useless creature.[4] But those that like their liberty and are not slaves to their religion content themselves with marrying when they are afraid of dying. This is a piece of theology very different from that which teaches nothing to be more acceptable to God than a vow of perpetual virginity. Which divinity is most rational I leave you to determine.

I have already made some progress in a collection of Greek medals. Here are several professed antiquaries who are ready to serve anybody that desires them, but you can't imagine how they stare in my face when I inquire about 'em, as if nobody was permitted to seek after medals till they were grown a piece of antiquity themselves. I have got some very valuable of the Macedonia kings, particularly one of Perseus, so lively I fancy I can see all his ill qualities in his face.[5] I have a porphyry head finely cut of the true Greek sculpture, but who it represents is to be guessed at by the learned when I return, for you are not to suppose these antiquaries (who are all Greeks) know anything. Their trade is only to sell. They have correspondents at Aleppo, Grand Cairo, in Arabia, and Palestine, who send them all they can find, and very often great heaps that are only fit to melt into pans and kettles. They get the best price they can for any of 'em, without knowing those that are valuable from those that are not. Those that pretend to skill generally find out the image of some saint in the medals of the Greek cities. One of them,

3. Although this was true, other travellers remarked that the husband usually chose a friend whose tactful continence he could rely on.

4. But according to Muslim doctrine matrimony does not affect the spiritual fate of women; and a widow is forbidden to remarry for a period of four months and ten days.

5. Perseus, last king of the Macedonians, had his brother murdered.

View of a Constantinople kebab house done by an anonymous Greek artist; the Golden Horn can be seen in the background. Soup, considered a good cure for a hangover, is being served.

Caravanserai at Kuskhuk-Czemege by Luigi Mayer. This was a small village where Lady Mary stayed en route from Adrianople to Constantinople in 1717: 'we lay the ... night ...at Küyük Çekmece ...in a very pleasant lodging, formerly a monastery of dervishes, having before it a large court encompassed with marble cloisters with a good fountain in the middle'.

146

showing me the fiture of a Pallas with a victory in her hand on a reverse, assured me it was the Virgin holding a crucifix. The same man offered me the head of a Socrates on a sardonyx, and to enhance the value gave him the title of St Augustine. I have bespoke a mummy, which I hope will come safe to my hands, notwithstanding the misfortune that befell a very fine one designed for the King of Sweden.[6] He gave a great price for it, and the Turks took it into their heads that he must certainly have some considerable project depending upon't. They fancied it the body of God knows who, and that the fate of their Empire mystically depended on the conservation of it. Some old prophecies were remembered upon this occasion, and the mummy committed prisoner to the Seven Towers, where it has remained under close confinement ever since. I dare not try my interest in so considerable a point as the release of it, but I hope mine will pass without examination. — I can tell you nothing more at present of this famous city. When I have looked a little about me you shall hear from me again. I am, sir, etc.

6. Charles XII of Sweden, after being defeated in 1709, remained near Adrianople until 1714 as a 'guest' of the Turks.

To Alexander Pope — *Belgrade Village 17 June 1717*

I hope before this time you have received two or three of my letters. I had yours but yesterday, though dated the third of February, in which you suppose me to be dead and buried. I have already let you know that I am still alive, but to say truth I look upon my present circumstances to be exactly the same with those of departed spirits. The heats of Constantinople have driven me to this place which perfectly answers the description of the Elysian fields. I am in the middle of a wood consisting chiefly of fruit trees, watered by a vast number of fountains famous for the excellency of their water, and divided into many shady walks upon short grass, that seems to me artificial but I am assured is the pure work of nature, within view of the Black Sea, from whence we perpetually enjoy the refreshment of cool breezes that makes us insensible of the heat of the summer. The village is wholly inhabited by the richest amongst the Christians, who meet every night at a fountain forty paces from my house to sing and dance, the beauty and dress of the women exactly resembling the ideas of the ancient nymphs as they are given us by the representations of the poets and painters. But what persuades me more fully

Turkish Encampment at Daud Pasha by Luigi Mayer. The Turkish army is about to leave on campaign. 'The appearance of the army tents is indeed very magnificent. Those of the great men are rather like palaces than tents, taking up a great compass of ground and being divided into a vast number of apartments.' (Letter of 17 May.)

Mosque of Sultan Achmet by
Luigi Mayer. Lady Mary
visited mosques in both
Adrianople and Constantinople
(see her letters to the Abbé
Conti on 17 May 1717 and to
Lady Bristol on 10 May 1718).

of my decease is the situation of my own mind, the profound ignorance I am in of what passes amongst the living, which only comes to me by chance, and the great calmness with which I receive it. Yet I have still a hankering after my friends and acquaintance left in the world, according to the authority of that admirable author,

> That spirits departed are wondrous kind
> To friends and relations left behind,
> Which nobody can deny,

of which solemn truth I am a dead instance. I think Virgil is of the same opinion, that in human souls there will still be some remains of human passions.

— Curae non ipsa in morte relinquunt;[1]

and 'tis very necessary to make a perfect Elysium that there should be a River Lethe, which I am not so happy to find. To say truth, I am sometimes very weary of this singing and dancing and sunshine, and wish for the smoke and impertinencies in which you toil, though I endeavour to persuade myself that I live in a more agreeable variety than you do, and that Monday setting of partridges, Tuesday reading English, Wednesday studying the Turkish language (in which, by the way, I am already very learned), Thursday classical authors, Friday spent in writing, Saturday at my needle, and Sunday admitting of visits and hearing music, is a better way of disposing the week than Monday at the Drawing Room,[2] Tuesday Lady Mohun's, Wednesday the opera, Thursday the play, Friday Mrs Chetwynd's,[3] etc: a perpetual round of hearing the same scandal and seeing the same follies acted over and over, which here affect me no more than they do other dead people. I can now hear of displeasing things with pity and without indignation. The reflection on the great gulf between you and me cools all news that comes hither. I can neither be sensibly touched with joy or grief when I consider that possibly the cause of either is removed before the letter comes to my hands; but (as I said before) this indolence does not extend to my few friendships. I am still warmly sensible of yours and Mr Congreve's and desire to live in your remembrances, though dead to all the world beside.

1. 'Even in death the pangs leave them not' (*Aeneid*).

2. At St James's Palace.

3. Mary Chetwynd was the wife of a Member of Parliament; her house was well known as a centre of gossip.

The Fountain of Ahmed III by
William Page. It was to the
Court of Ahmed III that
Wortley was appointed
Ambassador.

Aqueduct near Belgrade by
Luigi Mayer. Belgrade Forest
was a country spot north of
Constantinople, where
prosperous families came to
escape the worst of the
summer heat; Lady Mary
describes the area, which was
so named in celebration of a
Turkish victory over Austria at
Belgrade, Serbia, in her letter
to Alexander Pope of 17 June
1717 (see pages 147 - 151). The
aqueduct formed part of the
originally Byzantine system of
water-supply to the city, which
the Turks maintained and
improved.

View of the Second Court of the Topkapi Saray, the Sultan's Palace, by an anonymous Greek artist. Janissaries (soldiers) can be seen running to collect their pay, contained in small yellow purses. The first janissary to retrieve a purse, and show it to his senior officer received a small reward. Lady Mary saw as much of the Palace as she could. 'I believe there is no Christian king's palace half so large. There are six large courts in it all built round and set with trees, having galleries of stone.'

To Lady _____ — *Belgrade Village 17 June 1717*

I heartily beg your ladyship's pardon, but I really could not forbear laughing heartily at your letter and the commissions you are pleased to honour me with. You desire me to buy you a Greek slave who is to be mistress of a thousand good qualities. The Greeks are subjects and not slaves. Those who are to be bought in that manner are either such as are taken in war or stole by the Tartars from Russia, Circassia or Georgia, and are such miserable, awkward, poor wretches, you would not think any of 'em worthy to be your house-maid. 'Tis true that many thousands were taken in the Morea, but they have been most of them redeemed by the charitable contributions of the Christians or ransomed by their own relations at Venice. The fine slaves that wait upon the great ladies, or serve the pleasures of the great men, are all bought at the age of eight or nine year old and educated with great care to accomplish 'em in singing, dancing, embroidery, etc. They are commonly Circassians, and their patron never sells them except it is as a punishment for some very great fault. If ever they grow weary of 'em, they either present them to a friend or give them their freedoms. Those that are exposed to sale at the markets are always either guilty of some crime or so entirely worthless that they are of no use at all. I am afraid you'll doubt the truth of this account, which I own is very different from our common notions in England, but it is not less truth for all that.

Your whole letter is full of mistakes from one end to t'other. I see you have taken your ideas of Turkey from that worthy author Dumont,[1] who has writ with equal ignorance and confidence. 'Tis a particular pleasure to me here to read the voyages to the Levant, which are generally so far removed from truth and so full of absurdities I am very well diverted with 'em. They never fail giving you an account of the women, which 'tis certain they never saw, and talking very wisely of the genius of the men, into whose company they are never admitted, and very often describe Mosques, which they dare not peep into. The Turks are very proud, and will not converse with a stranger they are not assured is considerable in his own country. I speak of the men of distinction, for as to the ordinary fellows, you may imagine what ideas their conversation can give of the general genius of the people.

As to the balm of Mecca,[2] I will certainly send you some, but it is not so easily got as you suppose it, and I cannot in conscience advise you to make use of it. I

1. Jean Dumont, in *Nouveau Voyage au Levant* (1694).

2. Balm extracted from opobalsamum bushes and credited with extensive healing powers; the balm was a monopoly of the Sultan and the extraction method was kept secret.

know not how it comes to have such universal applause. All the ladies of my acquaintance at London and Vienna have begged me to send pots of it to them. I have had a present of a small quantity (which I'll assure you is very valuable) of the best sort, and with great joy applied it to my face, expecting some wonderful effect to my advantage. The next morning the change indeed was wonderful; my face was swelled to a very extraordinary size and all over as red as my lady's. It remained in this lamentable state three days, during which you may be sure I passed my time very ill. I believed it would never be otherwise, and to add to my mortification Mr Wortley reproached my indiscretion without ceasing. However, my face is since in *statu quo*. Nay, I am told by the ladies here that 'tis much mended by the operation, which I confess I cannot perceive in my looking glass. Indeed, if one was to form an opinion of this balm from their faces, one should think very well of it. They all make use of it and have the loveliest bloom in the world. For my part, I never intend to endure the pain of it again; — let my complexion take its natural course and decay in its own due time. I have very little esteem for medicines of this nature; but do as you please, madam, only remember before you use it that your face will not be such as you'll care to show in the drawing room for some days after.

If one was to believe the women in this country, there is a surer way of making oneself beloved than by becoming handsome, though you know that's our method. But they pretend to the knowledge of secrets that by way of enchantment gives them the entire empire over whom they please. For me, that am not very apt to believe in wonders, I cannot find faith for this. I disputed the point last night with a lady who really talks very sensibly on any other subject, but she was downright angry with me that she did not perceive she had persuaded me of the truth of forty stories she told me of this kind, and at last mentioned several ridiculous marriages that there could be no other reason assigned for. I assured her that in England, where we were entirely ignorant of all magic, where the climate is not half so warm nor the women half so handsome, we were not without our ridiculous marriages; and that we did not look upon it as anything supernatural when a man played the fool for the sake of a woman. But my arguments could not convince her against (as she said) her certain knowledge, though she added that she scrupled making use of charms herself, but that she could do it whenever she pleased and, staring in my face, said (with a very learned air) that no enchantments would have their effect upon me, and that there were some people exempt from their power,

The Slave Merchant, Constantinople by Thomas Allom. It is likely that Turkish sensitivities would have prevented Allom from visiting the slave market, and thus this scene is probably largely imaginative. Lady Mary writes about slaves, who were generally of Greek or Caucasian origin, in her letter of 17 June 1717 to Lady — (see page 154), and again in her letter of 10 April 1718 to Lady Bristol (see page 186): 'I cannot forbear applauding the humanity of the Turks to those creatures [slaves]. They are never ill used and their slavery is in my opinion no worse than servitude all over the world.'

*The main gate of Topkapi Saray,
the Sultan's palace, with the
fountain built by Ahmed III on
the right:* view by an
anonymous Greek artist. It
was during Ahmed III's reign
that Lady Mary visited
Constantinople.

but very few. You may imagine how I laughed at this discourse, but all the women here are of the same opinion. They don't pretend to any commerce with the devil, but that there are certain compositions to inspire love. If one could send over a shipload of them I fancy it would be a very quick way of raising an estate. What would not some ladies of our acquaintance give for such merchandise?

Adieu my dear Lady_____,I cannot conclude my letter with a subject that affords more delightful scenes to imagination. I leave you to figure to yourself the extreme court that will be made to me at my return if my travels should furnish me with such a useful piece of learning. I am, dear madam, etc.

To Miss Anne Thistlethwayte — *Pera of Constantinople 4 January 1718*

I am infinitely obliged to you, dear Mrs Thistlethwayte, for your entertaining letter. You are the only one of my correspondents that have judged right enough to think I would gladly be informed of the news amongst you. All the rest of 'em tell me (almost in the same words) that they suppose I know everything. Why they are pleased to suppose in this manner, I can guess no reason except they are persuaded that the breed of Muhammad's pigeon still subsists in this country and that I receive supernatural intelligence.[1] I wish I could return your goodness with some diverting accounts from hence, but I know not what part of the scenes here would gratify your curiosity or whether you have any curiosity at all for things so far distant. To say the truth, I am at this present writing not very much turned for the recollection of what is diverting, my head being wholly filled with the preparations necessary for the increase of my family, which I expect every day.[2] You may easily guess at my uneasy situation; but I am, however, in some degree comforted by the glory that accrues to me from it, and a reflection on the contempt I should otherwise fall under.

You won't know what to make of this speech, but in this country 'tis more despicable to be married and not fruitful than 'tis with us to be fruitful before marriage. They have a notion that whenever a woman leaves off bringing chil-

1. A pigeon was said to have been taught by Muhammad to pick corn out of his ear, which the vulgar took to be the whispering of the Holy Ghost.

2. A daughter, the future Countess of Bute, was born on 19 January and christened Mary.

dren, 'tis because she is too old for that business, whatever her face says to the contrary, and this opinion makes the ladies here so ready to make proofs of their youth (which is as necessary in order to be a received beauty as it is to show the proofs of nobility to be admitted Knight of Malta) that they do not content themselves with using the natural means, but fly to all sort of quackeries to avoid the scandal of being past child-bearing and often kill themselves by 'em. Without any exaggeration, all the women of my acquaintance that have been married ten year have twelve or thirteen children, and the old ones boast of having had five-and-twenty or thirty a piece and are respected according to the number they have produced. When they are with child, 'tis their common expression to say they hope God will be so merciful to 'em to send two this time, and when I have asked them sometimes how they expected to provide for such a flock as they desire, they answer that the plague will certainly kill half of 'em; which, indeed, generally happens without much concern to the parents, who are satisfied with the vanity of having brought forth so plentifully. The French Ambassadress is forced to comply with this fashion as well as myself. She has not been here much above a year and has lain in once and is big again. What is most wonderful is the exemption they seem to enjoy from the curse entailed on the sex. They see all company the day of their delivery and at the fortnight's end return visits, set out in their jewels and new clothes. I wish I may find the influence of the climate in this particular, but I fear I shall continue an English woman in that affair as well as I do in my dread of fire and plague, which are two things very little feared here, most families having had their houses burnt down once or twice, occasioned by their extraordinary way of warming themselves, which is neither by chimneys nor stoves, but a certain machine called a *tandir* the height of two foot, in the form of a table, covered with a fine carpet or embroidery. This is made only of wood, and they put into it a small quantity of hot ashes and sit with their legs under the carpet. At this table they work, read, and very often sleep; and if they chance to dream, kick down the *tandir* and the hot ashes commonly sets the house on fire. There was five hundred houses burnt in this manner about a fortnight ago, and I have seen several of the owners since who seem not at all moved at so common a misfortune. They put their goods into a bark and see their houses burn with great philosophy, their persons being very seldom endangered, having no stairs to descend.

But having entertained you with things I don't like, 'tis but just I should tell you something that pleases me. The climate is delightful in the extremest degree. I

Hamal, or porter, carrying a bag of charcoal; from *The Costume of Turkey* by William Miller.

Interior of a Turkish Caffinet,
Constantinople by Thomas
Allom. This coffee house was
decorated in an elaborate
Baroque style.

am now sitting, this present fourth of January, with the windows open, enjoying the warm shine of the sun, while you are freezing over a sad sea-coal fire; and my chamber is set out with carnations, roses and jonquils, fresh from my garden. I am also charmed with many points of the Turkish law, to our shame be it spoken, better designed and better executed than ours, particularly the punishment of convicted liars (triumphant criminals in our country, God knows). They are burnt in the forehead with a hot iron, being proved the authors of any notorious false-hood. How many white foreheads should we see disfigured? How many fine gentlemen would be forced to wear their wigs as low as their eyebrows were this law in practice with us? I should go on to tell you many other parts of justice, but I must send for my midwife.

To Lady Mar — *Pera of Constantinople 10 March 1718*

I have not writ to you (dear sister) these many months, a great piece of self-denial, but I knew not where to direct or what part of the world you were in. I have received no letter from you since your short note of April last in which you tell me that you are on the point of leaving England and promise me a direction for the place you stay in, but I have in vain expected it till now, and now I only learn from the *Gazette* that you are returned, which induces me to venture this letter to your house at London. I had rather ten of my letters should be lost than you imagine I don't write, and I think 'tis hard fortune if one in ten don't reach you. However, I am resolved to keep the copies as testimonies of my inclination to give you (to the utmost of my power) all the diverting part of my travels while you are exempt from all the fatigues and inconveniences.

In the first place I wish you joy of your niece, for I was brought to bed of a daughter five weeks ago. I don't mention this as one of my diverting adventures, though I must own that it is not half so mortifying here as in England, there being as much difference as there is between a little cold in the head, which sometimes happens here, and the consumptive coughs so common in London. Nobody keeps their house a month for lying-in, and I am not so fond of any of our customs to retain them when they are not necessary. I returned my visits at three weeks' end, and about four days ago crossed the sea which divides this place from Constantinople to make a new one, where I had the good fortune to pick up many curiosities.

I went to see the Sultana Hafise, favourite of the last Emperor Mustafa, who, you know (or perhaps you don't know), was deposed by his brother, the reigning Sultan, and died a few weeks after, being poisoned, as it was generally believed.[1] This lady was immediately after his death saluted with an absolute order to leave the Seraglio and choose herself a husband from the great men at the Porte. I suppose you imagine her overjoyed at this proposal. Quite contrary; these women, who are called and esteem themselves queens, look upon this liberty as the greatest disgrace and affront that can happen to them. She threw herself at the Sultan's feet and begged him to poniard her rather than use his brother's widow with that contempt. She represented to him in agonies of sorrow that she was privileged from this misfortune by having brought five princes into the Ottoman family, but all the boys being dead and only one girl surviving, this excuse was not received and she compelled to make her choice. She chose Ebubekir Effendi, then secretary of state, and above fourscore years old, to convince the world that she firmly intended to keep the vow she had made of never suffering a second husband to approach her bed, and since she must honour some subject so far as to be called his wife she would choose him as a mark of her gratitude, since it was he that had presented her at the age of ten year old to her lost lord. But she has never permitted him to pay her one visit, though it is now fifteen years she has been in his house, where she passes her time in uninterrupted mourning with a constancy very little known in Christendom, especially in a widow of twenty-one, for she is now but thirty-six. She has no black eunuchs for her guard, her husband being obliged to respect her as a queen and not enquire at all into what is done in her apartment, where I was led into a large room, with a sofa the whole length of it, adorned with white marble pillars like a *ruelle*, covered with pale *bleu* figured velvet on a silver ground, with cushions of the same, where I was desired to repose till the Sultana appeared, who had contrived this manner of reception to avoid rising up at my entrance, though she made me an inclination of her head when I rose up to her. I was very glad to observe a lady that had been distinguished by the favour of an Emperor to whom beauties were every day presented from all parts of the world.

1. Mustafa II, deposed in August 1703, died four months later — of dropsy.

162

But she did not seem to me to have ever been half so beautiful as the fair Fatima I saw at Adrianople, though she had the remains of a fine face more decayed by sorrow than time.

But her dress was something so surprisingly rich I cannot forbear describing it to you. She wore a vest called *dolaman*, and which differs from a caftan by longer sleeves, and folding over at the bottom. It was of purple cloth strait to her shape and thick set, on each side down to her feet and round the sleeves, with pearls of the best water, of the same size as their buttons commonly are. You must not suppose I mean as large as those of my Lord — but about the bigness of a pea; and to these buttons, large loops of diamonds in the form of those gold loops so common upon birthday coats. This habit was tied at the waist with two large tassels of smaller pearl, and round the arms embroidered with large diamonds; her shift fastened at the bosom with a great diamond shaped like a lozenge; her girdle as broad as the broadest English riband entirely covered with diamonds. Round her neck she wore three chains which reached to her knees, one of large pearl at the bottom of which hung a fine coloured emerald as big as a turkey egg, another lively green, perfectly matched, every one as large as a half-crown piece and as thick as three crown pieces, and another of small emeralds perfectly round. But her earrings eclipsed all the rest; they were two diamonds shaped exactly like pears, as large as a big hazel nut. Round her *talpack* she had four strings of pearl, the whitest and most perfect in the world, at least enough to make four necklaces every one as large as the Duchess of Marlborough's, and of the same size, fastened with two roses consisting of a large ruby for the middle stone, and round them twenty drops of clean diamonds to each. Besides this, her headdress was covered with bodkins of emeralds and diamonds. She wore large diamond bracelets and had five rings on her fingers, all single diamonds, (except Mr Pitt's) the largest I ever saw in my life.[2] 'Tis for jewellers to compute the value of these things, but according to the common estimation of jewels in our part of the world, her whole dress must be worth above £100,000 sterling. This I am very sure of, that no European queen has half the quantity, and the Empress's jewels (though very fine) would look very mean near hers.

She gave me a dinner of fifty dishes of meat, which (after their fashion) was placed on the table but one at a time, and was extremely tedious, but the magnificence of her table answered very well to that of her dress. The knives were of gold, the hafts set with diamonds, but the piece of luxury that grieved my eyes was

2. Thomas Pitt, an East India merchant, owned an enormous diamond of almost 140 carats; in 1717 he sold it to the French Regent.

the table cloth and napkins, which were all tiffany embroidered with silks and gold in the finest manner in natural flowers. It was with the utmost regret that I made use of these costly napkins, as finely wrought as the finest handkerchiefs that ever came out of this country. You may be sure that they were entirely spoilt before dinner was over. The sherbet (which is the liquor they drink at meals) was served in china bowls, but the covers and salvers, massy gold. After dinner, water was brought in a gold basin and towels of the same kind of the napkins, which I very unwillingly wiped my hands upon, and coffee was served in china with gold *soucoupes*.

The Sultana seemed in very good humour, and talked to me with the utmost civility. I did not omit this opportunity of learning all that I possibly could of the Seraglio, which is so entirely unknown amongst us. She assured me that the story of the Sultan's throwing a handkerchief is altogether fabulous, and the manner upon that occasion no other but that he sends the Kuzlir Aga to signify to the lady the honour he intends her. She is immediately complimented upon it by the others, and led to the bath where she is perfumed and dressed in the most magnificent and becoming manner. The Emperor precedes his visit by a royal present and then comes into her apartment. Neither is there any such thing as her creeping in at the bed's feet. She said that the first he made choice of was always after the first in rank, and not the mother of the eldest son, as other writers would make us believe. Sometimes the Sultan diverts himself in the company of all his ladies, who stand in a circle round him, and she confessed that they were ready to die with jealousy and envy of the happy she that he distinguished by any appearance of preference. But this seemed to me neither better nor worse than the circles in most Courts, where the glance of the monarch is watched and every smile waited for with impatience and envied by those that cannot obtain it.

She never mentioned the Sultan without tears in her eyes, yet she seemed very fond of the discourse. 'My past happiness,' said she, 'appears a dream to me, yet I cannot forget that I was beloved by the greatest and most lovely of mankind. I was chosen from all the rest to make all his campaigns with him. I would not survive him if I was not passionately fond of the Princess, my daughter, yet all my tenderness for her was hardly enough to make me preserve my life when I lost him. I passed a whole twelvemonth without seeing the light. Time has softened my despair, yet I now pass some days every week in tears devoted to the memory of my Sultan.' There was no affectation in these words. It was easy to see she was in a

Portrait by an anonymous Greek artist of a Palace confectioner, one of several hundred who worked in Topkapi Saray.

The Royal Sultana portrait after Jean-Baptiste Vanmour. The exact identity of this royal favourite is not known, but this is likely to be an accurate portrait.

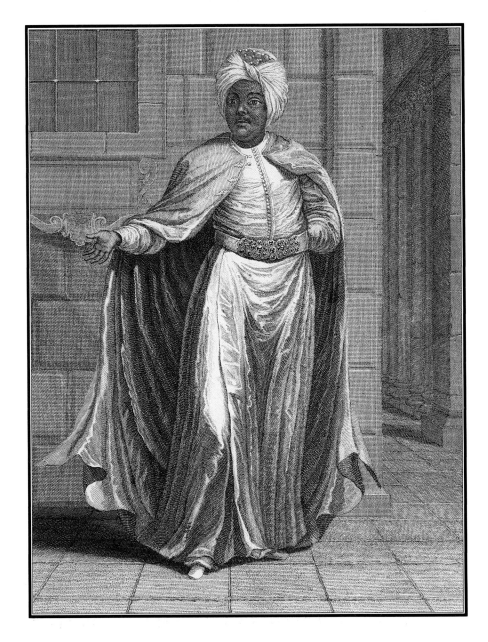

The Kisslar Agassi, or Chief Black Eunuch, after Jean-Baptiste Vanmour. Vanmour was employed principally by the French and other European ambassadors to Constantinople in the early part of the 18th century; his work represents almost the only extant visual evidence of Constantinople at the time of Lady Mary's visit.

deep melancholy, though her good humour made her willing to divert me.

She asked me to walk in her garden, and one of her slaves immediately brought her a *pélisse* of rich brocade lined with sables. I waited on her into the garden, which had nothing in it remarkable but the fountains, and from thence she showed me all her apartments. In her bed chamber her toilet was displayed, consisting of two looking-glasses, the frames covered with pearls, and her night *talpack* set with bodkins of jewels, and near it three vests of fine sables, every one of which is at least worth 1,000 dollars, £200 English money. I don't doubt these rich habits were purposely placed in sight, but they seemed negligently thrown on the sofa. When I took my leave of her I was complimented with perfumes as at the Grand Vizier's, and presented with a very fine embroidered handkerchief. Her slaves were to the number of thirty, besides ten little ones, the eldest not above seven years old. These were the most beautiful girls I ever saw, all richly dressed; and I observed that the Sultana took a great deal of pleasure in these lovely children, which is a vast expense, for there is not a handsome girl of that age to be bought under £100 sterling. They wore little garlands of flowers, and their own hair braided, which was all their head-dress, but their habits all of gold stuffs. These served her coffee kneeling, brought water when she washed, etc. 'Tis a great part of the business of the older slaves to take care of these girls, to learn them to embroider and serve them as carefully as if they were children of the family.

Now do I fancy that you imagine I have entertained you all this while with a relation that has (as least) received many embellishments from my hand. This is but too like (says you) the Arabian tales; these embroidered napkins, and jewel as large as a turkey's egg! — You forget, dear sister, those very tales were writ by an author of this country and (excepting the enchantments) are a real representation of the manners here. We travellers are in very hard circumstances. If we say nothing but what has been said before us, we are dull and we have observed nothing. If we tell anything new, we are laughed at as fabulous and romantic, not allowing for the difference of ranks, which afford difference of company, more curiosity, or the changes of customs that happen every twenty year in every country. But people judge of travellers exactly with the same candour, good nature, and impartiality they judge amongst you, I am so well acquainted with the morals of all my dear friends and acquaintance, that I am resolved to tell them nothing at all, to avoid the imputation (which their charity would certainly incline them to) of my telling too much. But I depend upon your knowing me enough to believe whatever I seriously assert for truth, though I give you leave to be surprised at an account so new to you. But what would you say if I told you that I have been in a harem where the winter apartment was wainscoted with inlaid work of mother of pearl, ivory of different colours and olive wood, exactly like the little boxes you have seen brought out of this country; and those rooms designed for summer, the walls all crusted with Japan china, the roofs gilt, and the floors spread with the finest Persian carpets. Yet there is nothing more true; such is the palace of my lovely friend, the fair Fatima, who I was acquainted with at Adrianople. I went to visit her yesterday, and (if possible) she appeared to me handsomer than before. She met me at the door of her chamber, and, giving me her hand with the best grace in the world: 'You Christian ladies,' said she with a smile that made her as handsome as an angel, 'have the reputation of inconstancy, and I did not expect, whatever goodness you expressed for me at Adrianople, that I should ever see you again; but I am now convinced that I have really the happiness of pleasing you, and if you knew how I speak of you amongst our ladies, you would be assured that you do me justice if you think me your friend.' She placed me in the corner of the sofa, and I spent the afternoon in her conversation with the greatest pleasure in the world.

The Sultana Hafise is what one would naturally expect to find a Turkish lady, willing to oblige but not knowing how to go about it, and 'tis easy to see in her manner that she has lived excluded from the world. But Fatima has all the politeness and good breeding of a court, with an air that inspires at once respect and tenderness; and now I understand her language, I find her wit as engaging as her beauty. She is very curious after the manners of other countries and has not that partiality for her own so common to little minds. A Greek that I carried with me who had never seen her before (nor could have been admitted now if she had not been in my train) showed that surprise at her beauty and manner which is unavoidable at the first sight, and said to me in Italian: 'This is no Turkish lady; she is certainly some Christian.' Fatima guessed she spoke of her, and asked what she said. I would not have told, thinking she would have been no better pleased with compliment than one of our court beauties to be told she had the air of a Turk. But the Greek lady told it her and she smiled, saying: 'It is not the first time I have heard so. My mother was a Poloneze taken at the siege of Camieniec,[3] and my father used to rally me, saying he believed his Christian wife had found some

3. A Polish fortress captured by the Turks in 1672.

The Sultan in the Seraglio with the Kisslar Agassi by Jean-Baptiste Vanmour. The Sultan is holding the handkerchief which, it was widely believed in Europe, he used to indicate his choice of nocturnal companion from the ladies of the *seraglio*; in fact, the Kuzlir Aga, or Chief Black Eunuch, was sent to the girl to signify to her the honour the Sultan intended her. She was immediately complimented upon it by the others (her companions in the *seraglio*) and led to the bath where 'she is perfumed and dressed in the most magnificent and becoming manner.'

Christian gallant, for I had not the air of a Turkish girl.' I assured her that if all the Turkish ladies were like her, it was absolutely necessary to confine them from public view for the repose of mankind, and proceeded to tell her what a noise such a face as hers would make in London or Paris. 'I can't believe you,' replied she agreeably; 'if beauty was so much valued in your country as you say, they would never have suffered you to leave it.'

Perhaps (dear sister) you laugh at my vanity in repeating this compliment, but I only do it as I think it very well turned and give it you as an instance of the spirit of her conversation. Her house was magnificently furnished and very well fancied, her winter rooms being furnished with figured velvet on gold grounds, and those for summer with fine Indian quilting embroidered with gold. The houses of the great Turkish ladies are kept clean with as much nicety as those in Holland. This was situated in a high part of the town, and from the windows of her summer apartment we had the prospect of the sea and the islands and the Asian mountains. My letter is insensibly grown so long, I am ashamed of it. This is a very bad symptom. 'Tis well if I don't degenerate in a downright story-teller. It may be, our proverb that knowledge is no burden, may be true as to one's self, but knowing too much is very apt to make us troublesome to other people.

To Lady _____ — *Pera of Constantinople 10 March 1718*

I am extremely pleased (my dear lady) that you have at length found a commission for me that I can answer without disappointing your expectation, though I must tell you that it is not so easy as perhaps you think it, and that if my curiosity had not been more diligent than any other stranger's has ever yet been, I must have answered you with an excuse, as I was forced to do when you desired me to buy you a Greek slave. I have got for you, as you desire, a Turkish love-letter, which I have put in a little box, and ordered the Captain of the Smyrniote to deliver it to you with this letter.[1] The translation of it is literally as follows. The first piece you should pull out of the purse is a little pearl, which is in Turkish called *ingi*, and should be understood in this manner:

1. The merchantman *Smyrniote* arrived at Smyrna (Izmir) from England on 24 February 1718 and stopped there again on its way home on 16 April; she must therefore have been in Constantinople in mid-March. She reached England in October.

Pearl Ingi	Sensin Uzellerin gingi Fairest of the young
Caremfil a clove	Caremfilsen cararen Yok conge gulsun timarin yok Benseny chok tan severim Senin benden haberin Yok You are as slender as this clove; You are an unblown rose; I have long loved you, and you have not known it.
Pul a jonquil	derdime derman bul Have pity on my passion.
Kihat paper	Biîlerum sahat sahat I faint every hour.
ermut pear	ver bize bir umut Give me some hope.
sabun soap	Derdinden oldum Zabun I am sick with love.
chemur coal	ben oliyim size umur May I die, and all my years be yours!
Gul a rose	ben aglarum sen gul May you be pleased, and all your sorrows mine!
hazir a straw	Oliîm sana Yazir Suffer me to be your slave.
Jo ha cloth	ustune bulunmaz Paha Your price is not to be found.

Portrait after Jean-Baptiste Vanmour of a Jewish woman who sold embroidery, sweetmeats and other similar items to young Turkish ladies confined to their homes. Such ladies, who did not have a good reputation, would also have carried secret messages and *billets-doux* in verse. Lady Mary reproduces examples of such verses in her letter of 16 March 1718 to Lady —- (see pages 171- 173). 'There is no colour, no flower, no weed, no fruit, herb, pebble, or feather that has not a verse belonging to it; and you may quarrel, reproach, or send letters of passion, friendship, or civility, or even of news, without ever inking your fingers.'

tartsin	sen ghel ben chekeim senin hargin
cinnamon	But my fortune [estate] is yours.
Gira	esking-ilen oldum Ghira
a match	I burn, I burn, my flame consumes me.
Sirma	uzunu benden ayirma
gold thread	Don't turn away your face.
Satch	Bazmazun tatch
hair	Crown of my head
Uzum	Benim iki Guzum
grape	My eyes.
tel	uluyorum tez ghel
gold wire	I die — come quickly.

And by way of postscript:

biber	Bize bir dogru haber
pepper	Send me an answer.[2]

You see this letter is all verses, and I can assure you there is as much fancy shown in the choice of them as in the most studied expressions of our letters, there being (I believe) a million of verses designed for this use. There is no colour, no flower, no weed, no fruit, herb, pebble, or feather that has not a verse belonging to it; and you may quarrel, reproach, or send letters of passion, friendship, or civility, or even of news, without ever inking your fingers.

I fancy you are now wondering at my profound learning, but alas, dear madam, I am almost fallen into the misfortune so common to the ambitious: while they are employed on distant, insignificant conquests abroad, a rebellion starts up at home. I am in great danger of losing my English. I find it is not half so easy to me to write in it as it was a twelve-month ago. I am forced to study for expressions, and must leave off all other languages and try to learn my mother tongue. Humane

2. Lady Mary's Turkish vocabulary and orthography are given here verbatim; neither was absolutely correct. Here is an accurate translation:

Pearl: You are the pearl of beauties (fairest of the fair maidens)

Carnation: You are the carnation inconstant. You are the budding rose inattentive. I have long loved you. You have had no word (of it) from me.

Jonquil: Find the remedy for my passion.

Paper: I faint hourly.

Pear: Give me some hope.

Soap: I am weak with passion for you.

Coal, charcoal: Let me live for you.

Rose: I weep. You laugh.

Straw mat: Let me be your slave.

Cloth: Your price is not to be found.

Cinnamon: Come let me bear your expenses.

Torch: I have become a torch with your passion.

Gold thread: Turn not your face from me.

Hair: Crown of my head.

Grape: My two eyes.

Silver or gold wire: I am dying. Come quickly.

Pepper: (Send) me a true answer.

understanding is as much limited as humane power or humane strength. The memory can retain but a certain number of images, and 'tis as impossible for one humane creature to be perfect master of ten different[1] languages as to have in perfect subjection ten different kingdoms, or to fight against ten men at a time. I am afraid I shall at last know none as I should do. I live in a place that very well represents the Tower of Babel; in Pera they speak Turkish, Greek, Hebrew, Armenian, Arabic, Persian, Russian, Slavonian, Walachian, German, Dutch, French, English, Italian, Hungarian; and, what is worse, there is ten of these languages spoke in my own family. My grooms are Arabs; my footmen French, English and Germans; my nurse an Armenian; my housemaids Russians; half a dozen other servants Greeks; my steward an Italian; my janissaries Turks, that I live in the perpetual hearing of this medley of sounds, which produces a very extraordinary effect upon the people that are born here. They learn all these languages at the same time and without knowing any of 'em well enough to write or read in it. There is very few men, women or children here that have not the same compass of words in five or six of 'em. I know myself several infants of three or four year old that speak Italian, French, Greek, Turkish, and Russian, which last they learn of their nurses, who are generally of that country. This seems almost incredible to you, and is (in my mind) one of the most curious things in this country, and takes off very much from the merit of our ladies who set up for such extraordinary geniuses upon the credit of some superficial knowledge of French and Italian. As I prefer English to all the rest, I am extremely mortified at the daily decay of it in my head, where I'll assure you (with grief of heart) it is reduced to such a small number of words, I cannot recollect any tolerable phrase to conclude my letter, and am forced to tell your Ladyship very bluntly that I am your faithful humble servant.

Portrait by an anonymous
Greek artist of a Court usher.

To Wortley — *23 March 1718*[1]

This day news is come of the Grey-hound's safe arrival at Smyrna. It has brought the minister for this place, and my money that was in my uncle's hands.[2] The Captain has writ that he met the Preston man of war at Cadiz having orders for Barbary and did not propose for this part of the world till July at soonest.[3] The Dutch madam[4] is a perfect mad woman. I sent a jeweller to her to offer her the money for her pearls and she would not take it, which she is very much in the right, for they are worth more; but 'tis very strange she should get a good bargain and complain of it. But she cheats the Ambassador. Her own vanity caused the discovery of her secret, which I kept very faithfully, and now he is (I suppose) angry at her laying her money out in ornaments. She would make him believe she did it to oblige me, and would seem glad to get rid of 'em, at the same time she won't part with them.

The boy was engrafted last Tuesday, and is at this time singing and playing and very impatient for his supper. I pray God my next may give as good an account of him. I suppose you know the allowance the King has made the Company on this occasion. I think you may with more justice insist on your extraordinaries which has never, yet been refused neither Sir R. Sutton nor no other ambassador.[5]

I cannot engraft the girl; her nurse has not had the small pox.

To Lady Bristol — *Pera of Constantinople 10 April 1718*

At length I have heard, for the first time, from my dear Lady Bristol, this present 10th of April 1718. Yet I am persuaded you have had the goodness to write before, but I have had the ill fortune to lose your letters. Since my last I have stayed quietly at Constantinople, a city that I ought in conscience to give your ladyship a right notion of, since I know you can have none but what is partial and mistaken from the writings of travellers. 'Tis certain there are many people that pass years here in Pera without having ever seen it, and yet they all pretend to describe it.

1. On this day Wortley arrived in Adrianople from Sofia to take leave of the Sultan's Court.

2. The *Greyhound* had left London in November 1717 and arrived in Smyrna on 7 or 8 March 1718. On board were the newly appointed English chaplain to Constantinople and also £1,600 worth of Spanish dollars, or pieces of eight, belonging to Lady Mary, which represented repayment of a loan she had made to her uncle.

3. The *Preston* was the warship sent to bring Wortley back to England on the termination of his appointment as ambassador. She set sail for Constantinople in January 1718, reached Cadiz Bay on 27 January, where she remained until 11 March, and arrived in Constantinople on 19 June.

4. Catharina de Bourg, wife of Count Jacob Colyer, Dutch Ambassador to Turkey.

5. Wortley had entered into the customary articles of agreement to stay in Constantinople at least five years, but since the King had recalled him so abruptly the Levant Company — who claimed the right to choose ambassadors to Turkey — asked for compensation of not less than £4,000, which they were granted in December 1717. Wortley's efforts to be paid for his 'extraordinaries' were unceasing; he petitioned King George II as late as 1747. In fact, the Levant Company, when informing him of his recall, allowed him £500 for his expenses, the same amount they had allowed Sir Robert Sutton, Wortley's predecessor, for his return.

Drinking Fountain at Pera by
Luigi Mayer. Pera was the
European quarter of
Constantinople, on the north
bank of the Golden Horn,
where Wortley lodged with his
wife and family.

Interior of the Sultan Ahmed Mosque by an anonymous Greek artist.

Pera, Tophana and Galata, wholly inhabited by Frank Christians (and which together make the appearance of a very fine town), are divided from it by the sea, which is not above half so broad as the broadest part of the Thames, but the Christian men are loath to hazard the adventures they sometimes meet with amongst the Levents or seamen (worse monsters than our watermen), and the women must cover their faces to go there, which they have a perfect aversion to do. 'Tis true they wear veils in Pera, but they are such as only serve to show their beauty to more advantage, and which would not be permitted in Constantinople. Those reasons deter almost every creature from seeing it, and the French Ambassadress will return to France (I believe) without ever having been there. You'll wonder, madam, to hear me add that I have been there very often. The *yaşmak*, or Turkish veil, is become not only very easy but agreeable to me, and if it was not, I would be content to endure some inconvenience to content a passion so powerful with me as curiosity; and indeed the pleasure of going in a barge to Chelsea is not comparable to that of rowing upon the canal of the sea here, where for twenty miles together down the Bosphorus the most beautiful variety of prospects present themselves. The Asian side is covered with fruit trees, villages and the most delightful landscapes in nature. On the European stands Constantinople, situated on seven hills. The unequal heights make it seem as large again as it is (though one of the largest cities in the world), showing an agreeable mixture of gardens, pine and cypress trees, palaces, mosques and public buildings, raised one above another with as much beauty and appearance of symmetry as your ladyship ever saw in a cabinet adorned by the most skilful hands, jars showing themselves above jars, mixed with canisters, babies and candlesticks. This is a very odd comparison, but it gives me an exact image of the thing.

I have taken care to see as much of the Seraglilo as is to be seen. It is on a point of land running into the sea: a palace of prodigious extent, but very irregular; the gardens a large compass of ground full of high cypress trees, which is all I know of them; the buildings all of white stone, leaded on top, with guilded turrets and spires, which look very magnificent, and indeed I believe there is no Christian king's palace half so large. There are six large courts in it all built round and set with trees, having galleries of stone: one of these for the guard, another for the stables, the fifth for the divan, the sixth for the apartment destined for audiences. On the ladies' side there is a least as many more, with distinct courts belonging to their eunuchs and attendants, their kitchens, etc.

View of the covered market in Constantinople(Left) by an anonymous Greek artist; silk-dealers are seated cross-legged on their booths. 'The exchanges are all noble buildings, full of fine alleys, the greatest part supported with pillars, and kept wonderfully neat. Every trade has their distinct alley, the merchandise disposed in the same order as in the New Exchange at London.'

Dervish dancer from *The Costume of Turkey* (Right) by William Miller. In her letter of 10 April 1718 to Lady Bristol, Lady Mary recounts a visit to a dervish monastery. 'While some (dervishes) play, the others tie their robe (which is very wide) fast round their waists and begin to turn with an amazing swiftness and yet with great regard to the music, moving slower or faster as the tune is played. This lasts above an hour without any of them showing the least appearance of giddiness.'

181

The next remarkable structure is that of St Sophia, which 'tis very difficult to see. I was forced to send three times to the Kaymakam (the Governor of the town), and he assembled the chief effendis or heads of the law and inquired of the Mufti whether it was lawful to permit it. They passed some days in this important debate, but I insisting on my request, permission was granted. I can't be informed why the Turks are more delicate on the subject of this Mosque than any of the others, where what Christian pleases may enter without scruple. I fancy they imagine that having been once consecrated, people on pretence of curiosity might profane it with prayers, particularly to those saints who are still very visible in mosaic work, and no other way defaced but by the decays of time, for 'tis absolutely false what is so universally asserted, that the Turks defaced all the images that they found in the city. The dome of St Sophia is said to be 113 foot diameter, built upon arches, sustained by vast pillars of marble, the pavement and stair-case marble. There is two rows of galleries supported with pillars of parti-coloured marble, and the whole roof mosaic work, part of which decays very fast and drops down. They presented me a handful of it. The composition seems to me a sort of glass or that paste with which they make counterfeit jewels. They show here the tomb of the Emperor Constantine,[1] for which they have a great venera-tion. This is a dull, imperfect description of this celebrated building, but I under-stand architecture so little that I am afraid of talking nonsense in endeavouring to speak of it particularly.

Perhaps I am in the wrong, but some Turkish Mosques please me better. That of Sultan Süleyman is an exact square with four fine towers on the angles, in the midst a noble cupula supported with beautiful marble pillars, two lesser at the ends supported in the same manner, the pavement and gallery round the Mosque of marble. Under the great cupula is a fountain adorned with such fine coloured pillars I can hardly think them natural marble. On one side is the pulpit of white marble, and on the other the little gallery for the Grand Signior. A fine stair case leads to it and it is built up with gilded lattices. At the upper end is a sort of altar where the name of God is written, and before it stands two candlesticks as high as a man, with wax candles as thick as three *flambeaux*. The pavement is spread with fine carpets and the Mosque illuminated with a vast number of lamps. The court leading to it is very spacious, with galleries of marble with green columns, covered with twenty-eight leaded cupolas on two sides, and a fine fountain of three basins

1. Lady Mary was mistaken; none of the Imperial tombs is or ever was in Santa Sophia.

View of Constantinople by A.I.
Melling. The city is seen from
the Asian side of the
Bosphorus; the Sultan's barges
are in the foreground.

The Bosphorus with the Castles of Europe and Asia by Thomas Allom. The Turks built the fortification in the foreground after they had gained a foothold on the European shore of the Bosphorus in 1452, the year before they took Constantinople. The castle in the background, on the Asian side, was of an earlier date. Both would have looked much like this in Lady Mary's time.

in the midst of it. This description may serve for all the Mosques in Constantinople; the model is exactly the same; and they only differ in largeness and richness of materials. That of the Valid is the largest of all, built entirely of marble, the most prodigious and (I think) the most beautiful structure I ever saw, be it spoke to the honour of our sex, for it was founded by the mother of Mehmet the 4th; (between friends) St Paul's Church would make a pitiful figure near it, as any of our squares would do near the Atmeydan or place of horses, *At* signifying a horse in Turkish.

This was the Hippodrome in the reign of the Greek Emperors. In the midst of it is a brazen column of three serpents twisted together with their mouths gaping. 'Tis impossible to learn why so odd a pillar was erected; the Greeks can tell nothing but fabulous legends when they are asked the meaning of it, and there is no sign of its having ever had any inscription. At the upper end is an obelisk of porphyry, probably brought from Egypt, the hieroglyphics all very entire, which I look upon as mere ancient puns. It is placed on four little brazen pillars upon a pedestal of square free stone full of figures in bas relief on two sides, one square representing a battle, another an assembly. The others have inscriptions in Greek and Latin. The last I took in my pocket book and is literally:

Difficilis quondam Dominis parere serenis
Iussus et extinctis palmam portare Tyrannis
Omnia Theodosio cedunt, sobolique perreni.[2]

Your Lord will interpret these lines. Don't fancy they are a love letter to him. All the figures have their heads on, and I cannot forbear reflecting again on the impudence of authors who all say they have not, but I dare swear the greatest part of them never saw them, but took the report from the Greeks, who resist with incredible fortitude the conviction of their own eyes whenever they have invented lies to the dishonour of their enemies. Were you to ask them, there is nothing worth seeing in Constantinople but Santa Sophia, though there are several larger Mosques. That of Sultan Ahmed has that of particular, its gates are of brass. In all these Mosques there are little chapels where are the tombs of the founders and their families, with vast candles burning before them.

The exchanges are all noble buildings, full of fine alleys, the greatest part supported with pillars, and kept wonderfully neat. Every trade has their distinct alley, the merchandise disposed in the same order as in the New Exchange at London. The Bedesten, or jewellers' quarter, shows so much riches, such a vast

2. Translated, the entire inscription, including two lines omitted by Lady Mary, reads; 'Of lords serene a stubborn subject once, bidden to bear the palm to tyrants also that have met their doom — all yields to Theodosius and his undying issue — so conquered I in thrice ten days and tamed, was under Proclus' judgeship raised to the skies above'.

quantity of diamonds and all kinds of precious stones, that they dazzle the sight. The embroiderers' is also very glittering, and people walk here as much for diversion as business. The markets are most of them handsome squares, and admirally well provided, perhaps better than in any other part of the world. I know you'll expect I should say something particular of that of the slaves, and you will imagine me half a Turk when I don't speak of it with the same horror other Christians have done before me, but I cannot forbear applauding the humanity of the Turks to those creatures. They are never ill used and their slavery is in my opinion no worse than servitude all over the world. 'Tis true they have no wages, but they give them yearly clothes to a higher value than our salaries to an ordinary servant. But you'll object men buy women with an eye to evil. In my opinion they are bought and sold as publicly and more infamously in all our Christian great cities. I must add to the description of Constantinople that the Historical Pillar is no more, dropped down about two years before I came.[3] I have seen no other footsteps of antiquity, except the aqueducts, which are so vast that I am apt to believe they are yet ancienter than the Greek Empire, tho' the Turks have clapped in some stones with Turkish inscriptions to give their nation the honour of so great a work, but the deceit is easily discovered.

The other public buildings are the hans and monastries, the first very large and numerous, the second few in number and not at all magnificent. I had the curiosity to visit one of them and observe the devotions of the dervishes, which are as whimsical as any in Rome. These fellows have permission to marry, but are confined to an odd habit, which is only a piece of coarse white cloth wrapped about 'em, with their legs and arms naked. Their order has few other rules, except that of performing their fantastic rites every Tuesday and Friday, which is in this manner. They meet together in a large hall, where they all stand with their eyes fixed on the ground and their arms across, while the imam, or preacher, reads part of the Koran from a pulpit placed in the midst; and when he has done, eight or ten of them make a melancholy consort with their pipes, which are no unmusical instruments. Then he reads again and makes a short exposition on what he has read, after which they sing and play till their Superior (the only one of them dressed in green) rises and begins a sort of solemn dance. They all stand about him in a regular figure; and while some play, the others tie their robe (which is very wide) fast round their waists and begin to turn round with an amazing swiftness and yet with great regard to the music, moving slower or faster as the tune is

3. Actually in 1695, having been weakened by earthquake and fire.

View of the interior of Santa Sophia Mosque done by an anonymous Greek artist. Lady Mary took great pains to visit this Mosque, applying no less than three times to the *Kaymakam*, or mayor, of the city. She wrote of her visit there in rather flat terms: 'this is a dull, imperfect description of this celebrated building, but I understand architecture so little that I am afraid of talking nonsense in endeavouring to speak of it particularly'.

The view is from the gallery, where women generally sat; the Sultan's seat and the *mimber* (pulpit) are visible.

played. This lasts above an hour without any of them showing the least appearance of giddiness, which is not to be wondered at when it is considered they are all used to it from infancy, most of them being devoted to this way of life from their birth, and sons of dervishes. There turned amongst them some little dervishes of six or seven years old who seemed no more disordered by that exercise than the others. At the end of the ceremony they shout out: there is no other God but God, and Muhammad is his prophet; after which they kiss the Superior's hand and retire. The whole is performed with the most solemn gravity. Nothing can be more austere than the form of these people. They never raise their eyes and seem devoted to contemplation, and as ridiculous as this is in description, there is something touching in the air of submission and mortification they assume. — This letter is of a horrible length, but you may burn it when you have read enough.

Mr Wortley is not yet here, but I may assure your Ladyship in his name of the respect he has for you. I give humble service to My Lord Bristol and Mr Hervey.

To The Countess of _____ *May 1718*

Your Ladyship may be assured I received yours with very great pleasure. I am very glad to hear that our friends are in good health, particulary Mr Congreve, who I heard was ill of the gout; I am now preparing to leave Constantinople, and perhaps you will accuse me of hypocrisy when I tell you 'tis with regret, but I am used to the air and have learnt the language. I am easy here, and as much as I love travelling, I tremble at the inconveniencies attending so great a journey with a numerous family and a little infant hanging at the breast. However, I endeavour upon this occasion to do as I have hitherto done in all the odd turns of my life, turn 'em, if I can, to my diversion. In order to this, I ramble every day, wrapped up in my *ferace* and *yaşmak*, about Constantinople and amuse myself with seeing all that is curious in it. I know you'll expect this declaration should be followed with some account of what I have seen, but I am in no humour to copy what has been writ so often over. To what purpose should I tell you that Constantinople was the ancient Byzantium; that 'tis at present the conquest of a race of people supposed Scythians; that there is five or six thousand Mosques in it; that Santa Sophia was founded by Justinian, etc? I'll assure you 'tis not want of learning that I forbear writing all these bright things. I could also, with little trouble, turn over Knolles and Sir Paul Rycaut to give you a list of Turkish Emperors,[1] but I will not tell you what you may find in every author that has writ of this country.

I am more inclined, out of a true female spirit of contradiction, to tell you the falsehood of a great part of what you find in authors; as, for example, the admirable Mr Hill, who so gravely asserts that he saw in Santa Sophia a sweating pillar very balsamic for disordered heads. There is not the least tradition of any such matter, and I suppose it was revealed to him in vision during his wonderful stay in the Egyptian catacombs, for I am sure he never heard of any such miracle here. 'Tis also very pleasant to observe how tenderly he and all his brethren voyage-writers lament the miserable confinement of the Turkish ladies, who are (perhaps) freer than any ladies in the universe, and are the only women in the world that lead a life of uninterrupted pleasure, exempt from cares, their whole time being spent in visiting, bathing, or the agreeable amusement of spending money and inventing new fashions. A husband would be thought mad that exacted any degree of economy from his wife, whose expenses are no way limited but by her own fancy. 'Tis his business to get money and hers to spend it, and this noble prerogative extends itself to the very meanest of the sex. Here is a fellow that carrys embroidered handkerchiefs upon his back to sell, as miserable a figure as you may suppose such a mean dealer, yet I'll assure you his wife scorns to wear anything less than cloth of gold, has her ermine furs, and a very handsome set of jewels for her head. They go abroad when and where they please. 'Tis true they have no public places but the *bagnios*, and there can only be seen by their own sex; however, that is a diversion they take great pleasure in.

I was three days ago at one of the finest in the town and had the opportunity of seeing a Turkish bride received there and all the ceremonies used on that occasion, which made me recollect the Epithilamium of Helen by Theocritus,[2] and it seems to me that the same customs have continued ever since. All the she-friends, relations and acquaintance of the two families newly allied meet at the *bagnio*. Several others go out of curiosity, and I believe there was that day at least two hundred women. Those that were or had been married, placed themselves round the room on the marble sofas, but the virgins very hastily threw off their clothes and appeared without other ornament or covering than their own long hair braided with pearl or riband. Two of them met the bride at the door, conducted by

1. Richard Knolles published his history of the Turks in 1603; Paul Rycaut wrote a continuation of it, the final volume of which was published in 1700. Lady Mary used both as sources.

2. In his *Idyll* xviii; an epithalamium is a nuptial song or poem in praise of the bride and bridegroom.

Turkish Woman Smoking on a Sofa after Jean-Baptiste Vanmour. Women smoked in the privacy of their own homes, generally preferring a milder, more aromatic, mixture than men.

relation. She was a beautiful maid of about
shining with jewels, but was presently reduced
o others filled silver gilt pots with perfume and
llowing in pairs to the number of thirty. The
wered by the others in chorus, and the two last
on the ground with a charming affectation of
ied round the three large rooms of the *bagnio*.
ie beauty of this sight, most of them being well
ll of them perfectly smooth and polished by the
'ing made their tour, the bride was again led to
io saluted her with a compliment and a present,
:uff, handkerchiefs, or little gallantries of that
for by kissing their hands.

aving seen this ceremony, and you may believe
: least as much wit and civility, nay, liberty, as
ame customs that give them so many oppor-
nations (if they have any) also puts it very fully
evenge them if they are discovered, and I don't
or their indiscretions in a very severe manner.
ound at day break not very far from my house
in, naked, only wrapped in a coarse sheet, with
side and another in her breast. She was not yet
itiful that there were very few men in Pera that
was not possible for anybody to know her, no
s supposed to be brought in dead of night from
here. Very little enquiry was made about the
murderer, and the corpse privately burned without noise. Murder is never
pursued by the King's officers as with us. 'Tis the business of the next relations to
revenge the dead person; and if they like better to compound the matter for money
(as they generally do) there is no more said of it. One would imagine this defect in
their government should make such tragedies very frequent, yet they are
extremely rare, which is enough to prove the people not naturally cruel, neither do
I think in many other particulars they deserve the barbarous character we
give them.

I am well acquainted with a Christian woman of quality who made it her choice to live with a Turkish husband, and is a very agreeable sensible lady. Her story is so extraordinary I cannot forbear relating it, but I promise you it shall be in as few words as I can possibly express it. She is a Spaniard, and was at Naples with her family when that kingdom was part of the Spanish dominion. Coming from thence in a felucca, accompanied by her brother, they were attacked by the Turkish Admiral, boarded and taken; and now, how shall I modestly tell you the rest of her adventure? The same accident happened to her that happened to the fair Lucretia so many years before her, but she was too good a Christian to kill herself as that heathenish Roman did. The Admiral was so much charmed with the beauty and long-suffering of the fair captive that as his first compliment he gave immediate liberty to her brother and attendants, who made haste to Spain and in a few months sent the sum of £4,000 sterling as a ransom for his sister. The Turk took the money, which he presented to her, and told her she was at liberty, but the lady very discreetly weighed the different treatment she was likely to find in her native country. Her Catholic relations, as the kindest thing they could do for her in her present circumstances, would certainly confine her to a nunnery for the rest of her days. Her infidel lover was very handsome, very tender, fond of her, and lavished at her feet all the Turkish magnificence. She answered him very resolutely that her liberty was not so precious to her as her honour, that he could no way restore that but by marrying her. She desired him to accept the ransom as her portion and give her the satisfaction of knowing no man could boast of her favours without being her husband. The Admiral was transported at this kind offer and sent back the money to her relations, saying he was too happy in her possession. He married her and never took any other wife, and (as she says herself) she never had any reason to repent the choice she made. He left her some years after one of the richest widows in Constantinople, but there is no remaining honourably a single woman, and that consideration has obliged her to marry the present Captain Pasha (i.e. Admiral), his successor.[3] I am afraid you'll think that my friend fell in love with her ravisher, but I am willing to take her word for it that she acted wholly on principles of honour, though I think she might be reasonably touched at his generosity, which is very often found amongst the Turks of rank.

'Tis a degree of generosity to tell the truth, and 'tis very rare that any Turk will assert a solemn falsehood. I don't speak of the lowest sort, for as there is a great deal of ignorance, there is very little virtue amongst them; and false witnesses are

3. The hero of Lady Mary's romantic tale was probably Ibrahim Pasha, who held office as Lord Admiral from 1706 to 1709 (when Naples was a Spanish possession) and again from February 1717 to February 1718. His successor was Süleyman Koca, who held office until 1721.

much cheaper than in Christendom, those wretches not being punished (even when they are publicly detected) with the rigour they ought to be. Now I am speaking of their law, I don't know whether I have ever mentioned to you one custom peculiar to this country. I mean adoption, very common amongst the Turks and yet more amongst the Greeks and Armenians. Not having it in their power to give their estates to a friend or distant relation to avoid its falling into the Grand Signior's treasury, when they are not likely to have children of their own they choose some pretty child of either sex amongst the meanest people, and carry the child and its parents before the kadi, and there declare they receive it for their heir. The parents at the same time renounce all future claim to it, a writing is drawn and witnessed, and a child thus adopted cannot be disinherited. Yet I have seen some common beggars that have refused to part with their children in this manner to some of the richest amongst the Greeks; so powerful is the instinctive fondness natural to parents! though the adopting fathers are generally very tender to these children of their souls, as they call them. I own this custom pleases me much better than our absurd following our name. Methinks 'tis much more reasonable to make happy and rich an infant whom I educate after my own manner, brought up (in the turkish phrase) upon my knees, and who has learnt to look upon me with a filial respect, than to give an estate to a creature without other merit or relation to me than by a few letters. Yet this is an absurdity we see frequently practised.

Now I have mentioned the Armenians, perhaps it will be agreeable to tell you something of that nation, with which I am sure you are utterly unacquainted. I will not trouble you with the geographical account of the situation of their country, which you may see in the map, or a relation of their ancient greatness, which you may read in the Roman history. They are now subject to the Turks, and, being very industrious in trade, and increasing and multiplying, are dispersed in great numbers through all the Turkish dominions. They were (as they say) converted to the Christian religion by St Gregory, and are (perhaps) the devoutest Christians in the whole world. The chief precepts of their priests enjoin the strict keeping of their Lents, which are at least seven months in every year and are not to be dispensed with on the most emergent necessity. No occasion whatever can excuse them if they touch any thing more than mere herbs or roots (without oil) and plain dry bread. This is their Lenten diet. Mr Wortley has one of his interpreters of this nation, and the poor fellow was brought so low with the severity of his fasts that his

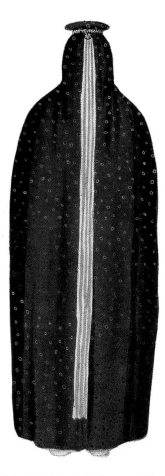

A Turkish lady in her wedding dress, as she appeared in the street, from *The Costume of Turkey* by William Miller. Lady Mary describes a ceremony at the Baths, when a new bride was received by her female friends and relations, in her letter of May 1718 to the Countess of -- .

life was despaired of, yet neither his master's commands or the doctor's entreaties (who declared nothing else could save his life) were powerful enough to prevail with him to take two or three spoonfuls of broth. Excepting this, which may rather be called custom than an article of faith, I see very little in their religion different from ours. 'Tis true they seem to incline very much to Mr Whiston's doctrine[4]; neither do I think the Greek church very distant from it, since 'tis certain the insisting on the Holy Spirit only proceeding from the Father is making a plain subordination in the Son. But the Armenians have no notion of transubstantiation, whatever account Sir Paul Rycaut gives of them (which account I am apt to believe was designed to compliment our Court in 1679), and they have a great horror for those amongst them that change to the Roman religion.

What is most extraordinary in their customs is their matrimony, a ceremony I believe unparalleled all over the world. They are always promised very young, but the espoused never see one another till three days after their marriage. The bride is carried to church with a cap on her head in the fashion of a large trencher, and over it a red silken veil which covers her all over to her feet. The priest asks the bridegroom whether he is contented to marry that woman, be she deaf, be she blind? These are the literal words, to which having answered yes, she is led home to his house accompanied with all the friends and relations on both sides, singing and dancing, and is placed on a cushion in the corner of the sofa, but her veil never lifted up, not even by her husband, till she has been three days married. There is something odd and monstrous in these ways that I could not believe them till I had enquired of several Armenians myself who all assured me of the truth of them, particularly one young fellow who wept when he spoke of it, being promised by his mother to a girl that he must marry in this manner, though he protested to me he had rather die than submit to this slavery, having already figured his bride to himself with all the deformities in nature.

I fancy I see you bless yourself at this terrible relation. I cannot conclude my letter with a more surprising story, yet 'tis as seriously true as that I am, dear sister, your, etc.

4. William Whiston (see note 5, page 99) upheld the Arian doctrine that Christ was not of the same essence or substance with God.

To The Abbé Conti — *Constantinople 19 May 1718*

I am extremely pleased with hearing from you, and my vanity (the darling frailty of humankind) not a little flattered by the uncommon questions you ask me, though I am utterly incapable of answering them, and indeed were I as good a mathematician as Euclid himself, it requires an age's stay to make just observations on the air and vapours.

I have not been yet a full year here and am on the point of removing; such is my rambling destiny. This will surprise you, and can surprise nobody so much as myself. Perhaps you will accuse me of laziness or dullness, or both together, that can leave this place without giving you some account of the Turkish Court. I can only tell you that if you please to read Sir Paul Rycaut you will there find a full and true account of the Viziers, the Belerbleys, the civil and spiritual government, the officers of the Seraglio, etc., things that 'tis very easy to procure lists of and therefore may be depended on, though other stories, God knows — I say no more — everybody is at liberty to write their own remarks. The manners of people may change or some of them escape the observation of travellers, but 'tis not the same of the government, and for that reason, since I can tell you nothing new I will tell nothing of it. In the same silence shall be passed over the arsenal and seven towers; and for Mosques I have already described one of the noblest to you very particularly; but I cannot forbear taking notice to you of a mistake of Gemelli (though I honour him in a much higher degree than any other voyage-writer).[1] He says that there is no remains of Calcedon. This is certainly a mistake. I was there yesterday and went cross the canal[2] in my galley, the sea being very narrow between that city and Constantinople. 'Tis still a large town, and has several mosques in it. The Christians still call it Calcedonia, and the Turks give it a name I forgot, but which is only a corruption of the same word. I suppose this an error of his guide, which his short stay hindered him from rectifying, for I have (in other matters) a very just esteem for his veracity.

Nothing can be pleasanter than the Canal, and the Turks are so well acquainted with its beauties, all their pleasure-seats are built on its banks, where they have at the same time the most beautiful prospects in Europe and Asia. There are near one another some hundreds of magnificent palaces. Humane grandeur being here yet more unstale than anywhere else, 'tis common for the heirs of a

1. Giovanni Francesco Gemelli Careriu, a Neapolitan doctor of civil law, the veracity of whose travel writings has been disputed.

2. The Bosphorus.

Portrait of a court official or minister by an anonymous Greek artist.

Portrait by an anonymous Greek artist of *Silahdar Aga*, sword-bearer to the Sultan.

great three-tailed Pasha not to be rich enough to keep in repair the house he built; thus in a few years they all fall to ruin. I was yesterday to see that of the late Grand Vizier who was killed at Peterwaradin. It was built to receive his royal bride, daughter of the present Sultan, but he did not live to see her there. I have a great mind to describe it to you, but I check that inclination, knowing very well that I cannot give you, with my best description, such an idea of it as I ought. It is situated on one of the most delightful parts of the Canal with a fine wood on the side of a hill behind it. The extent of it is prodigious; the guardian assured me there is eight hundred rooms in it. I will not answer for that number since I did not count them, but 'tis certain the number is very large and the whole adorned with a profusion of marble, gilding, and the most exquisite painting of fruit and flowers. The windows are all sashed with the finest cristaline glass brought from England, and all the expensive magnificence that you can suppose in a palace founded by a vain young luxurious man with the wealth of a vast Empire at his command. But no part of it pleased me better than the apartments destined for the *bagnios*. There are two exactly built in the same manner, answering to one another; the baths, fountains and pavements all of white marble, the roofs gilt, and the walls covered with Japan china; but adjoining to them two rooms, the upper part of which is divided into a sofa; in the four corners falls of water from the very roof, from shell to shell of white marble to the lower end of the room, where it falls into a large basin surrounded with pipes that throw up the water as high as the room. The walls are in the nature of lattices and on the outside of them vines and woodbines planted that form a sort of green tapestry and give an agreeable obscurity to these delightful chambers. I should go on and let you into some of the other apartments (all worthy your curiosity), but 'tis yet harder to describe a Turkish palace than any other, being built entirely irregular. There is nothing can be properly called front or wings, and though such a confusion is (I think) pleasing to the sight, yet it would be very unintelligible in a letter. I shall only add that the chamber destined for the Sultan, when he visits his daughter, is wainscoted with mother of pearl fastened with emeralds like nails; there are others of mother of pearl and olive wood inlaid, and several of Japan china. The galleries (which are numerous and very large) are adorned with jars of flowers and porcelain dishes of fruit of all sorts, so well done in plaster and coloured in so lively a manner that it has an enchanting effect. The garden is suitable to the house, where arbours, fountains, and walks are thrown together in an agreeable confusion. There is no ornament

The Palace of Beschik-Tasch by
A.I. Melling. This palace was
on the Bosphorus above
Constantinople. Lady Mary
remarked that: 'Nothing can
be pleasanter than the canal
(the Bosphorus), and the
Turks are so well acquainted
with its beauties, all their
pleasure-seats are built on its
banks, where they have at the
same time the most beautiful
prospects in Europe and Asia.
There are near one another
some hundreds of magnificent
palaces.'

wanting except that of statues.

Thus you see, sir, these people are not so unpolished as we represent them. 'Tis true their magnificence is of a different taste from ours, and perhaps of a better. I am almost of opinion they have a right notion of life; while they consume it in music, gardens, wine, and delicate eating, while we are tormenting our brains with some scheme of politics or studying some science to which we can never attain, or if we do, cannot persuade people to set that value upon it we do ourselves. 'Tis certain what we feel and see is properly (if anything is properly) our own; but the good of fame, the folly of praise, hardly purchased, and when obtained — poor recompense for loss of time and health! We die, or grow old and decrepit, before we can reap the fruit of our labours. Considering what short lived, weak animals men are, is there any study so beneficial as the study of present pleasure? I dare not pursue this theme; perhaps I have already said too much, but I depend upon the true knowledge you have of my heart. I don't expect from you the insipid railleries I should suffer from another in answer to this letter. You know how to divide the idea of pleasure from that of vice, and they are only mingled in the heads of fools — but I allow you to laugh at me for the sensual declaration that I had rather be a rich Effendi with all his ignorance, than Sir Isaac Newton with all his knowledge. I am, Sir, etc.

On 5 July 1718 Wortley sailed from Constantinople with his wife, children and their entourage, including nineteen servants, on board the *Preston*, a newly built warship which the English government had sent out to bring its ambassador home. It cannot have been a happy voyage. Wortley's diplomatic mission had been a failure, as he must now have been compelled to admit even to himself; the ambassadorship was the last government post he was to hold, and he spent much of the rest of his life in an irritable quest to win sufficient recompense for his dismissal and for the expenses he had incurred. Lady Mary must also have been bitterly disappointed, for she had by now developed a taste for travel and could have expected to remain in the East for at least another four years.

Perhaps because they were compiled with publication in mind rather than as a purely personal record, the *Embassy Letters* reveal little of Lady Mary's feelings. However, the course the *Preston* followed must have provided some compensation. It was a journey for which Lady Mary's extensive reading of classical authors had prepared her, and she enjoyed it to the full, as her exuberant letter to the Abbé Conti of 31 July shows. Having passed through the Dardanelles, the *Preston* entered the Aegean Sea and then dropped anchor off Troy. Lady Mary 'took the pain of rising at two in the morning' to view the ruins, and even hired an ass, the only transport available, to tour the ancient walls. Pressing onwards, the ship passed Mytilene, Lesbos and Cape Sounion and then cut across the ocean to Sicily, where Mount Etna could be seen in the distance, before turning south towards the coast of North Africa. A four-day halt here enabled Lady Mary to visit

Tunis, travelling by night since she found the heat of the sun quite intolerable, and the ruins of Carthage. For Wortley and Lady Mary, the final stretch of the sea voyage was across the Mediterranean to Livorno and Genoa. Here they disembarked, leaving the *Preston* to carry their two children and some of their servants back to London by sea; it proved a dangerous voyage — several hostile Spanish vessels were encountered, and many of the crew were struck down by disease — and the children did not reach home until the following January.

After being confined in quarantine for ten days in Genoa, a time spent pleasantly enough in a fine house in a fashionable suburb, Wortley and Lady Mary travelled north across the Alps to Lyons and then on to Paris. Here she was pleased to have an unexpected meeting with her sister Lady Mar, and together they enjoyed visiting the town and making excursions to Versailles and other palaces and gardens nearby. Then there was the Channel crossing from Calais (as on the outward crossing, rough seas threw the boat violently about) and the final journey from Dover to London.

From Dover, Lady Mary wrote to the Abbé Conti that she could not 'help looking with partial eyes on my native land'. Was it simple travel-weariness, and relief at her safe arrival after so long and rigorous a journey, that led her to comment that all we get by travelling is 'a fruitless desire of mixing the different pleasures and conveniences which are given to different parts of the world and cannot meet in any one of them'? At home again in London society, Lady Mary fell easily into her former routine of court assemblies and *soirées*, gossip and rivalries, reading and

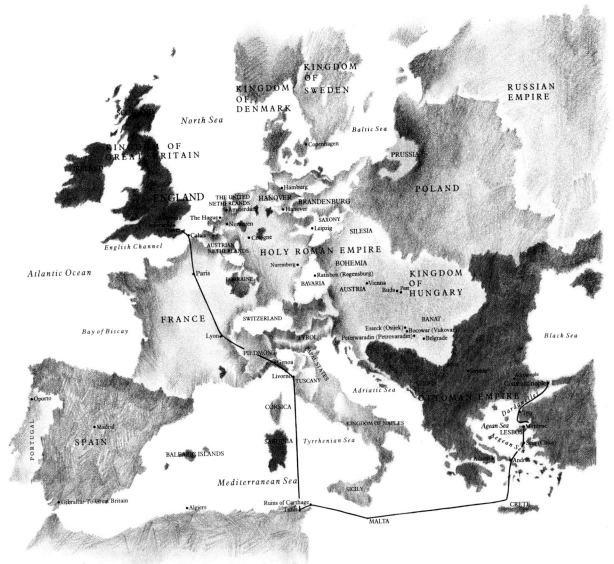

letter- and essay-writing. But the final chapter of her life, those two decades and more passed in voluntary exile in France and Italy, suggest that this journey to the East, with all its excitement and curiosities, had indeed stimulated in her a lifelong taste for the 'pleasures and conveniences' of other lands.

View of Constantinople by an anonymous Greek artist. Pera is on the hilltop in the background. In the foreground are the buildings of the Tophari canon foundry and the Kilic Ali Pasha Mosque built by Sinan in 1580.

To The Abbé Conti — *Tunis 31 July 1718*

I left Constantinople the 6th of the last month, and this is the first port from whence I could send a letter, though I have often wished for the opportunity that I might impart some of the pleasure I have found in this voyage through the most agreeable part of the world, where every scene presents me some poetical idea.

> Warm'd with Poetic transport I survey
> Th' immortal islands, and the well known sea,
> For here so oft the muse her harp has strung
> That not a mountain rears his head unsung.

I beg your pardon for this sally, and will (if I can) continue the rest of my account in plain prose. The second day after we set sail, we passed Gallipoli, a fair city, situated in the Bay of Chersonessus and much respected by the Turks, being the first town they took in Europe. At five the next morning we anchored in the Hellespont between the castles of Sestos and Abydos, now called the Dardanelles. There is now two little ancient castles, but of no strength, being commanded by a rising ground behind them which, I confess, I should never have taken notice of if I had not heard it observed by our captain and officers, my imagination being wholly employed by the tragic story that you are well acquainted with:

> The swimming lover and the nightly bride,[1]
> How Hero loved, and how Leander died.

Verse again! I am certainly infected by the poetical air I have passed through. That of Abydos is undoubtedly very amorous, since that soft passion betrayed the castle into the hands of the Turks in the reign of Orchanes,[2] who beseiged it. The Governor's daughter, imagining to have seen her future husband in a dream (though I don't find she had either slept upon bride cake or kept St Agnes' fast) fancied she afterwards saw the dear figure in the form of one of her beseigers and, being willing to obey her destiny, tossed a note to him over the wall with the offer

1. The second of these couplets comes from Addison's *Letter from Italy* (1703).

2. Orhan was the second Ottoman ruler (1324-59).

of her person and the delivery of the castle. He showed it to his General, who consented to try the sincerity of her intentions and withdrew his army, ordering the young man to return with a select body of men at midnight. She admitted him at the appointed hour; he destroyed the garrison, took her father prisoner, and made her his wife. This town is in Asia, first founded by the Milesians. Sestos is in Europe and was once the principal city in Chersonessus. Since I have seen this strait, I find nothing improbable in the adventure of Leander or very wonderful in the Bridge of Boats of Xerxes.[3] 'Tis so narrow, 'tis not surprising a young lover should attempt to swim it or an ambitious king try to pass his army over it. But then 'tis so subject to storms, 'tis no wonder the lover perished and the Bridge was broken. From hence we had a full view of Mount Ida,

> Where Juno once caressed her amorous Jove
> And the world's master lay subdued by love.

Not many leagues' sail from hence I saw the point of land where poor old Hecuba was buried, and about a league from that place is Cape Janissary, the famous promontory of Sigaeum, where we anchored; and my curiosity supplied me with strength to climb to the top of it to see the place where Achilles was buried and where Alexander ran naked round his tomb in his honour, which, no doubt, was a great comfort to his ghost. I saw there the ruins of a very large city, and found a stone on which Mr Wortley plainly distinguished the words of *Sigaeon polin*.[4] We ordered this on board the ship but were showed others much more curious by a Greek priest, though a very ignorant fellow that could give no tolerable account of anything. On each side the door of his little church lies a large stone about ten foot long each, five in breadth, and three in thickness. That on the right is very fine white marble, the side of it beautifully carved in bas relief. It represents a woman who seems to be designed for some deity sitting on a chair with a footstool, and before her another woman weeping and presenting to her a young child that she has in her arms, followed by a procession of women with children in the same manner. This is certainly part of a very ancient tomb, but I dare not pretend to give the true explanation of it. On the stone on the left side is a very fair inscription, which I am sure I took off very exactly, but the Greek is too ancient for Mr Wortley's interpretation. This is the exact copy. [*Here follow eleven double lines of Greek, apparently copied in another hand.*] I am very sorry not to

3. In the 480s BC, during the Persian Wars against Greece, the Persian Emperor Xerxes built a bridge of ships across the Hellespont.

4. 'City of Sigeum'. Having brought the stone to England, Wortley kept it in his London house; together with other Greek and Roman marbles acquired by Montagu during his Embassy, it was presented to Trinity College, Cambridge, after his death, and now forms part of the Trinity College Collection at the Fitzwilliam Museum, Cambridge.

have the original in my possession, which might have been purchased of the poor inhabitants for a small sum of money, but our captain assured us that without having machines made on purpose, 'twas impossible to bear it to the sea side, and when it was there his long boat would not be large enough to hold it.

The ruins of this great city is now inhabited by poor Greek peasants who wear the Sciote habit, the women being in short petticoats fastened by straps round their shoulders and large smock sleeves of white linen, with neat shoes and stockings, and on their heads a large piece of muslin which falls in large folds on their shoulders. One of my countrymen, Mr Sands[5] (whose book I do not doubt you have read, as one of the best of its kind), speaking of these ruins, supposes them to have been the foundation of a city begun by Constantine before his building at Byzantium, but I see no good reason for that imagination and am apt to believe them much more ancient. We saw very plainly from this promontory the River Simois rolling from Mount Ida and running through a very spacious valley. It is now a considerable river and called Simores, joined in the vale by the Scamander, which appeared a small stream half choked with mud, but is perhaps large in the winter. This was Xanthus amongst the Gods, as Homer tells us, and 'tis by that heavenly name the nymph Oenone invokes it in her epistle to Paris. The Trojan virgins used to offer their first favours to it by the name of Scamander, till the adventure which Monsieur de La Fontaine has told so agreeably abolished that heathenish ceremony.[6] When the stream is mingled with the Simois, they run together to the sea.

All that is now left of Troy is the ground on which it stood, for I am firmly persuaded whatever pieces of antiquity may be found round it are much more modern, and I think Strabo says the same thing. However, there is some pleasure in seeing the valley where I imagined the famous duel of Menelaus and Paris had been fought, and where the greatest city in the world was situated; and 'tis certainly the noblest situation that can be found for the head of a great Empire, much to be preferred to that of Constantinople, the harbour here being always convenient for ships from all parts of the world and that of Constantinople inaccessible almost six months in the year while the north wind reigns. North of the promontory of Sigaeum we saw that of Rhoeteum, famed for the sepulchre of Ajax. While I viewed these celebrated fields and rivers, I admired the exact geography of Homer, whom I had in my hand. Almost every epithet he gives to a

5. George Sandys, *Travels*, 1610.

6. The 'adventure' of an ingenuous maiden duped by a man masquerading as a river god is told by La Fontaine in 'La Fleuve Scamande'.

mountain or plain is still just for it, and I spent several hours in as agreeable cogitations as ever Don Quixote had on Mount Montesinos.[7] We sailed that night to the shore where 'tis vulgarly reported Troy stood and I took the pains of rising at two in the morning to view coolly those ruins which are commonly showed to strangers and which the Turks call eski-Stamboul, i.e. old Constantinople. For that reason, as well as some others, I conjecture them to be the remains of that city begun by Constantine. I hired an ass (the only *voiture* to be had there) that I might go some miles into the country and take a tour round the ancient walls, which are of a vast extent. We found the remains of a castle on a hill and another in a valley, several broken pillars, and two pedestals from which I took these Latin inscriptions. [*Here follow the two inscriptions of nine and twelve lines.*] I do not doubt but the remains of a temple near this place are the ruins of one dedicated to Augustus, and I know not why Mr Sands calls it a Christian temple, since the Romans certainly built hereabouts. Here are many tombs of fine marble and vast pieces of granite, which are daily lessened by the prodigious balls that the Turks make from them for their cannon.

We passed that evening the isle of Tenedos, once under the patronage of Apollo, as he gave it in himself in the particular of his estate when he courted Daphne. It is but ten mile in circuit, but in those days very rich and well peopled, still famous for its excellent wine. I say nothing of Tenes, from whom it was called, but naming Mytilene where we passed next, I cannot forbear mentioning Lesbos, where Sappho sung and Pittacus[8] reigned, famous for the birth of Alcaeus, Theophrastus, and Arion, those masters in poetry, philosophy, and music. This was one of the last islands that remained in the Christian dominion after the conquest of Constantinople by the Turks. But need I talk to you of Catucuseno,[9] etc.? princes that you are as well acquainted with as I am. 'Twas with regret I saw us sail swift from this Island into the Aegean Sea, now the archipelago, leaving Scio (the ancient Chios) on the left, which is the richest and most populous of these islands, fruitful in cotton, corn and silk, planted with groves of orange and lemon trees, and the Arvisian Mountain still celebrated for the nectar that Virgil mentions. Here is the best manufacture of silks in all Turkey. The town is well built, the women famous for their beauty, and show their faces as in Christendom. There are many rich families, though they confine their magnificence to the inside of their houses to avoid the jealousy of the Turks, who have a Pasha here. However, they enjoy a reasonable liberty and indulge the genius of their country,

7. Lady Mary means the cave of Montesinos, where Don Quixote passes about an hour so enchanted by his visions that when he is drawn up he thinks he has spent three days there.

8. Pittacus (*c.* 650-570 BC), one of the Seven Sages of Greece, reigned on Lesbos for about ten years.

9. Of the Cantacuzene family, John V (*c.* 1293-1383) ruled the Eastern Roman Empire during its decline.

And eat and sing and dance away their time,
Fresh as their groves, and happy as their clime.

Their chains hang lightly on them,[10] though 'tis not long since they were imposed, not being under the Turk till 1566; but perhaps 'tis as easy to obey the Grand Signior as the state of Genoa, to whom they were sold by the Greek Emperor. But I forget myself in these historical touches, which are very impertinent when I write to you.

Passing the strait between the island of Andros and Achaia (now Libadia) we saw the promontory of Sounion (now called Cape Colonna), where are yet standing the vast pillars of a Temple of Minerva.[11] This venerable sight made me think with double regret on a beautiful temple of Theseus, which I am assured was almost entire at Athens till the last campaign in the Morea, that the Turks filled it with powder and it was accidentally blown up.[12] You may believe I had a great mind to land on the famed Peloponessus, though it were only to look on the Rivers of Asopus, Peneus, Inachus, and Eurotas, the Fields of Arcadia and other scenes of ancient mythology. But instead of demi Gods and heroes, I was credibly informed 'tis now over run by robbers, and that I should run a great risk of falling into their hands by undertaking such a Journey through a desert country, for which, however, I have so much respect I have much ado to hinder myself from troubling you with its whole history from the foundation of Mycenae and Corinth to the last campaign there. But I check that inclination as I did that of landing, and sailed quietly by Cape Angelo, once Malea, where I saw no remains of the famous temple of Apollo. We came that evening in sight of Candia.[13] It is very mountainous; we easily distinguished that of Ida. We have Virgil's authority here was one hundred cities,

Centum urbes habitant magnas,[14]

the chief of them, Knossos, the scene of monstrous passions.[15] Metellus first conquered this birth place of his Jupiter.[16] It fell afterwards into the hands of _____. I am running on to the very siege of Candia,[17] and I am so angry at myself that I will pass by all the other islands with this general reflection, that 'tis impossible to imagine anything more agreeable than this journey would have been between two and three thousand years since, when, after drinking a dish of tea with Sappho, I might have gone the same evening to visit the temple of Homer in

10. In spite of her full description of the island and its inhabitants, Lady Mary did not stop there.

11. More recent excavations have shown that the ruin is a Temple of Poseidon.

12. The Parthenon was partially wrecked by a bomb when the Venetians besieged Athens in 1687.

13. Crete.

14. 'They dwell in a hundred great cities'.

15. Lady Mary refers to the legend connected with the birth of the Cretan Minotaur and his feasting on Athenian youths and maidens until he was slain by Theseus.

16. This Roman general conquered Crete in 67 BC; according to early legend Zeus was born here.

17. Heraklion, besieged by the Turks from 1648 until 1669 when it surrendered.

Chios, and have passed this voyage in taking plans of magnificent temples, delineating the miracles of statuaries and conversing with the most polite and most gay of humankind. Alas! Art is extinct here. The wonders of nature alone remain, and 'twas with vast pleasure I observed that of Mount Etna, whose flame appears very bright in the night many leagues off at sea, and fills the head with a thousand conjectures. However, I honour philosophy too much to imagine it could turn that of Empedocles, and Lucian shall never make me believe such a scandal of a man of whom Lucretius says

————vix humana videatur stirpe creatus.[18]

We passed Trinacria[19] without hearing any of the Sirens that Homer describes, and being neither thrown on Scylla nor Charibdis came safe to Malta, first called Melita from abundance of honey. It is a whole rock covered with very little earth. The Grand Master[20] lives here in the state of a sovereign prince, but his strength at sea is now very small. The fortifications are reckoned the best in the world, all cut in the solid rock with infinite expense and labour. Off of this island we were tossed by a severe storm, and very glad after eight days to be able to put into Porto Farina on the Africa shore, where our ship now rides.

We were met here by the English consul who resides at Tunis. I readily accepted of the offer of his house there for some days, being very curious to see this part of the world and particularly the ruins of Carthage. I set out in his *chaise* at nine at night; the moon being at full, I saw the prospect of the country almost as well as I could have done by daylight, and the heat of the sun is now so intolerable, 'tis impossible to travel at any other time. The soil is for the most part sandy, but everywhere fruitful in date, olive and fig trees, which grow without art, yet afford the most delicious fruit in the world. Their vineyards and melon fields are enclosed by hedges of that plant we call the Indian fig,[21] which is an admirable fence, no wild beast being able to pass it. It grows a great height, very thick, and the spikes or thorns are as long and sharp as bodkins. It bears a fruit much eaten by the peasants and which has no ill taste. It being now the season of the Turkish Ramadan (or Lent) and all here professing, at least, the Mohammedan religion, they fast till the going down of the sun and spend the night in feasting. We saw under the trees in many places companies of the country people, eating, singing, and dancing to their wild music. They are not quite black, but all mulattos, and the most frightful

18. 'He seems hardly to be born of mortal stock'. According to one legend, the philosopher and scientist Empedocles, driven by melancholy, committed suicide in the crater of Mount Etna.

19. Sicily.

20. This was Ramon Perellos y Roccaful, Grand Master of the Order of St John from 1697 to 1720.

21. The prickly pear, a native of North America which rapidly naturalized around the Mediterranean.

creatures that can appear in a human figure. They are almost naked, only wearing a piece of coarse serge wrapped about them, but the women have their arms to their very shoulders and their necks and faces adorned with flowers, stars and various sort of figures impressed by gunpowder; a considerable addition to their natural deformity, which is, however, esteemed very ornamental amongst them, and I believe they suffer a good deal of pain by it. About six mile from Tunis we saw the remains of that noble aqueduct which carried the water to Carthage over several high mountains the length of forty mile. There is still many arches entire. We spent two hours viewing it with great attention, and Mr Wortley assured me that of Rome is very much inferior to it. The stones are of a prodigious size and yet all polished and so exactly fitted to each other, very little cement has been made use of to join them. Yet they may probably stand one thousand years longer if art is not used to pull them down.

Soon after day break I arrived at Tunis, a town fairly built of a very white stone, but quite without gardens, which (they say) were all destroyed and their fine groves cut down when the Turks first took it. None having been planted since, the dry sand gives a very disagreeable prospect to the eye, and the want of shade contributing to the natural heat of the climate, renders it so excessive I have much ado to support it. 'Tis true here is every noon the refreshment of the sea breeze, without which it would be impossible to live, but no fresh water but what is preserved in the cisterns of the rains that fall in the month of September. The women in the town go veiled from head to foot under a black crepe, and, being mixed with a breed of renegades, are said to be many of them fair and handsome. This city was besieged 1270 by Lewis, King of France, who died under the walls of it of a pestilential fever. After his death, Philip, his son, and our Prince Edward, son of Henry the 3rd, raised the siege on honourable conditions. It remained under its natural African kings till betrayed into the hands of Barbarossa, admiral of Süleyman the magnificent. The Emperor Charles the 5th expelled Barbarossa, but it was recovered by the Turk under the conduct of Sinan Pasha in the reign of Selim the 2nd.[22] From that time till now it has remained tributary to the Grand Signior, governed by a Bey, who suffers the name of subject of the Turk, but has renounced the subjection, being absolute and very seldom paying any tribute. The Great City of Baghdad is at this time in the same circumstance, and the Grand Signior connives at the loss of these dominions for fear of losing even the titles of them.

22. Tunis, captured in 1534 by Barbarossa, was taken in 1535 by Charles V and retaken in 1574 by Kodja Sinan Pasha.

I went very early yesterday morning (after one night's repose) to see the ruins of Carthage. I was, however, half broiled in the sun, and overjoyed to be led into one of the subterranean apartments, which they called the stables of the elephants, but which I cannot believe were ever designed for that use. I found in many of them broken pieces of columns of fine marble and some of porphyry. I cannot think anybody would take the insignificant pains of carrying them thither, and I cannot imagine such fine pillars were designed for the ornament of a stable. I am apt to believe they were summer apartments under their palaces, which the heat of the climate rendered necessary. They are now used as granaries by the country people. While I sat here, from the town of tents not far off many of the woman flocked in to see me and we were equally entertained with viewing one another. Their posture in sitting, the colour of their skin, their lank black hair falling on each side their faces, their features and the shape of their limbs, differ so little from their own country people, the baboons, 'tis hard to fancy them a distinct race, and I could not help thinking there had been some ancient alliances between them. When I was a little refreshed by rest and some milk and exquisite fruit they brought me, I went up the little hill where once stood the castle of Birsa, and from whence I had a distinct view of the situation of the famous city of Carthage, which stood on an isthmus, the sea coming on each side of it. 'Tis now a marshy ground on one side where there is salt ponds. Strabo calls Carthage forty mile in circuit. There is now no remains of it but what I have described, and the history of it too well known to want my abridgement of it.

You see that I think you esteem obedience more than compliments. I have answered your letter by giving you the accounts you desired and have reserved my thanks to the conclusion. I intend to leave this place tomorrow and continue my journey through Italy and France. In one of those places I hope to tell you by word of mouth that I am your humble servant.

To Lady Mar — *Genoa 28 August 1718*

I beg your pardon (my dear sister) that I did not write to you from Tunis (the only opportunity I have had since I left Constantinople), but the heat there was so excessive and the light so bad for the sight, I was half blind by writing one letter to the Abbé Conti and durst not go on to write many others I had designed, nor indeed, could I have entertained you very well out of that barbarous country. I am now surrounded with objects of pleasure, and so much charmed with the beauties of Italy I should think it a kind of ingratitude not to offer a little praise in return for the diversion I have had here. I am in the house of Mrs Davenant at San Pietro d'Arena[1] and should be very unjust not to allow her a share of that praise I speak of, since her good humour and good company has very much contributed to render this place agreeable to me. Genoa is situated in a very fine bay, and being built on a rising hill, intermixed with gardens and beautified with the most excellent architecture, gives a very fine prospect off at sea, though it lost much of its beauty in my eyes, having been accustomed to that of Constantinople. The Genoese were once masters of several islands in the archipelago and all that part of Constantinople which is now called Galata. Their betraying the Christian cause, by facilitating the taking of Constantinople by the Turk, deserved what has since happened to them, the loss of all their conquest on that side to those infidels[2]. They are at present far from rich, and despised by the French since their Doge was forced by the late King to go in person to Paris to ask pardon for such a trifle as the Arms of France over the house of the envoy being spattered with dung in the night (I suppose) by some of the Spanish faction, which still makes up the majority here, though they dare not openly declare it.[3]

The ladies affect the French habit and are more genteel than those they imitate. I do not doubt but the custom of *tetis beys [cicisbeismo]* has very much improved their airs. I know not whether you have ever heard of those animals. Upon my word, nothing but my own eyes could have convinced [me] there were any such upon earth. The fashion begun here and is now received all over Italy, where the husbands are not such terrible creatures as we represent them. There are none among them such brutes to pretend to find fault with a custom so well established and so politically funded, since I am assured here that it was an expedient first found out by the Senate to put an end to those family hatreds which tore their state to pieces, and to find employment for those young men who were forced to cut one another's throats *pour passer le temps,* and it has succeeded so well that since the institution of *tetis beys* there has been nothing but peace and good humour amongst them. These are gentlemen that devote themselves to the service of a particular lady (I mean a married one, for the virgins are all invisible,

1. A fashionable suburb, where the British envoy, Henry Davenant, and his wife lived.

2. When Mehmet II besieged Constantinople in 1453 the Genoese allowed him to carry his light boats across Galata and into the Golden Horn, thus evading the naval barrier.

3. In 1684, the French bombarded Genoa in retaliation; and in May of the following year, the Doge and four Senators travelled to Versailles to apologize to Louis XIV.

confined to convents). They are obliged to wait on her to all public places, the plays, operas, and assemblies (which are called here conversations), where they wait behind the chair, take care of her fan and gloves if she plays, have the privilege of whispers, etc. When she goes out they serve her instead of lackeys, gravely trotting by her chair. 'Tis their business to present against any day of public appearance, not forgetting that of her name. In short, they are to spend all their time and money in her service who rewards them according to her inclination (for opportunity they want none), but the husband is not to have the impudence to suppose 'tis any other than pure plutonic friendship. 'Tis true they endeavour to give her a *tetis bey* of their own choosing, but when the lady happens not to be of the same taste (as that often happens) she never fails to bring it about to have one of her own fancy. In former times one beauty used to have eight or ten of these humble admirers but those days of plenty and humility are no more; men grow more scarce and saucy, and every lady is forced to content herself with one at a time. You see the glorious liberty of a republic, or more properly an aristocracy, the common people here as arrant slaves as the French but the old nobles pay little respect to the Doge, who is but two years in his office, and at that very time his wife assumes no rank above another noble lady. 'Tis true the family of Andrea Doria (that great man who restored them that liberty they enjoy) has some particular privileges; when the Senate found it necessary to put a stop to the luxury of dress, forbidding the wear of jewels and brocades, they left them at liberty to make what expense they pleased. I looked with great pleasure on the statue of that hero which is in the court belonging to the house of Duke Doria.[4]

This puts me in mind of their palaces, which I can never describe as I ought. Is it not enough that I say they are most of them of the design of Palladio? The street called Strada Nova here is perhaps the most beautiful line of building in the world. I must particularly mention the vast palace of Durazzo, those of two Balbi joined together by a magnificent (colonnade), that of the Imperiali at this village of San Pietro d'Arena, and another of the Doria. The perfection of architecture and the utmost profusion of rich furniture is to be seen here, disposed with most elegant taste and lavish magnificence, but I am charmed with nothing so much as the collection of pictures by the pencils of Raphael, Paulo Veronese, Titian, Carracci, Michelangelo, Guido, and Correggio, which two I mention last as my particular favourites. I own I can find no pleasure in objects of horror, and in my opinion the more naturally a crucifix is represented the more disagreeable it is. These, my

4. A naval commander, Doria expelled the French from Genoa in 1528 and re-established the Republic.

beloved painters, show nature and show it in the most charming light. I was particularly pleased with a Lucretia in the House of Balbi. The expressive beauty of that face and bosom gives all the passion of pity and admiration that could be raised in the soul by the finest poem on that subject. A Cleopatra of the same hand deserves to be mentioned, and I should say more of her if Lucretia had not first engaged my eyes. Here are also some inestimable ancient bustos. The Church of St Lawrence is all black and white marble, where is kept that famous plate of a single emerald,[5] which is not now permitted to be handled since a plot which (they say) was discovered to throw it on the pavement and break it, a childish piece of malice which they ascribe to the King of Sicily, to be revenged for their refusing to sell it to him. The Church of the Annunciata is finely lined with marble, the pillars of red and white marble, that of St Ambrose very much adorned by the Jesuits; but I confess all those churches appeared so mean to me after that of Santa Sophia, I can hardly do them the honour of writing down their names; but I hope you'll own I have made good use of my time in seeing so much, since 'tis not many days that we have been out of the quarantine from which nobody is exempt coming from the Levant; but ours was very much shortened and very agreeably passed in Mrs Davenant's company in the village of San Pietro d'Arena, about a mile from Genoa in a house built by Palladio, so well designed and so nobly proportioned 'twas a pleasure to walk in it. We were visited here only in the company of a noble Genoese commissioned to see we did not touch one another. I shall stay here some days longer and could almost wish it for all my life, but mine (I fear) is not destined to so much tranquillity.

5. This emerald was said to be a present from the Queen of Sheba to Solomon. The scepticism of many travellers proved to be well founded when it was taken to Paris during the Napoleonic wars and analysed as glass-paste.

To Lady Mar — *Turin 12 September 1718*

I came in two days from Genoa through fine roads to this place. I have already seen what is showed to strangers in the town, which indeed is not worth a very particular description, and I have not respect enough for the holy handkerchief[1] to

Letter 52
1. The Holy Shroud of Turin, for which a special chapel had been built.

speak long of it. The Church is handsome and so is the King's palace, but I have lately seen such perfection of architecture I did not give much of my attention to these pieces. The town itself is fairly built, situated in a fine plain on the banks of the Po. At a little distance from it we saw the palaces of La Venerie and La Valentin, both very agreeable retreats. We were lodged in the Piazza Royale, which is one of the noblest squares I ever saw, with a fine portico of white stone quite round it. We were immediately visited by the Chevalier _____, whom you knew in England, who with great civility begged to introduce us at Court, which is now kept at Rivoli about a league from Turin. I went thither yesterday, and had the honour of waiting on the Queen,[2] being presented to her by her first Lady of Honour. I found Her Majesty in a magnificent apartment, with a train of handsome ladies all dressed in gowns, amongst which it was easy to distinguish the fair Princess of Carignan.[3] The Queen entertained me with a world of sweetness and affability and seemed mistress of a great share of good sense. She did not forget to put me in mind of her English blood, and added that she always felt in her self a particular inclination to love the English. I returned her civility by giving her the title of Majesty as often as I could, which perhaps she will not have the comfort of hearing many months longer.[4] The King has a great vivacity in his eyes, and the young Prince of Piedmont[5] is a very handsome youth, but the great devotion which this Court is at present fallen into does not permit any of those entertainments proper for his age. Processions and masses are all the magnificences in fashion here, and gallantry so criminal that the poor Count of _____, who was our acquaintance at London, is very seriously disgraced for some small overtures he presumed to make to a maid of honour. I intend to set out tomorrow to pass those dreadful Alps, so much talked of. If I come alive to the bottom you shall hear of me.

2. Anne, wife of Victor Amadeus II, Duke of Savoy and King of Sicily; her mother was Henrietta, daughter of Charles I. England had no diplomatic representative to Savoy at this time, and so the Wortley Montagus could not be presented by a British ambassador.

3. Maria Anna, the natural daughter of Victor Amadeus II, who married the Prince of Carignan in 1714.

4. Victor Amadeus had been awarded the Kingdom of Sicily by the Treaty of Utrecht in 1713, but Spain had invaded the island during the summer of 1718.

5. Lady Mary seems dazzled by royalty. Although the late Prince of Piedmont (d.1715) had been handsome, intelligent and charming, his brother Charles Emanuel III was ugly, hunchbacked and clumsy of understanding.

To Miss Anne Thistlethwayte — *Lyons 25 September 1718*[1]

1. The dates of this letter, and of all the following ones, are several weeks out. Lady Mary arrived in Paris on 18 September and in London on 2 October.

I received at my arrival here both your obliging letters, and from many of my other friends, designed to Constantinople and sent me from Marseilles hither, our merchant there knowing we were upon our return.

I am surprised to hear my sister Mar has left England. I suppose what I writ to her from Turin will be lost, and where to direct I know not, having no account of her affairs from her own hand. For my own part, I am confined to my chamber, having kept my bed till yesterday ever since the seventeenth that I came to this town, where I have had so terrible a fever I believed fore some time that all my journeys were ended here, and I do not at all wonder that such fatigues as I have passed should have such an effect. The first day's journey, from Turin to Nova-lese, is through a very fine country, beautifully planted, and enriched by art and nature. The next day we begun to ascend Mount Cenis, being carried in little seats of twisted osiers fixed upon poles, on men's shoulders, our chaises taken to pieces and laid upon mules. The prodigious prospect of mountains covered with eternal snow, clouds hanging far below our feet, and the vast cascades tumbling down the rocks with a confused roaring would have been solemnly entertaining to me if I had suffered less from the extreme cold that reigns here, but the misty rain, which falls perpetually, penetrated even the thick fur I was wrapped in, and I was half dead with cold before we got to the foot of the mountain, which was not till two hours after 'twas dark. This hill has a spacious plain on the top of it, and a fine lake there, but the descent is so steep and slippery, 'tis surprising to see these chairmen go so steadily as they do, yet I was not half so much afraid of breaking my neck as I was of falling sick, and the event has showed that I placed my fears in the right place. The other mountains are now all passable for a chaise, and very fruitful vines and pastures; amongst them is a breed of the finest goats in the world. Aiguebelette is the last, and soon after we entered Pont-de-Beauvoisin, the frontier town of France, whose bridge parts this kingdom and the dominion of Savoy. The same night we arrived late at this town, where I have had nothing to do but to take care of my health. I think myself already out of any danger, and am determined that the sore throat, which still remains, shall not confine me long. I am impatient to see the antiquities of this famous city and more impatient to continue my journey to Paris, from whence I hope to write you a more diverting letter than 'tis possible for me to do now, with a mind weakened by sickness, a head muddled with spleen, from a sorry inn, and a chamber crammed with the mortifying objects of apothecary's vials and bottles.

To Lady Rich — *Paris 10 October 1718*

I cannot give my dear Lady Rich a better proof of the pleasure I have in writing to her than choosing to do it in this seat of various amusements, where I am *accablé* with visits, and those so full of vivacity and compliment that 'tis full employment to hearken whether one answers or not. The French Ambassadress at Constantinople has a very considerable and numerous family here, who all come to see me and are never weary of making inquiries. The air of Paris has already had a good effect on me, for I was never in better health, though I have been extreme ill all the road from Lyons to this place. You may judge how agreeable the journey has been to me, which did not need that addition to make me dislike it. I think nothing so terrible as objects of misery, except one had the God-like attribute of being capable to redress them, and all the country villages of France show nothing else. While the post horses are changed, the whole town comes out to beg, with such miserable starved faces and thin, tattered clothes, they need no other eloquence to persuade [one of] the wretchedness of their condition.

This is all the French magnificence till you come to Fontainebleau. There you begin to think the kingdom rich when you are showed 1,500 rooms in the King's hunting palace. The apartments of the royal family are very large and richly gilt, but I saw nothing in the architecture or painting worth remembering, The Long Gallery, built by Henry the Fourth, has prospects of all the King's houses on its walls, designed after the taste of those times, but appears now very mean. The park is indeed finely wooded and watered, the trees well grown and planted, and in the fish ponds are kept tame carp, said to be some of them eighty years of age. The late King passed some months every year at this seat; and all the rocks round it, by the pious sentences inscribed on them, show the devotion in fashion at his Court, which I believe died with him. At least I see no exterior marks of it at Paris, where all people's thoughts seem to be on present diversion. The Fair of St Lawrence is now in season. You may be sure I have been carried thither, and think it much better disposed than ours of Bartholomew. The shops being all set in rows so regularly well lighted, they made up a very agreeable spectacle. But I was not at all satisfied with the *grossièreté* of their harlequin, no more than with their music at the opera, which was abominable grating after being used to that of Italy. Their house is a booth compared to that of the Haymarket, and the playhouse not so neat as that in Lincoln's Inn Fields; but then it must be owned to their praise, their tragedians are much beyond any of ours. I should hardly allow Mrs Oldfield[1] a better place than to be confidant to La [Desmares]. I have seen the tragedy of *Bajazet* so well represented, I think our best actors can be only said to speak, but these to feel, and 'tis certainly infinitely more moving to see a man appear unhappy than to hear him say that he is so, with a jolly face and a stupid smirk in his countenance. Apropos of countenances, I must tell you something of the French ladies. I have seen all the beauties, and such (I can't help making use of the coarse word) nauseous _____, so fantastically absurd in their dress! so monstrously unnatural in their paint! their hair cut short and curled round their faces, loaded with powder that makes it look like white wool, and on their cheeks to their chins, unmercifully laid on, a shining red japan that glistens in a most flaming manner, that they seem to have no resemblance to human faces, and I am apt to believe took the first hint of their dress from a fair sheep newly raddled. 'Tis with pleasure I recollect my dear pretty country women, and if I was writing to anybody else I should say that these grotesque daubers give me still a higher esteem of the natural charms of dear Lady Rich's auburn hair and the lively colours of her unsullied complexion.

I have met the Abbé Conti here, who desires me to make his compliments to you.

1. Anne Oldfield was the leading actress at Drury Lane.

2. Racine's *Bajazet* (whose Turkish subject was so appropriate to Lady Mary) was performed at the *Comédie française* while she was in Paris, with Charlotte Desmares as Roxanne.

To [Anne] Thistlethwayte — *Paris 16 October 1718*

You see I am just to my word in writing to you from Paris, where I was very much surprised to meet my sister Mar,[1] I need not add, very much pleased. She as little expected to see me as I her (having not received my late letters), and this meeting would shine under the hand of Mr de Scuderie,[2] but I shall not imitate his style so far as to tell you how often we embraced, how she enquired by what odd chance I returned from Constantinople? And I answered her by asking what adventure brought her to Paris? To shorten the story, all questions and answers and exclamations and compliments being over, we agreed upon running about together

1. Lady Mar had arrived in Paris on 1 October. She was on her way to Italy to join her husband, who with the Pretender and his Court had been expelled from France.

2. Georges de Scudery, a writer of extravagant plays.

and have seen Versailles, Trianon, Marl and St Cloûd. We had an order for the waters to play for our diversion, and I was followed thither by all the English at Paris. I own Versailles appeared to me rather vast than beautiful, and after having seen the exact proportions of the Italian buildings, I thought the irregularity of it shocking. The King's cabinet of antiques and medals is indeed very richly furnished. Amongst that collection none pleased me so well as the Apotheosis of Germanicus on a large agate, which is one of the most delicate pieces of the kind that I remember to have seen. I observed some ancient statues of great value, but the nauseous flattery and tawdry pencil of Le Brun[3] are equally disgusting in the gallery. I will not pretend to describe to you the great apartment, the vast variety of fountains, the theatre, the grove of Aesop's Fables,[4] etc., all which you may read very amply particularized in some of the French authors that have been paid for those descriptions. Trianon in its littleness pleased me better than Versailles, Marl better than either of them, and St Cloûd best of all, having the advantage of the Seine running at the bottom of the gardens. The great cascade, etc. You may find in the foresaid books, if you have any curiosity to know the exact number of the statues and how many foot they cast up the water. We saw the King's pictures in the magnificent house of the Duc d'Antin,[5] who has the care of preserving them till His Majesty is of age. There is not many, but of the best hands. I looked with great pleasure on the Archangel of Raphael, where the sentiments of superior beings are as well expressed as in Milton. You won't forgive me if I say nothing of the Tuilleries, much finer than our Mall, and the *Court*[6] more agreeable than our Hyde Park, the high trees giving shade in the hottest season. At the Louvre I had the opportunity of seeing the King, accompanied by the Duke Regent. He is tall and well shaped, but has not the air of holding the crown so many years as his grandfather.[7] And now I am speaking of the Court, I must say I saw nothing in France that delighted me so much as to see an Englishman (at least a Briton) absolute at Paris. I mean Mr Law,[8] who treats their dukes and peers extremely *de haut en bas,* and is treated by them with the utmost submission and respect. Poor souls! This reflection on their abject slavery puts me in mind of the Place des Victoires,[9] but I will not take up your time and my own with such descriptions, which are too numerous. In general, I think Paris has the advantage of London in the neat pavement of the streets, and the regular lighting of them at nights, the proportion of the streets, the houses being all built of stone, and most of those belonging to people of quality beautified by gardens; but we certainly may boast of a town very near twice as

3. The painter Charles le Brun.

4. The lead fountain-statues of Aesop's fabulous characters were designed by Le Nôtre in 1673.

5. The house of the Duc d'Antin, Superintendent of Works for the Crown since 1716, was filled not only with his own magnificent furniture but also with tapestries and pictures of great value belonging to the King, including a *Saint Michael* by Raphael.

6. The Cour de la Mayne consisted of three long alleys planted with high trees.

7. Louis XV, eight years old at this time, had succeeded his great-grandfather Louis XIV in 1715. Louis XIV's nephew Philippe duc d'Orléans acted as Regent.

8. John Law, a Scottish financier who organized the Mississippi Scheme, a French speculative venture.

9. Here on a white marble pedestal stood a tremendous gilt-bronze statue of Louis XIV with a captive slave in bronze at each corner.

large, and when I have said that, I know nothing else we surpass it in. I shall not continue here long. If you have anything to command me during my short stay, write soon, and I shall take pleasure in obeying you.

To The Abbé Conti — *Dover 31 October 1718*

I am willing to take your word for it that I shall really oblige you by letting you know as soon as possible my safe passage over the water. I arrived this morning at Dover after being tossed a whole night in the packet-boat in so violent a manner that the master, considering the weakness of his vessel, thought it prudent to remove the mail, and gave us notice of the danger. We called a little fisher boat, which could hardly make up to us, while all the people on board us were crying to heaven, and 'tis hard to imagine one's self in a scene of greater horror than on such an occasion; and yet, shall I own it to you? though I was not at all willing to be drowned, I could not forbear being entertained at the double distress of a fellow passenger. She was an English lady that I had met at Calais, who desired me to let her go over with me in my cabin. She had bought a fine point head[dress] which she was contriving to conceal from the custom-house officers. When the wind grew high and our little vessel cracked, she fell very heartily to her prayers and thought wholly of her soul; when it seemed to abate, she returned to the worldly care of her head-dress, and addressed herself to me. 'Dear Madame, will you take care of this point? if it should be lost — Ah Lord! we shall all be lost! Lord have mercy on my soul — pray, Madame, take care of this head-dress.' This easy transition from her soul to her head-dress, and the alternate agonies that both gave her, made it hard to determine which she thought of greatest value. But, however, the scene was not so diverting but I was glad to get rid of it and be thrown into the little boat, though with some hazard of breaking my back. It brought me safe hither, and I cannot help looking with partial eyes on my native land. That partiality was certainly given us by nature to prevent rambling, the effect of an ambitious thirst after knowledge which we are not formed to enjoy. All we get by it is a fruitless desire of mixing the different pleasures and conveniencies which are given to different parts of the world and cannot meet in any one of them. After having read all that is to be found in the languages I am mistress of, and having decayed my sight by midnight studies, I envy the easy peace of mind of a ruddy milkmaid who, undisturbed by doubt, hears the sermon with humility every Sunday, having not confused the sentiments of natural duty in her head by the vain inquiries of the schools, who may be more learned, yet after all must remain as ignorant. And after having seen part of Asia and Africa and almost made the tour of Europe I think the honest English squire more happy who verily believes the Greek wines less delicious than March beer, that the African fruits have not so fine a flavour as golden pippins, and the *beccafichi* of Italy are not so well tasted as a rump of beef, and that, in short, there is no perfect enjoyment of this life out of Old England. I pray God I may think so for the rest of my life, and since I must be contented with our scanty allowance of daylight, that I may forget the enlivening sun of Constantinople.

To Alexander Pope — *Dover 1 November 1718*

I have this minute received a letter of yours sent me from Paris. I believe and hope I shall very soon see both you and Mr Congreve, but as I am here in an inn where we stay to regulate our march to London, bag and baggage, I shall employ some of my leisure time in answering that part of yours that seems to require an answer.

I must applaud your good nature in supposing that your pastoral lovers (vulgarly called haymakers) would have lived in everlasting joy and harmony if the lightning had not interrupted their scheme of happiness[1]. I see no reason to imagine that John Hughes and Sarah Drew were either wiser or more virtuous than their neighbours. That a well-set man of twenty-five should have a fancy to marry a brown woman of eighteen is nothing marvellous, and I cannot help thinking that had they married, their lives would have passed in the common tract with their fellow parishioners. His endeavouring to shield her from the storm was a natural action and what he would have certainly done for his horse if he had been in the same situation. Neither am I of opinion that their sudden death was a reward of their mutual virtue. You know the Jews were reproved for thinking a

1. In his letter Pope had related a pathetic tale of two rustic lovers struck by lightning; evidently the man had tried to shield the woman. Pope's letter contained two epitaphs that treated the subject sentimentally.

village destroyed by fire more wicked than those that had escaped the thunder. Time and chance happen to all men. Since you desire me to try my skill in an epitaph, I think the following lines perhaps more just, though not so poetical as yours:

> Here lies John Hughes and Sarah Drew;
> Perhaps you'll say, what's that to you?
> On this poor couple that are dead.
> On Sunday next they should have married,
> But see how oddly things are carried.
> On Thursday last it rained and lightened;
> These tender lovers sadly frightened
> Sheltered beneath the cocking hay
> In hopes to pass the storm away.
> But the bold thunder found them out
> (Commissioned for that end no doubt)
> And seizing on their trembling breath,
> Consigned them to the shades of death.
> Who knows it 'twas not kindly done?
> For had they seen the next year's sun
> A beaten wife and cuckold swain
> Had jointly cursed the marriage chain.
> Now they are happy in their doom,
> For Pope has wrote upon their tomb.

I confess these sentiments are not altogether so heroic as yours, but I hope you will forgive them in favour of the two last lines. You see how much I esteem the honour you have done them, though I am not very impatient to have the same and had rather continue to be your stupid living humble servant than be celebrated by all the pens in Europe.

I would write to Mr Congreve but suppose you will read this to him if he inquires after me.

Notes from the Editor

In preparing this edition of the *Embassy Letters* for a general readership, I have relied on the authoritative text established by Professor Robert Halsband in his edition of Lady Mary's *Complete Letters*, published by the Clarendon Press between 1965 and 1967, and have also made extensive use of his annotations. The spelling, capitalization and punctuation of the letters has been modernized; names of people and places have generally been given in their current version. I have also provided notes to elucidate references to people and events which may be obscure to the present-day reader and to clarify the chronology of the Embassy. For reasons of space, some ten letters have been omitted; these are generally brief ones whose content is reproduced elsewhere.

I would like to thank Professor Halsband most warmly for his generosity in permitting me to use both his own modernization of some of the letters (these originally appeared in his *Selected Letters* published by St Martin's Press in New York in 1971 and by Penguin Books in 1986) and also the annotations contained in his complete edition. Professor Halsband has also given me enthusiastic encouragement and much valuable advice, for which I am most grateful.

I have also benefited enormously from the willing co-operation of Charles Newton of the Victoria & Albert Museum. Besides guiding me through the Searight Collection and advising on the choice of illustrations and on the wording of the captions, he has checked Lady Mary's Turkish orthography and has willingly helped me to find the answers to many obscure questions about Ottoman Turkey.

Christopher Pick
London, October 1987

The Searight Collection

The great majority of illustrations in this book have been taken from the Searight Collection in the Victoria & Albert Museum. This collection is an extensive visual and literary record of scenes, events and personalities in North Africa and the Near East. It reflects the range of European interest and activity, between the sixteenth and twentieth centuries, in a large geographical area. The emphasis is on those parts most frequented by travellers — Turkey, Syria and Egypt — but the less accessible areas, such as Afghanistan and Arabia, are also covered.

The Collection contains about 2,000 water colours and drawings, several thousand prints and several hundred illustrated travel books. Over 500 artists and travellers are represented. The works are mainly by British artists but there is a large French contribution, and also examples by German, Italian, Scandinavian, Swiss, Maltese and other European artists. In addition, there is a fringe of American, Russian and 'Levantine' artists.

Among the well-known artists represented are John Frederick Lewis, David Roberts, Edward Lear, David Wilkie, William Muller, Owen Jones, Carl Haag, Prosper Marilhat, Adrien Dauzats, Alexandre Decamps, Carl Werner and Amadeo Preziosi. An additional and special characteristic of the Collection is the large number of little-known or amateur artists whose work is rarely represented in other public collections.

The Collection was formed by Rodney Searight, a former director of Shell International Petroleum Company, who worked in the Near East for many years. He began collecting in the early 1960s when there was little interest in orientalist artists, and his enthusiasm has been instrumental in focusing attention on this now popular field of study.

Illustration Acknowledgements

There are few illustrations of Turkey at the time of Lady Mary's visit; Jean-Baptiste Vanmour seems to have been the only European artist working in Constantinople while Turkish works do not exist. The majority of the illustrations reproduced in this book date from the century following Wortley's embassy. Turkish society changed so little in those years that, to all intents and purposes, they can be taken as evidence of what life was like in 1717 and 1718.

The aquatints by Luigi Mayer are from the book *Views in the Ottoman Dominions*, 1810. Mayer was employed by Sir Robert Ainslie, ambassador to Constantinople, from 1776 to 1794 and travelled throughout the Turkish Empire, Thomas Allom (1804-72) was an architect and topographical draughtsman who travelled to Turkey and Palestine in about 1838. The anonymous Greek artist was employed by Canning, when he served as ambassador to Turkey in 1809. Antoine Ignace Melling (1763-1831) travelled c.1782 to Italy, Egypt and Constantinople, where he worked as architect to the Sultana Hadice, and remained for about eighteen years; his *Voyage pittoresque de Constantinople et des rives du Bosphore* was published in 1819. Michel-Francois Preaulx (*fl.*1796-1827) went to Constantinople with a group of artists and artisans to construct naval and military buildings and installations for the Ottoman government; he received commissions from several British and French travellers, and in 1811 was appointed draughtsman to the French Embassy. The plates in William Miller's *The Costume of Turkey*, 1802 were done after drawings made by Octavien Dalvimart in Constantinople *c* 1798; Miller himself did not travel to Turkey.

Jean-Baptiste Vanmour (1671-1737) was a Flemish painter who accompanied the French ambassador to Constantinople *c* 1699 and then worked mainly for French and other ambassadors in Turkey, where he settled. The *Recueil de cent estampes représentant différentes nations du Levant*, with etchings after Vanmour's paintings, was first published in 1712.

Index

236937

B   MONTAGU
MONTAGU
   EMBASSY TO CONSTANTINOPLE

                              $30.00